LEIGH HOWARD
and the
Ghosts of
Simmons-Pierce Manor

Shawn M. Warner

Black Rose Writing | Texas

ISBN: 978-1-68513-073-2 (Paperback); 978-1-68513-353-5 (Hardcover)
PUBLISHED BY BLACK ROSE WRITING
www.blackrosewriting.com

Printed in the United States of America
Suggested Retail Price (SRP) $21.95 (Paperback); $25.95 (Hardcover)

Leigh Howard and the Ghosts of Simmons-Pierce Manor is printed in Garamond

*As a planet-friendly publisher, Black Rose Writing does its best to eliminate unnecessary waste to reduce paper usage and energy costs, while never compromising the reading experience. As a result, the final word count vs. page count may not meet common expectations.
Author Photograph by Lynn Michelle Photography

For Lizette

who gave me the freedom to dream,
the courage to try,
and the inspiration to always strive
for the best possible version of myself.

LEIGH HOWARD and the Ghosts of Simmons-Pierce Manor

Chapter One

Leigh felt like a pound-rescued mutt being paraded in front of new owners. Minutes ago, the limousine she rode in passed through what she could only describe as being a medieval castle's sentry gate. Riding beneath its arches, she glanced into the guard tower and caught sight of rifles lining the walls. Twisting around in the backseat, she stared out the window at the guards sealing the iron gates behind her. Instead of chain mail and swords, these men wore designer suits with concealed guns bulging beneath their jackets.

She jerked back around and faced forward. Her dad had been a cop and he taught her more about firearms than most adults know. He had taken her to the gun range on several occasions and she knew herself to be a pretty darned good shot. That abundance of weaponry stockpiled in one place still made her breath come in thin, panicked pants. Looking up, she watched her reflection in the limo's rear-view mirror nibble on a thumbnail. She balled her fingers into fists and dropped them into her lap.

It had taken five minutes for the big black machine to make it from the gate to the mansion, traveling at a steady thirty miles per hour. She'd checked the speedometer. Did the math. Thirty miles every sixty minutes made for half a mile a minute. Five minutes meant two and a half miles. The driveway, if that was what people like the Simmons-Pierces called it, was over two miles long.

Now, standing in front of her new family, she waited for them to pass judgment. She could see the doubt and hesitation in their eyes as they looked her over. They stared at her long black bangs dangling well over her eyes in a messy tussle, spiking in front of her exposed ears and tapering down to the nape of her neck. It didn't help that she wore neither make-up nor fingernail polish. In fact, she had no nails to speak of. She'd bitten them down to the quick.

With holes in her jeans and wearing a baggy tie-died hoodie, she imagined her cousin, Tristin Simmons, his wife Peg, and their daughter, Myra, silently asking themselves, "Will she chew on the furniture or pee on the rugs?"

Leigh couldn't bear to look them in the eye. Cheeks burning with embarrassment, she focused on the blue-ink doodles she had drawn on the toes of her red canvas high-tops. "I can't thank you enough for taking me in, Mrs. Simmons," she mumbled, trying to get their silent attention off her.

"Please," the lady of the manor cooed, "call me Aunt Peggy. Or just Peg, if you like."

Leigh turned her eyes to the castle in front of her. As far as she was concerned, that's what the house was. Enormous. Old. Built out of huge gray boulders with tiny flakes embedded in them that sparkled like shattered glass in the gutter. For two centuries, maybe more, green ivy had been storming those walls but still hadn't made it halfway across their face.

Tristin sauntered up beside her to share the view. "Impressive, isn't it? The ancestral home of the Simmons-Pierce family."

He made a sweeping gesture of pride. "For most of America's history, this house has stood at the center of it all. Presidents have signed treaties here. Generals came up with battle plans. Spies plotted. Philanthropists danced. This house isn't a monument to history. It *is* history."

"Dad, now isn't the time for all that. I'm sure Leigh is far more interested in *her* future than she is in our *home's* past."

Leigh turned and smiled at Myra Simmons. Cousin Myra.

They were all cousins. Myra. Peg. Tristin. Very distant cousins. Leigh's cynical side -- her only side -- told her that Peg and Tristin adopted the titles of "aunt" and "uncle" to make a statement. They were in charge. They'd be calling the shots.

Leigh held her smile steady. She didn't care. Not about them. Not about anything.

To come here she had to convince the psychiatrists she wasn't an immediate threat to herself. It was true enough; a fragile truth the weight of a falling eyelash would shatter. Tonight. Tomorrow. Sometime next week. Eventually, she'd try to kill herself again.

For now? Just keep smiling, Leigh told herself.

She turned that phony smile on Myra.

At nineteen, Myra was three years older than herself. She wore denim pants too expensive to be called jeans and a sweater whose battered look belied its lofty price tag. Her hair and nails were styled with meticulous care to make her look like everybody else. Leigh estimated that a thousand dollars, easily, went into making Myra Simmons look breathtakingly ordinary.

"You see that window?" Myra asked, pointing to the tower Leigh and Tristin were admiring. "Third one up? It's the only room on that floor. It's yours."

She leaned in as if to share a secret but spoke loud enough for all to hear. "Best room in the place, if you ask me."

"Why's that?" Leigh asked with halfhearted interest.

"Because of the ghosts!"

Leigh's heart revved up to three-quarters interest. "Ghosts? Cool!"

Myra laughed.

"Myra," Peg scolded, "don't fill Leigh's head with that nonsense."

"I'm sorry, Leigh," Peg went on. "She spends too much time in front of the TV."

"And too little time in front of her school books," Tristin added. "That's not going to cut it when you start college in the fall."

Peg groaned. "Myra, why don't you take Leigh up to her room before we end up having *that* conversation again. Dinner will be ready in twenty minutes."

"Sure," Myra said.

Looking over her mother's shoulder, Myra raised her eyebrows and pursed her lips playfully. "Love you, Daddy."

Tristin smiled, sighed, and shook his head in defeat. "Love you, too."

Myra hoisted Leigh's suitcase off the ground and led the way inside. Fulfilling her role as the loyal hound, Leigh jerked her duffel bag into her arms and obediently followed.

Inside, the manor was sealed with dark wood paneling. Leigh's eyes widened to see so many portraits hanging on the walls. Landscapes filled in what few gaps remained between portraits.

Leaning sideways she peered into the adjacent sitting room. Imitating the foyer, it too was full of paintings.

Gasping, Leigh dropped her duffel bag to the floor. Her heart pounded with irrational hope as she darted inside the room. Ignoring all other portraits, she went to stand in front of a woman's picture hanging on the wall closest to the window.

Sunlight shimmered off the gold leaf frame that surrounded the painting like a halo. The woman in the portrait wore a puffy blue cupcake dress from a long-gone era. She had curly auburn hair and a kind smiling face.

Myra moved to stand beside her. "Leigh? What's the matter?"

"This woman," Leigh said, pointing at the painting. "Who is she?"

"That's Rebecca Florence Pierce. She died in the early eighteen-hundreds. Why?"

Leigh fumbled inside her tie-dyed jacket, slipping her hand into a hidden pocket. She pulled out a photograph and gave it to Myra. "This is...was...my mother."

Myra took a moment to study the photo and compare it to the painting.

"Thanks," Myra said, handing it back. "I didn't want to ask. At least not straight away. About how you were related to us? That answer involves your parents, which makes the details yours to give when you're ready, not mine to try and take."

Leigh studied Myra, trying to see the person beneath the expensive exterior.

Myra was respecting her privacy, though she didn't know Leigh any better than some beggar panhandling on the street. Leigh decided this meant Myra respected everyone by default.

Leigh wasn't sure how long she'd stay at Simmons-Pierce Manor -- didn't know how long she'd stay alive. She wasn't looking to make friends, but that didn't mean she had to make enemies.

"It's okay," Leigh said. "At least you cared enough not to ask. Most don't. They seem to think that their being curious means I owe them an explanation."

Leigh blushed and looked at her shoes. Without thinking, she tugged the sleeves of her hoodie over the scars on her wrists, balling her fingertips around the cuffs making fists so tight her knuckles turned white. "About everything."

Myra's eyes fluttered as a tear rolled out of each corner.

Leigh's jaw clenched. She hated it when people felt sorry for her. Even more, she despised it when they tried to comfort her. All that meant was that her pain was making them uncomfortable and what they were really trying to do was make themselves feel better.

Myra was different. She wasn't doing any of that. She was letting her be, sharing in her sadness as best she could without denying it was there as if it were some kind of ugly carpet stain, or worse, trying to fix it. To fix *her*. Suffering was part of who she was and Myra wasn't trying to change that.

"Come on," Myra said as if sensing Leigh's gloomy thoughts. "You might like this."

"Doubtful," Leigh muttered to herself as she followed her cousin out of the room.

They went back across the foyer and into the library lay straight across from the sitting room where Rebecca Pierce's portrait hung.

The library wasn't adorned with near as many paintings as the sitting room. In their place, massive bookshelves claimed the wall space. What few portraits did cling to the paneling were clustered around a giant portrait over the fireplace mantle.

The painting was of a dour looking old man with a mustache-less beard. He was sitting in a chair and an Asian servant stood behind him and to the far left, almost out of the painting entirely. The seated man's face lacked any suggestion of warmth and his piercing eyes, glaring out into the room from beneath eyebrows that looked like gray hedges, made Leigh feel he was watching her every movement.

"These two," Myra said gesturing to a much smaller and happier painting, "are the twins Christian and Corinne Pierce. They were Rebecca's children."

Leigh blinked to shake off the effect of the old man's painted glare. In stunned amazement, she studied the pair Myra pointed out. Corinne looked more like her mother than Rebecca. Leigh's shoulders tightened as a shiver ran up her spine. Seeing so much of her mother, and of herself, in these long dead faces was a morbid kind of eerie she wasn't ready to embrace.

"So," Myra said pointing to the man in the painting, "our cousin Christian was due to inherit the family's business. Until that happened, he determined to spend at least one year in every port where our firm had offices. Corinne decided to go with Christian for the year he planned to spend in the British West Indies. Being a young woman of that era, she had even less to occupy her time than her brother did."

Myra snickered at her own joke. Leigh forced a smile onto her face.

"While she was there, she met Monroe." Myra paused, waiting for Leigh to ask the obligatory question.

Leigh dutifully played her part. "Who's Monroe?"

"He was a sugar cane farmer! Not even wealthy enough to claim he was a plantation owner. Just a meager farmer."

"Bet that went over well with the folks back home," Leigh said.

"It did not," Myra said emphatically. "What's more, Monroe was a native. He was black. Nowadays, no big deal. But in the early eighteen-hundreds? Scandalous!

"Well you can imagine what happened when Corinne announced their engagement. It was 'call off the wedding or be disowned.'"

"So, what'd she do?" Leigh asked feeling the unfamiliar twinge of interest pricking her. These were, after all, her ancestors.

"She told the entire Simmons-Pierce clan, along with all their money, to go to Hell and married Monroe anyway."

Leigh flashed a genuine smile at the portrait. "You go, girl!"

"I know!" Myra beamed a broad smile at the image of Corinne, notes of pride ringing in her voice. "I like her, too."

"What happened after that?" Leigh asked.

Myra turned to look at her, eyebrows knotted. "What do you mean?"

"To Corinne? What was her life like? Did she have any kids?"

"She must have," Myra said. "You're here."

Leigh stared at her, silently demanding a better answer.

Myra explained. "Today, we struggle to imagine any parent turning their back on their child. In those days, 'disowned' meant *disowned*. Corinne's marriage to Monroe was the last the family ever heard from her."

Growing quiet, Myra looked at the painting and, speaking as if she were miles away, said, "It's kind of weird. Growing up in this house, I naturally wondered about Corinne's family. Where her descendants might be."

She turned and smiled at Leigh. "I thought about you without knowing it was you I was thinking about. And now, here you are."

Leigh shrugged and grimaced. "Here I am. Hope I'm not too much of a disappointment."

Myra bounced her eyebrows and pursed her lips like she did at her father when they were still outside. "Not too much, no. At least not yet."

Suddenly Myra erupted with carefree laughter. Leigh was jealous of Myra's joy and her face flushed with shame.

Leigh needed to get her mind away from such dangerous territory. She pointed at the large portrait and asked, "And who is that?"

Myra threw her arms wide, as if embracing the huge painting of the scowling old man over the fireplace. "Bodie Pierce!"

Leigh sneered. "Bodie?"

"Well, that's what I call him. His real name was Ichabod."

Myra shook her head in dismay and pity. Speaking to the portrait, she asked, "What were your parents thinking?"

Both girls chuckled. Leigh startled at the unaccustomed sound of her own cheerfulness. "What's so special about Bodie?" she asked to put a stop to it.

Myra looked at her with delight gleaming in her eyes. "He's the ghost that haunts Simmons-Pierce Manor."

"Have you ever seen him?"

"No. And neither has anybody else in the family. Mom and Dad think it's a lot of nonsense. But there have been stories over the years. According to legend, the ghost of Big Bodie only comes out when the family is in serious trouble. Little Bodie is another matter, but I've never seen him, either."

Leigh cocked her head to the side like a puzzled pup. "Little Bodie?"

"Myra," Peg called from another part of the house, "are you planning to take Leigh up to her room? It's almost time for dinner."

Myra rolled her eyes. "I'll explain upstairs," she whispered.

Leigh followed Myra up the grand staircase. When they reached the second floor, Myra said, "Mom and Dad's room is over there."

She gestured to somewhere on the far side of the stairs, giving Leigh no real clue which of the many doors she was pointing to.

Myra turned and walked to the end of the hall. Leigh had no choice but to follow. The more she saw of the house, the more she felt like she had been transported to the set of some British television show, not anything she'd expect to see standing in a remote corner of Maryland. Every instinct she had told her she didn't belong here, but she had nowhere else to go.

Myra's image blurred as tears welled in Leigh's eyes. Using a rough corner of the duffel bag she hugged in her arms, Leigh dabbed them dry before Myra could notice.

"That's mine," Myra chirruped, pointing to a door that looked as old and boring as all the others.

Directly across the hall from Myra's room was a small domed landing. Inside the little cave was a very steep and narrow spiral staircase. Myra crossed over to it and started up.

Reaching the top, Leigh stood two steps down from Myra, who was standing on a small platform barely large enough to accommodate one person. In front of Myra was a peculiar wooden door, smaller than normal and shaped like a circle.

With a teasing lilt in her voice Myra asked, "Quite a climb, isn't it?"

"It is carrying this bag. Not sure how I feel about coming all this way every time I want to take something heavy to my room."

Myra's lips curled as she treated Leigh to a slow teasing smile. "Oh, there's an elevator that runs to the second floor, but I thought you might like a bit of exercise, being cooped up in a car all day."

Leigh's mouth dropped open. "A practical joke? Really?"

"Just a small one," Myra grinned. "I hope you aren't mad."

"Not mad, no. But I will get even," Leigh said.

Smiling even broader, Myra opened the little round door and went inside. Leigh crouched and followed. The moment she saw the layout, she fell in love.

The room was much bigger than she imagined it could be. The first thing Leigh noticed was that it, like the door, was circular. The second thing was that the sleeping, sitting, and dressing areas were all on different levels.

The twin bed, directly across from the door, was atop the thickest window ledge Leigh had ever seen. Technically, the sleeping area was a loft, but instead of empty space below, a solid foundation of rough-hewn rock, matching the outside of the castle, lay beneath.

Leigh dropped her duffel in the middle of the room and scrambled up the wooden stairs. The steps were so steep they seemed almost a ladder. Running parallel to the wall, they matched its curve and sounded hollow beneath her feet.

Reaching the top, Leigh found the little balcony provided plenty of room for the bed, a nightstand, and for her to move around without fear of falling off. Even so, the edge of the sill was fitted with a highly polished wooden railing. On the other side of the bed was a beautiful bay window running from floor to ceiling. The heavy curtains were pulled back, leaving only a thin gauze to cut the evening's glare. Looking out, Leigh could see for miles over the wooded countryside.

Descending the stairs to the main floor, Leigh crossed over to the sunken sitting area. This time no barrier stood in place to prevent her walking over the edge. She could either jump down into the three-foot depression or use the small flight of stairs. She chose the more dignified mode knowing full well that, whenever alone in the room, she'd take the direct route of jumping off the ledge.

Sunlight flooded through a rectangular window situated high up the wall at the far end of the sitting area. Making a small hop, she hooked her fingertips over the sill and pulled herself up. Looking out, she could see the driveway disappear into the wood line. She now had her bearings as to the orientation of the room in relation to the rest of the house. This was the same window Myra pointed out to her when they were still outside.

"Wow!" Myra said, still standing in the dressing area. "You did that pull-up like it was nothing."

Ignoring her, Leigh dropped from the window.

To Leigh's right were three stone steps leading into another room. Climbing them, she found herself standing in the bathroom. Another circular room, this one added an inner curved wall, making a circle within a circle, which functioned as a shower stall.

"Cozy, but not cramped," Myra said, having followed her down into the sitting area.

Leigh rushed out of the bathroom and leapt over the three stone stairs, landing on her toes and making a soft hop. She felt a warmth rush through her body that she hadn't felt in over a month. When she was told her parents were murdered, she iced over like the arctic sea. After spending a week locked in that prison of frigid loneliness, she slit her wrists. This was the greatest thaw of her depression since that horrific night.

"I think it's wonderful," she said. "Is this another joke or is this really mine?"

"All yours," Myra answered sweetly.

Over Myra's shoulder, Leigh noticed a solitary portrait hanging on the furthest wall. When she'd first come, she hadn't noticed it because her back had been to the painting. Leigh climbed out of the sitting area and moved to stand in front of it, studying it.

In the picture was the figure of a young boy who looked to be a few years younger than she was. His blond hair dangled in bangs over big, beautiful, blue eyes. The bulk of his tawny locks caressed his shoulders in what, Leigh knew, even for those times, would have been considered unfashionably long. His appearance wasn't disheveled, his clothes were clean and his ivory skin wasn't grubby, but his looks weren't crisp and neat, either.

His features were fine and thin. Delicate, even. Splashed across his cheeks and the bridge of his nose was a light dusting of freckles. Posed as he was, with his lips parted ever so slightly, Leigh could see the youthful hallmark of two adult front teeth bordered by baby teeth on either side. It appeared as if he had been trying to smile for the painter but fell a little short of the mark. The lips were a pale pink and curved up at their edges in a way that denied innocence but didn't quite suggest delinquency.

All boy, Leigh decided.

The longer she looked at the painting, a very different sense for who the boy might have been crept over Leigh. Taken individually, the boy's features were strikingly cute. Collectively, they worked together to make him appear sad. His melancholy mingled with her own and in the deepest corner of her soul Leigh sensed he was a kindred spirit -- someone who knew sorrow.

"That," Myra said, pulling Leigh out of her trance, "is Little Bodie."

"The second ghost in the house?"

"Not at all," Myra chuckled. "Big Bodie and Little Bodie are the same ghost."

Leigh blinked at Myra as she tried to work it out. "Little Bodie is actually Big Bodie? Just in younger form?"

"Exactly," Myra said.

"So how do you know they are the same ghost?"

Myra chuckled. With a voice dripping with mock disdain, she said, "Your ancestors and mine, dear cousin, hired Madam Some-Spooky-Witch to prove we had a ghost living with us. No one was surprised to learn it was Old Man Bodie skulking about the manor.

"It was what the medium had to say about Little Bodie that threw the family for a loop. She announced that in certain places, the ones where he was happiest in life, the soul of Ichabod Pierce manifested itself in his childlike form.

"Well, you can imagine what happened next. The medium wasted no time leaking the story to the press, who milked it for all it was worth. She manipulated the tale in order to launch herself into being one of the most famous mediums in the world. No one had ever heard of such a thing before and she made sure nobody ever forgot she was the one who discovered it. Her memoir is downstairs in the library somewhere. You should read it sometime."

Leigh had no intention of doing that. "So no one has ever seen either of these ghosts?" she asked.

"Not true," Myra objected. "I said *none of us* have seen them. There have been sightings in the past. Big Bodie was seen quite often during World War II and the Cold War. There was even a general who claimed to have had an all-night discussion with him about what could be expected should the U. S. decide to invade Japan. This general attributed his decision to campaign against that plan to Bodie's insights."

"You're making that up," Leigh accused.

Before she could answer, Peg's voice trickled up from below. "Myra? What are you two doing up there? Dinner's getting cold."

"We'd better go down," Myra said. "And no," she grinned at Leigh, "I'm not making any of it up."

Chapter Two

Leigh's mind was spinning with the idea of ghosts as she followed Myra downstairs. If she'd been asked a year ago whether or not she believed in ghosts she'd have said no. If asked if she could picture herself living in a mansion with one of the richest families in the world, she would have laughed. Yet, here she was, feeling confused and uncertain about everything, including ghosts.

The dining room Myra led her to was as ornate and elegant as the rest of the house. White curtains covered the windows and matched the snowy tablecloth too perfectly to be coincidence. The oak table was long enough to seat twelve, but they all sat clustered at one end with Tristin at the head. Leigh eyed the fancy platter of chicken. It looked like it came out of a five-star kitchen, showing no indication of being home cooked. The meal was beautiful to look at, delicious to taste but, to Leigh, it was sterile and unsatisfying.

The cook had prepared the meal with the goal of serving her employer something delicious. That was, after all, her job, but it clashed with Leigh's memories of the meals her parents churned out. They were often over cooked, too salty when Dad made them, but were created as love offerings. Flawed though they were, they tasted so much better. Leigh sat in her offered seat at the Simmons's table and picked at her food out of politeness.

"Not hungry, dear?" asked Peg.

"Sorry, no" Leigh mumbled to her plate. "It's really good, though."

Tristin's knife and fork made delicate tinkling sounds as they scraped across the delicate China. "If there are any dishes you'd like to have, just talk to Jenny. I'm sure she'd be happy to whip up anything you want."

"Jenny's our chef," Myra explained, "and she can cook anything. You name it!"

Leigh tried to picture her mother's meatloaf, smothered in a spicy sauce made out of canned tomato soup, frozen french-fries from a bag, with microwaved peas on the side, sitting on these fancy dishes. She imagined knock-off Coke fizzing in the crystal glasses. If not for the longing pain in her heart, she would have burst out laughing at the absurdity of it all.

"I told Leigh all about the ghosts of Big and Little Bodie," Myra said.

"Myra," Tristin snapped as he set his cutlery on his plate with a clatter. "For the last time, forget about that nonsense. You've wasted enough of your time chasing those phony phantoms and I won't stand for you wasting Leigh's time with it as well."

"But Dad!"

Tristin shot a scathing look at his daughter. His stare was so cold it frightened Leigh to her core.

She thought about her own dad and how he was so strict with his rules and his high expectations; everything anyone would expect from a former Marine turned cop. But he never scared her. Even when he raised his voice, which was seldom, he never came across as threatening. At least not to her.

Myra stared straight back at her father.

Leigh stretched her leg under the table and nudged Myra's foot. Flashing the same proud smile of respect that she'd given to the painting of Cousin Corinne, Leigh let Myra know she'd pushed Tristin far enough on her account.

Myra's lips quivered. Her body began to shake as she fought against it, but her giggles refused to be suppressed. Myra gave up trying and erupted in laughter.

Caught off guard, Tristin's eyes widened in surprise.

"Well, I never," Peg said, scandalized.

Leigh heard herself let out a soft laugh. The suddenness of it frightened her and she clamped her teeth down on it. "It's been a long day for me," she said. "If it's all the same to everyone, I think I'll turn in."

"This early?" Myra asked before adding, "Guess it has been a different kind of day for you. If it's all right with you, can I come up later to check on how you are doing?"

A few hours ago Leigh would have suspected Myra of being afraid she'd do something stupid during the night. The thought occurred to her now but, despite having just met Myra, that notion didn't seem to fit. Myra wasn't worried about anything Leigh might do, but about anything she might want or need.

Leigh's gloom buoyed slightly. "I'd like that."

Leigh excused herself from the table and made her way to the kitchen where Myra had told her the elevator was located. The lift had been installed, according to Myra, when one of the family members in the nineteen-teens could no longer navigate the stairs. Leigh didn't pay much attention to which ancestor Myra said needed the device nor to why they could no longer manage the stairs.

Like everything else, the elevator was an antique, complete with a folding screen to be pulled closed behind her. She pressed the brass button embossed with the number two and flinched as the rickety contraption jerked into motion.

As it rose, so too did Leigh's feelings of loneliness. Opening the elevator's manual door, she raced to her room and up the stairs to the loft. Throwing herself onto the bed, she sobbed until she fell into a fitful sleep.

Sadness and feelings of abandonment bubbled like a stew in Leigh's subconscious. The worst part was how alone she felt. Completely alone. Like no-one-else-existed-in-the-entire-universe alone.

Reaching her room, Leigh left a trail of clothes behind her as she shuffled up the stairs to her bed and huddled beneath her blankets. Despair wracked her sleeping mind, forcing it to churn out ugly nightmares. Trapped in a frightening dream of blackness, she felt as if she was swimming in pancake syrup in an enormous void. All around her lurked looming dark shapes she couldn't keep from bumping into. Some were hard as granite while others were sticky, like singed marshmallow. Some crashed over her like poorly stacked tires, threatening to crush her.

Terrified, she whimpered, tossed, and turned.

In her dream, a soft blue light shone off to one side. Struggling to turn and look at it, the light vanished as soon as she made it around and reappeared in her peripheral vision on the other side.

Timid and shy, a thin voice whispered, "Are you okay?"

Leigh was suddenly freezing. Both in her dream and in her bed, she curled into a ball and shivered to keep warm.

"Are you okay?" the small voice repeated.

Leigh felt as if she were drowning and moaned in horror.

The blue light turned a sickening burnt acid-purple. Like thunder, a deep and angry voice roared, "Are you okay?"

Leigh shot upright into a sitting position. Heart pounding, lungs churning, her skin was covered in goosebumps.

"Leigh?"

Myra was sitting on the edge her bed. "Leigh, are you okay?"

"I...I'm fine. I was dreaming."

"That was a nightmare, not just some dream," Myra said. "Do you want to tell me about it, before you forget it? I always forget my dreams if I don't write them down as soon as I wake up."

"You write down your dreams?"

"I do. Well, I used to. When I was twelve I kept a special dream diary for them. Night after night, I hoped Bodie would talk to me in my dreams. He never did, so I quit writing in the diary. Your dream must have been a doozy!"

"It was! And in it, I kept hearing someone asking if I was okay."

Myra's face looked guilty. "That might have been me. I came up to check on how you were doing. I did knock. I swear I did! I also called through the door, asking if you were okay. I must have asked two or three times before I came in, saw you were having a bad dream and came up here. It had to be my voice you were hearing in your dream. Sorry."

"Don't worry about it," Leigh said. "I was having rotten dreams long before I came here. If anything, you rescued me from a whole night of them."

Myra let out a playful chuckle. "Glad I could help."

Leigh could tell Myra was genuinely glad to offer any help she could. Cousin Myra, she decided, was one of the kindest people she'd ever met.

Cautiously, feeling as if she were taking a huge risk, Leigh asked, "Aren't you ever, I don't know, unhappy?"

"Sure I am," Myra said. "But why would anyone want to stay that way?"

A guilty look spread over Myra's face. "Oh! That was a thoughtless thing to say, wasn't it?"

"No," Leigh said. "It wasn't."

"You might as well know," Myra said, "I have a bad habit of saying what's on my mind before thinking about whose feelings I might hurt. I don't do it to be cruel. It's just that I can't hear how mean I sound until the words are already out."

"I'll be honest with you, too, Myra. Ever since my parents were killed, people have been so careful not to upset me. Treating me like I'm a fragile Christmas ornament. I know they're trying to be nice, but it feels so phony. You have been one of the few to just be themselves. Please don't stop. And I promise I'll always be honest with you."

For the first time since they met, Leigh witnessed Myra at a loss for words.

"So, are you? Okay?" Myra asked.

In keeping with their newly formed pact of honesty Leigh told her, "We both know I'm not," but said it in a tone of teasing irony.

"Gallows humor!" Myra nodded in approval. "I like it."

Leigh laughed. It felt good to have someone with whom she could share a morbid laugh without them getting all sourpussed and telling her that feeling so low wasn't a laughing matter.

"Listen," Leigh said, "I haven't unpacked or anything yet. Want to stick around and help me find places to put my stuff? I mean, after that dream, I'm not going to sleep anytime soon."

"Sure," Myra agreed.

Leigh crossed the room and entered the closet beneath the stairs.

"Ew! It's musty in here!" she groaned.

"Is it? I know Mom ordered the whole place scrubbed top to bottom," Myra said. "I'll tell her to have someone take a look at it tomorrow.

"As long as you're in there, crawl all the way to the front. You'll have to get down on your hands and knees."

"What for?"

"Just do it. Lay on your back and look up at the bottom of the second step."

Despite the odor, the floor in the closet looked clean enough. Leigh stooped and walked as far forward as she could. She turned and laid down with her head under the lower parts of the stairs. Using her shoulder blades to shuttle herself along, she inched under the stairs until her head tapped the first step and she could go no further.

Using the light on her phone, she found what she had been sent to see. Under the second step, inches away from her nose, the name Ichabod was carved into the wood with immaculate letters.

"You've got to be kidding me," Leigh yelled to Myra. "Even in this awkward position his handwriting is better than mine when I'm sitting at a desk!"

"Mine, too," Myra said. "The little brat."

Leigh began inching her way out again. The floorboards rattled beneath her.

"Did you know the floor is loose in there?" Leigh asked once she was back outside the closet.

"No, but the last time I was in there I was, like, thirteen. I may have noticed and forgotten."

"You've been ghost crazy for a long time, haven't you?"

"Ever since I found out about them. Now it's all fun and games, but when I was little, I was obsessed. It drove my parents nuts. Like you saw at dinner, it still makes them goofy. I think that's why I like to go on about it. It's so much fun to pull their chains."

"Especially our dads! I used to tell mine I was dating..."

The memory hurt and Leigh fell silent.

"It's okay, Leigh. You don't have to talk about your family if you don't want to."

"I *do* want to. And I don't. It's just that, when I do, I feel a weird unhappy kind of happy."

Myra smiled. "That was a poetic way of putting it. Still, if you're not ready, I'm not going to push."

"I was going to say," Leigh began again, "that, well, you know Dad was a cop, right?"

"Yeah!"

"So, my school wasn't the greatest, and kids there would get into trouble all the time. Whenever one of the boys got hauled in by the police, I'd ask Dad for details, telling him the kid was my boyfriend. Dad would flip out!"

"Oh! You are awful. So, what did he do when your real boyfriend came around?"

Leigh gathered the split ends of the hair dangling in front of her eyes into her hands and studied them. "I haven't had a boyfriend yet."

"Seriously? You're beautiful. How can you not have had a boyfriend?"

Leigh felt the heat of her face turning pink. Myra wasn't being kind. She was speaking her mind again. It made Leigh uncomfortable. "Never felt the need, I guess."

Pushing the focus onto Myra, she asked, "What about you?"

"Boyfriends? A fair few, but nothing serious. I was doing research, mostly."

Leigh's nose crinkled. "Research?"

"Yeah. The first time I kissed a boy I was about your age. It sounds awful, but I wasn't all that into him. I mean I was but...wasn't. You know? Anyway, I wanted to see what it was like. What all the fuss was about.

"The second boy I kissed was to find out if different guys kiss in different ways. They do, in case you are wondering."

Leigh shared in a scandalous laugh.

"Well I had to make sure that second kiss wasn't a fluke or anything, so there had to be a third, right?"

"And I'm guessing a fourth and maybe even a fifth," Leigh snarked.

"Hey," Myra objected, "I like kissing, okay?"

She jabbed a playful finger at Leigh, "Just kissing!"

"I wasn't suggesting otherwise!" Leigh laughed.

The more Leigh talked to Myra the more she forgot that she was supposed to be in despair. Hours later, with moonlight seeping through the windows, Myra fell asleep on the couch while Leigh moved back up to the bed.

The afternoon sun beaming through her window woke Leigh. She blinked at the clock beside her bed and was surprised to see it was past two o'clock. Myra was gone. Leigh lounged for another twenty minutes before easing herself up and moving toward the shower. Last night's sleep was the best she'd had in a long time. She felt refreshed and, while not looking forward to the day, she wasn't dreading it either.

A wicked thought made her stop halfway across the room. Not giving herself a chance to change her mind, she ran toward the ledge separating the sitting area from the rest of the room and jumped off. Landing with a thud that sent pain shooting into the soles of her feet in no way made her regret her decision.

Leigh's door flew open.

"What on earth was that?" Peg asked.

"What was what?" Leigh asked, whipping around and looking guilty.

"You jumped off the ledge, didn't you?"

"Who? Me?"

Peg smiled and wagged a scolding finger, but was clearly not mad. "Yes, you. Myra used to do the same thing. But she was a good deal younger than you are now. You should know better."

"Heard the thump," Myra said as she came into the room behind her mother, her face beaming with pride. "Thought I'd better come see if there were any broken bones."

"You both heard that?" Leigh asked.

"Well, I was on my way up anyway, so it's not like I was terribly far from your room. It is after two you know," Peg explained. "I wanted to check on you."

"And I was downstairs about to go for a walk," Myra said. "I should have warned you, there's something about that floor. If you jump hard enough, the entire house rattles."

"What the devil is going on up there?" Tristin's voice boomed from far below. "I was on the phone with our New York office."

"Nothing, dear," Peg called down, grinning at Leigh and Myra. "Us girls got a little rambunctious up here."

"I'm expecting a call from our Panamanian shipyard at any moment," Tristin shouted back. "Please don't bring the whole place crashing down around my ears while I'm on the phone."

"Thanks, Mom," Myra said with a grin.

"Yeah. Thanks Peg," Leigh said. "Sorry I disturbed everyone."

"Nonsense!" pooh-poohed Peg. "You live here now. We'll just have to get used to the occasional rumble.

"But it might be best," she went on, "to wait until you know your Uncle Tristin is out of the house before leaping off that ledge again."

"I'll remember that. Thanks again!"

"Why don't you get dressed and join me on my walk?" Myra suggested. "I can show you around the grounds and we'll be out of Dad's way."

"So where are we going?" Leigh asked when she joined Myra outside the front door.

"I thought I'd take you to the river," Myra said. "It's one of my favorite places."

They headed off across the lawn until they reached the point where the manicured grass ended and dense forest began. With expert familiarity, Myra led the way to a well-worn trail. It twisted and turned, but eventually wound away from the house and downhill.

Leigh could hear the river before she saw it. The swift moving water looked deep and dangerous in the middle but far tamer near the shoreline. Countless trees were growing several feet away from the bank. One stood out from the others by being the closest tree to the water and by marking the point where the trail ended at the river's edge.

It had a great fat trunk that angled away from the bank and over the water. Seeing where the bark was worn smooth, Leigh imagined countless centuries of bare feet climbing up into the tree's branches and jumping off into the water.

Myra sat on the sandy ground beneath the tree, stretching her legs out in front of her. Tilting her head back, she inhaled the rich earthy air deep in through her nose. Her mouth opened and she let the air in her lungs empty with a whoosh, matching the sounds of rustling leaves overhead. Leigh envied how peaceful her cousin seemed to be. She sank onto the sand beside Myra and tried to let some of her cousin's contentment seep into her.

"Mom and Dad hate me coming down here," Myra said at last.

Leigh flicked a pebble into the stream. "Why? It's so calm here."

Myra pointed to the tree overhanging the river. "That tree nearly killed me."

Leigh shot Myra a shocked look. "What? Okay, you can't say something like that without telling the whole story, you know that, right?"

"I was much younger than you," Myra said. "Ten maybe? Back then, I went skinny-dipping down here every chance I got."

Leigh scoffed at the idea.

"Don't look so shocked," Myra teased. "You'll do it at some point. I guarantee it."

Leigh's nose wrinkled and her lip curled nastily, "Not flipping likely."

Myra chuckled. "We'll see. Anyway, I came down here to swim and climbed that tree to jump into the water."

She pointed to the highest branch. Her voice took on a somber tone as if she were reliving the moment as she was describing it. "Walking out on that limb, I slipped and banged my head before I fell into the water. I mean I cracked my noggin good. I don't even remember hitting the water. I was already out cold."

Leigh's heart skipped a beat. "Don't take this the wrong way, but how did you not drown?"

"I have no idea. The next thing I remember was waking up in my bed three days later with my head bandaged like an Egyptian mummy."

"No!" Leigh shouted, "You can't skip the middle like that. What happened?"

"Don't have a stroke," Myra teased. "I don't know what happened. Neither does anybody else. I know I was down here, naked as the day I was born, then, so I'm told, Dad finds me outside the doors leading to the garden, dressed in my clothes, with blood flowing out of my head."

"Maybe you were so out of it you don't remember walking back on your own," Leigh suggested.

"Doctors said that was impossible. I'd have died half way back."

"Somebody must have carried you up to the house then. Who?"

"I told you, we don't know. Here's the weird bit..."

"Because up to this point, this story hasn't been creepy enough?" Leigh asked.

"Just listen. So, while I'm lying in bed unconscious, Dad hires people to start investigating. They get down here and there's blood all over the limb." Myra pointed to the branch again.

"There was blood all over my clothes and on the doorstep where I ended up. There was blood on the trunk and the sand beneath it. Thing is, no one found so much as a drop of blood between the river and the house."

Leigh's face scrunched in thought. "That's not possible. Even if you were carried, there would have been some drops of blood. I mean, heads bleed more than other parts of the body. Something to do with there being more blood vessels."

"Well there's a fun fact," Myra said in mock revulsion.

"Point is," Leigh groaned, "there should have been something."

"Well, there wasn't."

"So, what do you think happened?" Leigh asked as if challenged.

"I used to think Little Bodie carried me back. It's rumored he loved swimming in the river. Now? I suppose somebody was trespassing on the grounds and pulled a Good Samaritan Act, but didn't want to get busted for whatever they were up to."

Leigh pulled her legs tight against her chest and pressed her chin into the crease formed by her knees. "Maybe."

Myra's cell phone buzzed in her jeans' back pocket. Leaning on her side, she slid it into her hand and said, "Has to be."

Myra read her text message. "It's Dad. He wants us back at the house ASAP."

"Why?" Leigh asked.

Myra pushed to her feet and dusted sand off her rear before offering her hand to Leigh. "Something you need to know about Dad. He runs the biggest shipping company in the world. He gives orders, not explanations."

"Nice," Leigh said as she allowed herself to be pulled to her feet.

"Oh, don't get me wrong. He's super awesome, kind and sweet -- lets mom and me walk all over him most of the time. A great dad! But when he's serious he's all business."

Chapter Three

They walked back through the forest without speaking. The silence of the woods made it feel like a sacred place demanding a reverence that even the sounds of their voices would desecrate. Silence was usually a dangerous thing for Leigh. It allowed her mind too much free space -- space she filled with thoughts of how alone she felt and ways she could put a permanent end to that loneliness.

This quiet was different. Her mind was just as empty, but it felt natural, like it was how it was supposed to be in a place like this. The void was not filling with anything toxic.

Alternating patches of sun and shade spilled over her face. She felt the breeze caressing her hair. She felt alive.

Clearing the tree line, she saw a familiar, midnight blue, nineteen-sixty-nine Chevrolet Camaro convertible parked in front of the house.

"Ty!" she screamed out, breaking into a run.

"Who?" Myra called after her.

"Tyrone Milbank. One of my dad's friends. He's a cop."

Leigh burst into the house. Assuming Ty was here on business, she headed straight for Tristin's home office. Without bothering to knock, she pushed open the door and bolted inside.

Tristin jumped to his feet. "Leigh! You can't just barge into my office!"

She ignored him and bounded over to Ty, wrapping her arms around him.

"It's so good to see you!" she said.

"Good to see you, too. How's life here treating you?"

"So far so good. Tristin and Peg have been great. And Cousin Myra is just the best."

"Well, you do look a whole lot better since the last time I saw you."

Leigh felt her skin flush and tussled her long bangs with her fingertips to hide her eyes. The last time Ty saw her, she was in a psychiatric hospital drugged out of her skull on anti-depressants and sedatives and was sporting bandages on both her wrists, covering the gashes she made in them. It would be impossible to look worse.

Leigh felt deeply ashamed of herself and wanted to flee but she stayed, forcing an embarrassed smile to appear on her face. "So, what brings you all the way out here?"

Ty shifted on his feet. "I wanted to ask you a few questions. If you feel up to it. No pressure."

"About Mom and Dad?"

"Yeah, sweetie. About your parents. You good with that?"

"I guess so."

"Good girl."

Ty cast an unwelcoming glance in Tristin's direction. Leigh's look was far less subtle. They both wanted him out of the room.

"Oh! Eh-hem. Well," Tristin stammered, "Detective Milbank, I understand that you have a history with the family. With Leigh. And, if this were a personal visit, which you are welcome to make as often and whenever you like," he added in a flustered rush, "I wouldn't hesitate to give you as much privacy as you'd like."

Leigh watched him as he calculated very carefully what he was going to say. "On the other hand, as I understand it, this is a professional interview and, since we are Leigh's guardians..."

Ty waved away the rest of whatever Tristin was about to say. "Perfectly understandable, Mr. Simmons. Matter of fact, I'm encouraged that you take your role as guardian so seriously. Of course you are welcome to stay, Leigh being a minor and all."

Leigh was not happy about the situation. Not having a voice in the matter filled her with resentment. But the adults had spoken and, as much as she hated it, her lot as a kid was to lump it.

"Here," Ty said as if sensing her fury, "why don't we sit down?"

Leigh took a seat on the couch Ty gestured to. He moved to sit beside her while Tristin took the armchair across from them. Leigh mused, *The last time a roomful of adults showed me this much consideration was the day they told me my parents were murdered.*

Ty's voice pulled her out of her memories. "Leigh? I want you to think back. Take as much time as you need. Think about any conversations you might have overheard between your mom and dad. Or maybe on the phone. Try to remember if you ever saw your dad writing things down."

Leigh narrowed her eyes as if in deep concentration. In reality she was choking down the horror she felt and that was making it impossible for her to speak. She was a cop's daughter. She knew the ropes. If Ty was coming to her asking for eavesdropped nuggets of information, that could only mean they've got nothing else to go on. No evidence. No leads. *If they're coming to me looking for clues, they're desperate.*

"I can't think of anything, Ty. But you knew Dad. If it weren't for the fact that he left every morning wearing a badge and a gun, I'd have never known he was a policeman." She shrugged. "That's just how it was, you know?"

"I do know. I keep my boys in the dark, too."

"Maybe he talked about the job with Mom," she said meekly, staring at her shoes, "but never when I was around."

"As it should be, sweetheart." Ty patted her knee. "As it should be." He sighed.

"And what about you, Mr. Simmons? Can you think of any reason why the murders took place at your shipyards?"

"What!" Leigh shouted.

"Detective Milbank!" snapped Tristin. "That was both unprofessional and insensitive of you!"

Ty looked as if he'd been slapped across the cheek. "I thought you knew," he said to Leigh.

"I knew they were killed down at the docks!"

She turned on Tristin. "Nobody said they were *your* docks."

Leigh let out a loud growl of frustration. "Nobody wants to share any details with me."

She clenched her teeth, forcing herself to settle down. Tugging at the cuffs of her hoodie she said softly, "I guess there are obvious reasons for that. But still...it's frustrating."

"Well, I'm sorry I blurted it out like that. It's just a routine question, Leigh. Simmons-Pierce Shipping owns over eighty percent of the docks. It's impossible for much of anything to happen there that doesn't go down on their property. We're all pretty sure it's just a coincidence."

Leigh nodded. "I understand."

The logic in Ty's reasoning didn't make the news any easier to take.

"How'd I end up here?" she asked, surprising herself that she said it aloud.

"I'm sorry?" Ty asked.

"You're family," Tristin said.

"I know that now, but I didn't know we were family before Mom and Dad were killed. Nothing personal, Tristin, but I doubt you knew we were part of the family before then, either. So, I mean, how did you find out about me?"

"As Simmons-Pierce conducted its own investigation into what happened, it was discovered we were related. On your mother's side," Tristin explained. "After talking to Peg about it, we decided to offer to become your guardians."

Ty turned to look at Tristin. "How'd you find that out?"

"After the bodies...I'm sorry Leigh. It was cruel of me to say it like that...after Leigh's parents were discovered, our security branch began a special investigation to look into the matter. We asked all employees to come in on their day off, offering triple overtime, so we could interview each and every person who was working the shifts twenty-four hours before and after they were discovered. Unfortunately, we didn't learn anything new.

"What we *did* find out was that Leigh's mother left a single document with an attorney who often represents our interests but is not on staff. In that letter, Leigh's mother traced the connection between her family and ours."

Tristin faced Leigh. "I set some people to work on it and confirmed the fact that your mother and I, and therefore you, Leigh, are distant cousins."

Ty bristled. "Why weren't the police notified of these interviews?"

"What for? No new information came to light."

"That's for us to decide," Ty said in a harsh tone. "I want access to the transcripts of those interviews as well as any other documentation you have."

"I'll have the interviews waiting for you this afternoon, at our offices. As for any other documents, they will have to be gone over by our legal team first. I'll let you know when they are ready. It could take several weeks. And we will need the appropriate court orders."

"Why the obstruction?" Ty asked.

Leigh thought she heard the tones of accusation or suspicion in his voice. Tristin just have heard it, too, because he fidgeted in his seat before answering.

"Please understand, Officer Milbank," Tristin said, "Simmons-Pierce is a multi-billion-dollar company. Our clients include some of the wealthiest of individuals as well as nations, including our own. None of them would be comfortable with our turning over sensitive data without following proper procedure. The potential for legal action against us is far too great a risk, no matter how worthy the cause. I promise, if you dot so much as half the I's and cross a third of the T's, you'll find Simmons-Pierce more than willing to provide anything you wish to review."

Ty continued to pry while Tristin deflected his efforts. Leigh thought they'd forgotten about her and that Ty would never leave. She felt lousy over wishing him away. The fact that she liked Ty and, more importantly, her dad liked him, ate at her. All she could do was bunch the cuffs of her hoodie into her fists and ride it out until Tristin and Ty concluded their business.

"Can I have a few moments to visit with Leigh before I go?" Ty finally asked.

Tristin gave him a dubious look.

"I promise," Ty said, "I'll leave the badge in my pocket. Purely a visit from a friend of the family."

"That'll be fine," Tristin chuckled as if embarrassed by his hesitation.

"Leigh?" Ty asked, "Want to show me around a bit?"

"If you want," Leigh said with no enthusiasm.

She led him outside and into the gardens.

"So, what's it like here?" he asked, a lilt of disbelief ringing in his voice.

"It's not like some kind of fairytale, if that's what you're thinking," she said.

"I bet not. Still, they treating you OK?"

"Oh, yeah. Everyone's great. Especially Myra."

"Myra. She's the daughter, right?"

"Yeah. She's sweet."

"Well, I'm glad you made a friend," Ty said.

They walked together in silence. Leigh assumed Ty's lack of conversation was because he had nothing more to say, confirming her suspicions that the police hit a dead-end in their investigation.

Ty finally said, "It's going to take time for you to get used to life without your mom and dad in it."

"I know," Leigh said feeling tired. This was not a topic she wanted to discuss, but it seemed to her everyone else did.

"You *don't* know," Ty insisted. "Just like you don't know I had a daughter."

Leigh stopped and stared at him.

"Yeah," Ty said. "She'd be about your age. Died when she was two days, five hours, and forty-two minutes old. Something called anencephaly, if you're interested in the technical stuff."

"I'm...I'm sorry," Leigh said, wondering why he was telling her this.

"Thing is," he said ignoring Leigh's apology, "I think of her every day. She isn't here, but I still think of her. The world I have to live in is a world where she isn't. I've had to accept that and to learn how to live in that world. How to be happy in that world."

Leigh dug the toe of her sneaker into the grass. "How'd you do it?"

"Time, mostly. Minute-by-minute till I could manage day-by-day. People helped, too. Like my wife and your mom and dad. I let them in and they helped me out."

"I know I can count on you, Ty," Leigh said.

"It isn't a competition, Leigh," Ty said in a chuckle. "I don't care if it's me, Myra, or the gardener. I assume, place like this, there's a gardener?"

Leigh shrugged and came close to smiling.

"Point is," Ty went on, "find the right ones to let in. The ones that fit you, like your folks fit me 'cause them scars on your wrists? They aren't about what you lost. They're about what you haven't found."

"And what's that?" Leigh whispered, wishing he'd say what he had to say then shut up.

"Yourself. Your place in this world. Most importantly, people to share the good and the crap with. People who fit. Most young people slide into that over time. You, baby girl? You got thrown into the deep end with no warning. Sucks, but there it is. Thing is, it isn't being chucked into the pool that matters. It's whether you choose to swim or drown."

Leigh needed to mull that over.

"When you coming back?" she asked.

"Soon as I can. I promise."

"Ty, promise me something else?"

"What's that?"

"That you'll keep me up to date on how the investigation is going. That you won't try to protect me from bad news. No matter how bad?"

He looked at her through squinty eyes. "Don't ask for much, do you?"

She stuck her pinkie out in his direction. "The people who fit me are the ones who don't try to protect me. They're the ones who help me deal. To cope."

Ty hooked his little finger around hers. "Promise."

Long past the point in the drive where a curve took Ty's blue Camaro behind the tree line, Leigh stood in the pea gravel in front of the house staring after it. She was overwhelmed by all he'd said. Information kept churning in her mind. As soon as she shook off one dreadful fact, another one circled around on a carousel of misery.

Knowing her parents' killers were going to get away with murder clawed at her mercilessly. There would be no closure. No justice. Their deaths were just another one of those awful things you hear about on the evening news. Tragic. Pointless. But still ahead, weather and sports. Life goes on. Unless, of course, it didn't.

The people she was living with owned the property where her parents were killed. She was surrounded by more comfort and wealth than she ever could have dreamed of, and all for the price of her parents' lives. It somehow felt dishonest. She didn't choose it, but it still felt gross.

With slow labored steps, Leigh made her way to her room. Her feet felt like wooden logs as she labored to lift them to the next step on the spiral staircase. She felt sick, but not the kind that made her want to throw up. Hers was an illness of the heart.

Filled with nothing but loneliness and emptiness, she convinced herself she did something wrong, that everything was her fault. The worst part was the guilt she felt for not wanting to be alive, knowing that's the one thing her parents would want for her.

Leigh made it to her room and shut the door behind her without making a sound. Not strong enough to reach her bed, she took three steps inside before falling to the floor in a tearful heap. She bit into her arm to stifle her sobs lest Myra, the only one sensible and caring enough to come check on her, should hear.

Outside, the sounds of an approaching storm forced their way through the window's glass. Their muffled moans sounded like a love song sung to the immaculate hedges as they swayed like drunken dancers. Lifting her head to look out the huge window, she saw blue-green clouds had collected in the sky like foam in a pot of noodles about to boil over. The scene outside was as threatening and tumultuous as she felt inside.

Overwhelmed with fatigue, Leigh used the last of her energy to crawl up into the loft and lay on her mattress. She pulled her quilt over her head. If she couldn't be dead, she could at least escape into the next best thing, the nightmare-riddled mini-death of sleep.

Chapter Four

Leigh shot up in bed, her heart thumping hard against her ribs. On the other side of her massive window lightning flashed like a strobe light. Thunder roared, imitating cannons on a battlefield. Between the blinding flashes and deafening booms, pitch black consumed the night and rain pelted the glass sending sheets of water cascading down.

Her room burst white in a bright flash. The thunderclap that followed shook the gargantuan house to its foundations. Little Bodie's portrait rattled on the wall. On her nightstand, the framed photo of her parents jumped a full inch, threatening to fall off. Seconds later the already heavy rain turned torrential.

Having nothing but the window between her and tempest terrified Leigh, but the power of the storm kept her a mesmerized prisoner. She watched in horrified fascination as the trees at the far end of the lawn whipped and bowed in protest to the howling wind. Somewhere in that black chaos Leigh heard one lose the fight, giving a high-pitched crack as though shrieking in pain. The low booming thunder rumbled on in complete indifference.

The room exploded with light again and its accompanying blast vibrated the full-length window panes with so much violence Leigh thought they were going to shatter. Fear jolted her into action. Throwing her pillow and heavy quilt over the banister, she scrambled down to drag them over to the couch where the window was smaller and she was farther away from it. If she weren't an orphan, she'd have sprinted to the safety of her parents' bed, shivering against them like a three-year-old.

Lightning and thunder shattered the darkness the very instant she had that thought. Leigh threw the blanket over her head and cowered on the couch. The idea of sprinting down to Myra's room and jumping beneath her covers flashed in her mind with as much force as the weather blustering outside. As badly as she wanted to, she forced herself to dismiss the idea as ridiculous.

Another crash reverberated through the house. Leigh's door flew open. With a start, Leigh bounded off the couch. In the flash of another lightning bolt she saw Myra standing in her doorway.

"Oh, um, hi," Myra said inching her way into the room. "I wanted to check on you. You know. Make sure you were okay with the storm and all."

Myra tacked on a nervous laugh at the end of her sentence.

"I'm all right," Leigh lied.

Light and sound shook the room yet again. Leigh whirled around to look out the window. Myra rushed down the stairs to stand beside her.

"Are you sure? I could hang out with you, I mean, if you'd like."

Leigh looked at her, calling her bluff.

"Okay! You got me. Can I hang out with you? Please!"

"Of course you can," Leigh said. "Anytime you want."

Myra sat down on the couch and helped herself to one end of Leigh's blanket. "I'm not usually afraid of storms. It's just that, the way this one makes the house rattle every time the thunder hits. It's unnerving."

Leigh slid under the opposite end of the blanket. "I feel the same way. Does it happen often?"

"I can't remember one this bad," Myra said. "I mean, we've had big storms before, but the whole house never shook."

"Do you ever get, I don't know, like tornadoes, here?"

"Never," Myra reassured her. "We don't even get tornado warnings, except maybe once every three or four years."

A cold draft rolled through the room bringing with it a low moaning sound. When Myra entered, she'd left Leigh's door open. It slammed shut.

Lightning bolted across the skies outside. Seconds after, the house shuddered with thunder.

Leigh and Myra ducked their heads beneath the blanket.

Popping their heads out, Leigh's ears and cheeks pricked with the cold.

"That's weird," Myra said.

"What's weird," Leigh told her, "is that I can see your breath as you talk."

"That's what I'm talking about. It wasn't this cold a second ago."

"I wonder if a window broke somewhere," Myra said. "That would explain the draft."

A scream from downstairs tore through the house.

"What was that?" Myra shrieked.

"I've no idea," shouted Leigh, already on her feet and moving to the door.

Expecting the door to fly open at her first yank, it stood firm. Her shoulder jarred in its socket.

Lightning flashed and thunder roared. Another frantic cry filled the air.

Using both hands, Leigh pulled with all her might, but the door refused to yield. She was trapped.

Steam left her mouth as she panted out her breaths. A dull ache stabbed in her side while her heart fluttered with unbelievable speed.

"What is wrong with this stupid door!" Leigh shouted, yanking and tugging furiously.

Myra ran up beside her. "The wood must have swelled from all the moisture in the air."

Placing her hands over Leigh's, both girls gave a mighty heave against the door. Failing, they tried again. On their third attempt the door ripped open, sending both girls sprawling to the floor, one on top of the other.

Scrambling to her feet, Leigh shoved her hand down to lift Myra. "Let's go!"

Leigh and Myra raced down the twisting stairs, their bare feet thudding against the steps. Making as much noise as the thunder outside, they bounded through the hallway, Myra shouting for her mom and dad the whole way. The main staircase leading to the front door was wide enough for them to hurtle along side-by-side.

Peg was standing in the doorway of Tristin's office.

She grabbed Leigh and Myra yelling, "You can't go inside! The window has shattered and a whirlwind has blown in!"

Peering over Peg's shoulder, Leigh saw a tempest raging in the office. Papers were flying madly. Heavy books were being blown off shelves. Pens and knickknacks sailed through the air. Furniture was rocking and sliding. The chaos was terrifying to witness.

"Where's Dad?" screamed Myra.

"He went in to see if there was anything he could do," Peg shouted over the devastation.

Leigh peered around Peg. Tristin was standing in the middle of the chaos being pelted by debris.

"I see him!" she shouted. "He's all turned around."

Pushing away from Peg with all her might, she lunged into the maelstrom.

Behind her, Peg and Myra screamed for her to come back.

Trash battered Leigh's face. Glass cut into the soles of her bare feet. Ducking her head, she drove forward to where Tristin stood in the center of the room being pummeled with debris. Leigh reached out her arm and grabbed him by his sleeve to drag him from the room. As soon as she made contact with the cloth of his shirt, a torturous cold gripped Leigh at the core of her being.

Everything came to a halt. Heavier objects fell crashing to the floor while papers floated down in see-saw motions. The sudden quiet was unnerving. The storm outside moved on as well, leaving behind a gentle sprinkle.

The arctic hand that seemed to hold Leigh's soul in its iron grip released her. Like everything else in the room, she dropped to the floor.

"Daddy! Leigh!" Myra screamed.

"Tristin? Are you all right?" Peg shouted.

"I'm...I'm OK. I think," he stammered.

"Pick Leigh up and the two of you get out of there!" Peg demanded.

Dazed, Leigh felt herself being scooped into Tristin's arms and carried out of the office. Peg snapped the doors closed behind them as Tristin lowered Leigh onto the steps of the main staircase.

Myra pounded her fists against the banister. "Leigh! What were you thinking, rushing into the storm like that?"

Leigh turned her head to face Myra. Exhausted, she managed to sigh, "No child should lose a parent. Not ever," before passing out.

Leigh's eyes fluttered open again and were assaulted by pink, white and chocolate striped wallpaper brightly reflecting the morning's light. Turning her head, she caught sight of Myra sitting in a wicker bowl chair across the room reading a gossip magazine, unaware she was awake.

"I've died and gone to Hell, haven't I?" Leigh croaked.

Dropping her magazine to the floor Myra darted to her bedside. "Why would you say such a thing?"

"Because, whenever I picture Hell in my mind, it's decorated in this wallpaper."

Myra folded her arms across her body and sucked her teeth. "Your first visit to my room, and that's all you have to say?"

Leigh turned her head and checked out the room. It looked more like a small European apartment than a teen girl's bedroom. The furniture was, unlike the rest of the house, modern and fresh. Myra's unique personality reflected off every inch of it, except the wallpaper.

Drawing back her upper lip in derision Leigh snarked, "Well, yeah!"

Leigh watched as Myra clamped her lips between her teeth to keep from busting out laughing. Being too much to take, Leigh sputtered out a chuckle. Myra lost control and belted out laughter.

"So, how's your dad?" Leigh asked.

"He's fine. Well, he was. He's downstairs with Mom, cleaning up the mess. I got myself banished when I put forward the theory that Big Bodie was throwing a tantrum over something."

"You are terrible," Leigh said through a chortle.

"Yeah, I am. How about you? How do you feel?"

"I'm fine. Don't know why I passed out."

Myra sat on the edge of the bed and began ironing the blanket laying over Leigh with her palms. "That was very brave of you, rushing in like that."

"I don't think so. Brave would have been if I thought about it first. I didn't. I just ran in."

Myra smiled at her. "And you don't see how that makes it an even braver thing to have done?"

Leigh's face became warm. She adjusted herself against the pillow. "Why don't we go down and help with the clean-up?" she said.

"Are you sure you're up to it?"

"Anything's better than sitting here looking at this wallpaper."

Myra eased herself off the bed and offered her hand. Leigh gingerly put her feet on the floor and, with Myra's help, straightened her legs. Pain shot across the bottoms of her feet as if she stepped on an electric hot plate.

"Why not wait till later?" Myra suggested.

Hurting too much to say anything, Leigh shook her head and tried again. Myra hovered close until Leigh found her balance.

"There," Leigh breathed out, her taught shoulders relaxing. "I think I've got it now. I'll go and you follow. Sound good?"

Despite Leigh's best efforts, she couldn't keep from walking with short stumpy steps. The cuts on the bottoms of her feet weren't severe, but they were painful. Leigh set the pace and every time she winced, she heard Myra suck in a sympathetic breath.

When they appeared in the study's doorway, Peg's eyes bloomed with concern. "What on earth are you doing out of bed?"

"I wanted to help," Leigh said. "I can't stand lying there knowing everyone else is working."

"Good girl," Tristin said. "How about you sit at the desk and see if you can sort out that disaster."

He turned on Myra. "As for you, young lady. One word out of you about flipping ghosts and you'll be in your room until Christmas dinner. Understood?"

Leigh noticed the tone he was using because, for the first time since arriving at the manor, Myra deferred to him without so much as a hint of sass. Feeling awkward over the exchange between Tristin and Myra, Leigh hobbled to the desk, avoiding making eye contact with them both.

Using her forearm like an earth-mover, Leigh plowed smaller items to the edges of the desk. Lifting the small lamp and a fancy two pen stand off the floor, she returned them to their rightful places. Stumping around to the chair, she fell into it more than sat.

Adjusting the pen holder's location on the desk, Leigh spied a corner of a sticky-note caught beneath it. Flipping it over, she found it was a thin slip of paper intentionally taped to the bottom. Written on it was a curious collection of letters and numbers. Recognizing the scrawl as a safe's combination, she tossed surreptitious glances about the room looking for the safe, itself.

Like the rest the house, an ample number of paintings usually plastered the walls of Tristin's office. However, in the aftermath of the storm, they were now either knocked to the floor or hung askew. If a safe were concealed behind any one of them it'd be visible. Built in bookcases ran from floor to ceiling. Dozens of books lay strewn across the wooden floor, giving her clear sight to most of the shelves' back panels. They looked uniform and solid.

She had no idea where the safe might be.

Tristin dropped a heavy box of jumbled papers onto the desk.

Leigh's heart thumped as she snapped her head back, flinching away from the noise.

"You okay?" Tristin asked. "Your mind seems to be a thousand miles away."

She blinked up at him, her guilt making her believe Tristin knew what she'd been doing. Studying his face she saw more concern in his eyes than distrust or accusation.

In a breath of relief she said, "I'm fine. I was just trying to remember what made me lose consciousness."

He smiled at her. "There's no way to know. It must have been a horrifying experience. You were incredibly brave. I suspect that, once the danger passed, you were simply wiped out, nothing more."

His intent to reassure her was clear enough, but Leigh felt she'd just been called emotionally weak. Her cheeks burned.

"Don't worry too much about trying to put these documents back in order," Tristin said sliding the box he laid on the desk toward her. "I'll have somebody come by and do that tomorrow. But, if you would, maybe sort them by type, you know, spreadsheets in one stack, letters in another. And these sticky-notes? You can line them up one on top of the other along the edge of the desk," he said pressing the gummy strip of one in the top corner. "That'd be a great help."

"No problem," Leigh said, trying to hide how boring she found the task, but it had to be done.

If she was going to live here, her sense of duty told her she should chip in without complaining. At least that's what her mom always told her when she griped about doing chores. Thinking about her mom and dad made her heart ache and she threw herself into the job at hand to try to make her mind stop ruminating over how badly she missed them.

"How's it coming?" Tristin asked after what seemed like hours.

"Almost done. I was able to put a couple of reports together because they had the same title on every page. Most of them I sort of lumped together in a stack."

"Fantastic," Tristin said. "Couldn't ask for more."

Leigh bit her lip, staring at a single sticky-note she kept separate from the others. "Um, Uncle Tristin?"

Her use of the word Uncle, along with her tremulous voice made Tristin stop what he was doing and cross the room to stand beside her.

"I wanted to ask about this note. It's dated July twenty-second of this year. And beneath the date it says thirty-eight thousand dollars. It's just that, well, the twenty-second of July was the day my parents were killed."

Myra and Peg froze. They stared at her. Leigh could tell her face burned red as a pomegranate. She kept her eyes glued to the desktop. It took all the nerve she could muster to ask about the scrap of paper. She had none left to fend off their shocked expressions.

"Oh!" stammered Tristin. "I see."

Myra and Peg turned their focus onto him.

"Daddy?" Myra prodded.

Tristin faced Myra. "A shipping container out of Bahrain," he explained turning back to look at Leigh. "That's in the middle east. It came in and certain contents were sent on to the local client. That morning, the twenty-second, the client reported to us that part of the shipment was missing.

"Bahrain is famous for their pearls. A box that was supposed to contain thirty-eight thousand dollars' worth of pearls wasn't in the container, but it was on the shipping list."

"Does Ty know about it?" Leigh asked.

"I doubt it. It's unrelated. The container's security seals were set before it left Bahrain. They were inspected and signed off as being still intact when the container was delivered to the local client. Either the pearls never got put inside the container or they were taken out by the client here and were misplaced."

Tristin's voice held the same tone as when he admonished Myra not to mention ghosts. Leigh knew he was done discussing the matter, but she was a long way from letting it go. Pearls going missing on the same night that her parents were killed was too much of a coincidence for her liking. The first chance she had, she would share that information with Ty.

Keeping quiet, she went back to making herself useful in the clean-up. As she worked, she read as much as she could of all the papers, ledgers, receipts, and notes being piled up on the desk without being too obvious. None of it made much sense to her aside from dollar amounts that staggered her imagination. Simmons-Pierce Shipping was worth billions.

The crashing sound of Peg tipping a dustpan of debris into a large trashcan made Leigh jump.

"That's the fourth pass I've made with the broom and I'm still picking up trash," she exclaimed.

"The floor looks great, Peg," Tristin said. "Though why you didn't get someone in to do it for you is beyond me."

"Our mess. Our problem," Peg answered. "Besides, there are too many sensitive documents lying about."

"That's why I asked Marcus Figueroa to come out tomorrow. He can sort all this mess out better than I can."

"Maybe Leigh and I can go shopping or something," Myra groaned.

"What is it with you and Marcus?" Peg asked.

"He's such a phony," Myra exclaimed.

"He is not," said Tristan, pique ringing out loud and clear in his voice. "Unless you consider being interested in the good of the company being 'phony'."

"Who's Marcus Figueroa?" Leigh asked.

Chapter Five

The next morning, Leigh woke to the sound of a helicopter landing on the lawn. Gazing out the window beside her bed, she watched the chopper settle onto the grass as if it were a scene from a movie. It was so surreal that it made her wonder if she were still asleep, dreaming it all up.

The well-dressed pilot clambered out of his machine. His roguishly long hair, though not long enough to be seen as a statement of defiance, fluttered in the rotor's wake.

Unlike the movies, Marcus Figueroa, for that is who Leigh assumed the man was, walked tall and proud, unconcerned about the slowing spinning blade over his head. Crossing the lush lawn, he shook hands with Tristin before giving Peg a kiss on either cheek. Slipping her arm through his, Peg escorted him to an awaiting service tray of coffee and pastries that had been laid out on the back-garden patio.

"So that's Marcus Figueroa," Leigh mused to herself.

As if in answer, a cold and unfriendly draft wheezed through the house.

Yesterday, Myra had explained to her that Marcus was, in title, the head of global security for Simmons-Pierce Shipping. "The truth is," Myra went on to say, "he's Dad's right-hand-man. Marcus travels the world, inspecting and spot-checking mostly, but whenever an incident takes place, Marcus Figueroa always arrives in person to supervise the investigation."

Myra's tones of admiration soured. "He takes himself far too seriously for my liking, especially for how young he is. He's only a couple of years older than me. He thinks no one but himself can do the job right. Still, he's good at it. Apparently, he's some kind of whiz-kid when it comes to corporate security. Illegal activities, smuggling and organized crime, that sort of thing? It all dropped since he took over as head of security."

"Wow," Leigh exclaimed. "Is all that real?"

"You're darn right it is," Myra said. "In a company the size of ours, with connections all over the globe, we are a prime target for all sorts of nastiness."

Last night, Myra's words pestered Leigh's mind like a swarm of gnats and she lay awake for hours wondering if that nastiness was what got her parents murdered. When she did finally drift into sleep, it was fitful and nightmare leaden.

This morning, seeing Mr. Figueroa in the flesh filled her with an unaccustomed sense of interest that bordered on hope. She sprang out of bed and dressed in a rush. She determined to meet him and, given half the chance, find out what he knew about her parents' murders. Hustling through the house as best she could, her feet still bandaged and sore, she refused to miss the opportunity to be introduced to this man by Peg and Tristin.

Pausing at the French doors leading to the garden patio, Leigh took a deep breath to collect herself. She pushed the doors open and forced her lips into a smile.

"Good morning," she greeted the party.

"Is it?" Tristin said, looking at his watch, checking to make sure it was, in fact, still morning.

Leigh let the tease go unanswered. What mattered was that she was in the presence of Simmons-Pierce's chief of security; the man who potentially held the answers.

"Hi," she said, holding her hand out. "You must be Marcus Figueroa. I'm Leigh."

Marcus got to his feet and took her hand in his. "Ms. Howard. Nice to meet you. My deepest sympathy for your loss."

Like an orchid exposed to an unexpected frost, Leigh's smile withered and died.

Marcus was easy on the eyes, just as Myra described. Everything about him was pure European chic. His suit was, Leigh assumed, custom made and crisp. His shoes, highly polished tan leather. His dark skin and wiry hair one-hundred percent pure Italian. It was his tone of voice that bothered her.

Despite what he had said, Marcus didn't sound sorry at all. She'd heard that tone so often she wanted to scream. It was the one people used to say something they feel they are supposed to, given the circumstances, but not something they actually feel.

Protocol.

"Thank you," Leigh whispered though she didn't know what she was thanking him for.

"Pull up a chair and join us," Peg invited. "Help yourself to a sweet."

Leigh chose a cream filled doughnut and tried to be inconspicuous. She hoped Tristin and Marcus would go back to talking about whatever it was they were talking about before she arrived and maybe let something slip.

"I was just telling Marcus about the freak storm in my office," Tristin said.

"Yes," Marcus said. "Very peculiar. And I understand your actions were quite heroic."

Leigh tried to dodge being the center of attention by saying, "It was nothing, really."

"I beg to differ," Peg insisted. "Tristin could have been killed in there and you didn't hesitate at all. Ran straight in without even considering the risk to yourself."

Changing the subject Leigh said, "I understand you are the head of security, Mr. Figueroa. That must be a fascinating job."

Marcus flashed one of those insincere smiles that appear to be humble but is dripping with arrogance. "Please, do call me Marcus. As for my exciting job? Not as dashing and daring as you might think. Paperwork and research, mostly. See, it's the paper trail that does in the villains. More crooks are brought down by the accountant's pen than the policeman's gun."

"Then why do criminals keep documents at all?" Leigh asked.

"Because, my dear, crime is big business. It's organized. Efficient. Often more so than legal enterprises. In order to function on such a large scale, it is, like any other organization, bloated with records, contracts, and receipts."

"You sound like you approve," Leigh couldn't stop herself from saying.

"Admire, perhaps. But not approve. Just as I can admire the awesome power of a great white shark while not approving of its eating people."

Leigh agreed with Myra. She didn't care much for Marcus, but she wanted what he had -- information about the night her parents were killed. As long as Peg and Tristin were hovering around, drinking coffee and treating her like a porcelain doll every time the conversation became serious, she wasn't going to get any information out of him. Somehow, she had to corner Marcus while he was alone.

"Tristin told me you're here to work on the mess in his office. If there's anything I can do, I'd like to help," she offered.

Peg cooed. "Didn't I tell you she was the sweetest thing ever?"

"So I see," murmured Marcus as he eyed Leigh with misgivings. "Unfortunately, there wouldn't be much you could do. We need someone familiar with the day-to-day operations of the company to make sense of all the documents and ledgers. It would take longer to show you what to do than it would to do it myself. Sorry."

Once again, despite what he was saying, Marcus didn't sound sorry at all.

"But I want to help," Leigh insisted. "I mean, I am part of this family, aren't I?"

She flashed a glance at Tristin and Peg. Fire blazed in her cheeks as she lowered her eyes. She couldn't help but think about how her mother taught her better than to be so openly rude.

"Of course you are," Peg insisted, her fingers nervously toying with the gold pendant that hung around her neck.

"Well, then," Leigh continued, trying to sound confident while, at the same time feeling ashamed of her bluntness, "I want to learn the family's business. I mean, I can't be part of the family without being part of the business. From what I can tell, the two are one and the same."

"Well said," Tristin declared. "And, if that is what you want, I'm sure we can begin working on it. But you'll have start at the bottom and work your way up. Quite impossible to begin at the top and drill down. There are so many subtleties and even small mistakes can lead to millions in losses."

"I understand," Leigh said not wanting to tip her hand. "Still, I'll be around if you think of anything I can do to help."

She excused herself, leaving her untouched pastry on its plate. As she left, she heard the group titter. Whether the laughter was derisive or appreciative of her offer to help, Leigh neither knew nor cared. All that mattered was that her plan to be alone with Marcus so she could question him failed.

Back in her room, sitting on her bed and glowering through her window at the small garden party going on below her, she wracked her brain for a plan-B. All she came up with was a repackaged plan-A, which was to keep trying to catch Marcus on his own.

As she sat waiting for her chance, she saw Peg excuse herself from the table. Leigh sat paralyzed with indecision. Was this her moment? Her heart pulsed and, as hot blood coursed through her body, it carried along with it tingling pinpricks of anxiety.

Tristin remained and showed no signs of leaving so, no, this wasn't her opportunity. Breathing deeply, she continued waiting, watching, and plotting.

The two men rose and came inside. Leigh knew they were headed to the office. In giddy excitement, she wanted to bound downstairs and watch them. Taking a deep breath, she forced herself to remain calm. To play it cool. She had all day. Rushing things, being too obvious, was the surefire way to get busted.

Pacing in her room occupied Leigh for less than ten minutes. Pinching her lips as she crossed and recrossed the floor, she whipped her mind into a lather. Marcus, the man who had the answers she wanted so bad it made her heart ache was right here, right now, but he might just as well have been on Jupiter.

Leigh froze in the middle of her room and glared at her door. Clenching her jaws, she struggled against the temptation to rush out, storm into Tristin's office, and demand she be given answers. Letting out an audible growl, she forced herself to be patient, spun around, and began pacing again.

Too pensive to jump off the ledge into the sitting area, she slouched down the stairs and collapsed onto the couch. She felt she was somehow betraying her parents by not being more aggressive but didn't know what else to do. Tears began to slide over her cheeks.

The old mansion creaked. A faint draft breathed through her room. From the direction of her staircase-closet something rattled so softly she wasn't sure she heard anything at all. Bodie's name carved beneath the bottom step came to her mind.

Pushing her face into the crook of her elbow, she used her sleeve to dry her eyes. Heaving herself to her feet, she picked up the notebook that was on the coffee table. Taking up a pencil, she entered the closet under the stairs. To pass the time, she intended to make a rubbing of Little Bodie's name.

Wriggling beneath the stairs, the loose board again rocked beneath her shoulder blades. She grimaced. Peg asked one of the maintenance people to take a look at it after Myra reported the loose board. According to Peg, the man fails to find anything wrong with the floor inside the closet. Leigh would have to show him where it was herself.

Maneuvering her body in the cramped space beneath the stair was awkward work. Pressing a sheet of paper against the underside of the stair she spread her fingers wide to hold it in place. Rubbing the side of her pencil lead over the grooves of the carved name made her body wobble left and right. The phone she'd laid on her chest, the only light she had to work by, kept sliding off and she was forced to hold it in place by pressing down with her chin. Her elbows became stiff and the muscles of her forearms began to ache from the combined effort of holding the paper in place while, at the same time, rubbing with the pencil.

"At least it's not stuffy under here," she said, surprised at how cool and fresh the air felt. It was very different from her first day at the manor, when Myra told her where to find Bodie's graffiti.

Taking a break from her scratchy rubbing, a humming like the buzz of a bee came to her ear. She stopped breathing, terrified of being stung.

Listening intently, she realized the hum was a conversation, but the words were unintelligible and the speakers unidentifiable.

Sliding closer to the wall the staircase was built against, she pressed her ear to its cold surface. Muffled and faint, she strained to make out Tristin's words.

"I've got to take a call from Taiwan. Will you be okay for an hour or so on your own?"

"Of course," Marcus said. Even muted, his tone sounded arrogant.

Leigh squirmed from beneath the stairs. Slipping her top off, she shook it like a small rug to remove any dust she might have collected. Pulling it back on as she walked, she opened her door and made her way down the spiral staircase. Peering around the wall, she crept into the hallway like a timid mouse.

Looking over the banister of the second floor, she saw Tristin making his way up from the first. She darted behind a thick square pillar and hid until she heard one of the many doors open and shut.

Abandoning caution, she pelted down the stairs and presented herself at the entry to Tristin's office. Not wanting to burst in panting and breathless, she paused and waited for her heart and lungs to calm down.

"How's it coming?" she asked with casual politeness when she entered.

Marcus didn't bother to look up at her.

He was standing over a box of papers and books, leafing through them and sorting them into separate piles on a long table.

Leigh didn't think he'd heard her until he grunted, "Fine."

She inched her way in and sat at Tristin's desk, making broad swivels left and right in the chair.

"Still nothing I can do?"

"You can keep out of the way."

"I'm not in the way," she said cheerily.

For the first time he raised his head and looked at her. "I suppose not. Just don't mess with those stacks of papers. I spent all morning sorting them."

He set down the ledger he was reading on the top of a stack beside him. Picking up an identical looking volume, he returned to scanning the contents.

Leigh's outward calm belied her nervousness. She had no idea how to be subtle when bringing up the topic of murder. With nothing else coming to mind, she decided the best action would be to get it over with.

"Mr. Figueroa?"

"You can call me Marcus. And the answer is yes."

"Answer to what?" Leigh asked, caught off guard.

"Yes, Tristin told me that your police officer friend, Milbanks was it? That he wanted transcripts of the interviews we made while looking into the murder of your parents. I've put some people to work on it. As soon as he delivers the court order, I'll deliver the documents."

"How did you know I was going to ask about that?"

"It was either that or some other question about your parents. Why else would you have tried to con your way into working with me earlier? Or is it a coincidence that as soon as Tristin left, you showed up?"

Her ears burned. He made her feel like a fool. She resented being called out so easily and his smug arrogance as he did it made her furious. Marcus's personality worked her emotions over like sandpaper. Whatever reasons Myra had for not liking him, she now had her own. Marcus was a jerk.

"So, what did your investigation turn up?" she asked.

"Nothing," he said while lifting two ledgers off the stack in order to put the one he'd been reading in third position, "so far."

"So far? You're not giving up then?"

Marcus sat with half his butt on a table and folded his arms across his chest as if posing for a fashion magazine. "No."

"I think the police are about to," she said.

"I should think so. They've got nothing to go on."

She balked. His words were cold and hard, like a boxer punching her. Unwilling to give up she pressed on. "Do you?"

"Not yet. But a dead police officer and his wife found in our dockyard is too suspicious, too dangerous to the company, to not follow through."

"Dangerous to the company? How?"

He stared at her long and hard. She felt uneasy but refused to look away. If this is what it took to know the truth she would endure.

At long last Marcus said, "Nothing I can tell you will make any difference. I don't know who killed your parents and I don't know why. Even if I did, and I told you, your parents will still be gone. Never coming back. That's cruel, I know, but that's how it is. You've got to find some way to move on."

Leigh drew herself up straight in her chair, her chin thrust out. "I'll never stop looking for the truth. I'm going to keep pushing until I find out who did this to Mom and Dad. To me. And then? I'm going to see to that they pay for it. If everyone else quits, I'll take up the investigation on my own!"

Marcus's hips came off the table. "What you're going to do is get yourself killed, just like your parents. You want the truth? Okay. Here it is.

"Your parents weren't caught in a wrong-place/wrong-time random incident. They were targeted. Executed. Shot in the back of the head. From the angle of the wounds, they were on their knees. After they were killed, the whole place was sanitized. Not a trace of evidence could be found.

"That tells me this was a professional job. Organized crime is involved. It means some mob either already has or desperately wants to get their hooks into Simmons-Pierce. Hooks they are willing to kill to keep in place. That includes killing you."

Tears pooled in her eyes, but Marcus wasn't finished with her.

"I have a small army working on this and so far, we've come up empty. So have the police. What are you, a little girl who's so wounded by grief she tried to kill herself, going to do against the Mafia? Or the Yakuza? Or whoever the hell this is? Nothing. That's what. I say this for your own good: focus on rebuilding your life and leave finding answers to those who know what they are doing."

Leigh covered her mouth to keep from howling. Her tears ran in torrents, dripping off her cheeks and onto her hoodie. Bolting to her feet, she ran from the office. Racing to her room she huddled in her closet, biting hard into her forearm to keep from screaming.

Chapter Six

The morning sun glowed a lemon meringue yellow. Still too early to blaze at full heat, the air was filled with its pleasant warmth as it inched over the treetops. Landscapers were out in force, taking full advantage of the comfortable morning.

On the far side of the lawn a woman, wearing a khaki uniform, was steering a riding mower in a systematic pattern back and forth. Small groups of two or three, all in olive and khaki uniforms, weeded flowerbeds. One man, atop a ladder, sloshed a squeegee into a bucket that was hanging on a hook beside him. Using a rag, he was polishing the second floor windows.

Leigh wandered across the grass not going anywhere in particular. She'd spent another night not so much sleeping but dozing on and off, fading in and out of nightmare tortured unconsciousness. It had been three days since Marcus bawled her out and told her to mind her own business.

As if the murder of my parents isn't my business.

Marcus was long gone. The hurt he'd caused lingered. She hadn't done anything to deserve the treatment she received. All she did was ask questions. She was struggling to understand why Marcus was so cruel to her.

"Ms. Howard," a voice yelled out.

Turning automatically, without feeling any real interest, she scanned the grounds until deciding the man on the ladder was the one who was calling to her. He was a dark and handsome young man with black hair and eyes who sported a five o'clock shadow at eight in the morning. His dark complexion made Leigh suspect that either he or his family hailed from somewhere in South America.

She turned her steps in his direction as he made his way to the ground.

"I'm Nacho," he said when they met.

Leigh's left eyebrow lifted of its own accord. "You mean, like the snack?"

Nacho laughed and gave a shrug. "Yep. My real name is Ignacio Dominguez. People call me Nacho."

In monotone Leigh said, "I'm Leigh. People call me Leigh."

Nacho's face faltered slightly. "Right. Well, Ms. Howard..."

"Leigh."

"Sorry. Leigh. Mrs. Simmons told me you're still having trouble with a loose board in your closet? I took a second look and couldn't find any problems."

"I'll show it to you," Leigh said sounding unenthusiastic. "Whenever you have time."

Nacho smiled at her. "I have time now. Windows can wait."

Leigh took in a deep breath and let it rush out her nose. She wasn't headed anywhere in particular but was annoyed over not being allowed to get there.

"Okay," she said. "Let's go."

With plodding steps, she led Nacho inside. The elevator ride to the third floor was made in silence. It occurred to Leigh that she should say something.

She glanced at Nacho out of the corner of her eye. His lips were pursed and he was shifting his weight from the balls of his feet to his heels and back again. She assumed the silence must feel awkward to him, too, but she couldn't muster the energy to speak.

"It's in the closet under the stairs," Leigh said once they reached her room.

She opened the door and began kicking shoes and unhung clothes out into the center of her room. "You have to go all the way to the back, almost to where the second step is."

"I'll take a look," Nacho said as he brushed past her and entered the closet.

He crouched down on his hands and knees and, as he neared the back, began thumping the floor with his fist.

"So, was it more to the left or the right?"

Leigh felt frustrated. It was obvious which board was loose. It wiggled at the slightest touch.

"It's the one a little off center, to the right," she said.

More thumping.

"Hmmm," Nacho grunted and began thumping again.

Crawling back out he told her, "Couldn't find it."

Leigh clamped her teeth together to keep from saying something rude.

Nacho dug into a cargo pocket of his trousers and pulled out a pen. "Here, take this and lay it on top of the board that's loose. When you come out, I'll go back in and take another look."

Heaving a great sigh, Leigh took the pen and followed his suggestion. She knew which board was loose and was frustrated because it was so obvious. Reaching the board, she pressed down on it for certainty's sake but the board didn't budge.

She pressed again.

Nothing.

Like Nacho, she balled her fist and hammered.

The board didn't move.

Leigh gave up.

"I don't get it," she said when she stood beside Nacho.

He smiled at her as if indulging the fantasy of a toddler.

"You don't believe me?" she asked.

"Eh," he said with a shrug. "This house is over three hundred years old. Things shift around; shrink and swell all the time. That's why I was hired. There's always something needs fixing."

"Sorry I wasted your time."

"Yeah, because I was having such a good time cleaning the windows."

Leigh looked at the floor. More to herself than to Nacho she said, "Not so long ago, I would have thought that funny."

Nacho took a rag out of his back pocket and began wiping his hands. "I bet a lot of things seemed funny not so long ago. Understandable why they aren't anymore."

Her head shot up and she glared at him.

Of course he knew. Everyone working here knew. Most of Maryland knew. The murder of cop and his wife was a big story, and anybody following the news with any degree of interest would know what she tried to do, too.

"Sorry," Nacho said. "None of my business."

"That's okay. It's not like I can pretend it didn't happen."

Nacho nodded his head. "True."

He wasn't that much older than Myra -- twenty-one. Maybe twenty-three? Yet his eyes made Leigh think that he'd seen a lot. Suffered a lot.

Taking a chance, she asked, "So who did you lose?"

"Me? Everyone. I'm from Guatemala. When the Zetas took over my village, anyone who didn't join them was killed."

She gave him an accusing look. "You're still alive."

"I'm also not in Guatemala anymore."

He laughed. "I'm not a member of the Zeta Cartel, if that's what you're thinking."

"Of course you're not," Leigh said. "Sorry. I'm not at the top of my game these days."

Nacho didn't say anything to that, but asked, "So, do the police know anything?"

"No," Leigh answered. "They're about to give up. I think that's why I've been so down lately."

"They've gotta have some leads?"

Leigh shook her head.

"What about Simmons-Pierce security? Does Mr. Figueroa have anything?"

Leigh gave him another suspicious look. "You're pretty well up on things, for a handyman."

Another shrug. "Ever since what happened with the Zetas, I've learned to keep my eyes and ears open."

That made sense to Leigh and she nodded.

"Marcus suspects organized crime," she said. "That's all he would say before telling me in no uncertain terms to keep my nose out of it."

"Maybe you should."

"What did you say?"

Nacho shifted on his feet. "So, it's not my place, but, I mean, nothing's going to change what happened. Let's say they catch the guy who killed your parents. So what? The people who hired him would still be free. And let's say that those people get busted, too. Si? In less than a week some lieutenant will take over and it's back to business as usual. Trust me. I know these things."

Tears pooled in Leigh's eyes. "It somehow seems so wrong, you know? To let them win like that."

"Hey," Nacho said, "you make a happy life for yourself and nobody but you and your parents win. Isn't that what they would have wanted for you?"

"Well, yeah."

Nacho shrugged, smiling at her. "Then your parents win."

Leigh looked at Nacho, seeing him as being a lot like Myra. Both were honest and direct with her. Both accepted her as bruised, not broken. Ty's words, "Let the right ones in and they'll help you out," blew through her mind like a soft breeze. Maybe Nacho, like Myra, was one of the right ones.

"I'll think about it," she said.

"If you ever want to talk, I'm always around somewhere. And if that board comes loose again, I'll..."

Leigh forced herself to smile. "You'll be around."

Nacho grinned. "Yeah. I've got to get back to my windows, if you're okay?"

"I'm fine. No problem. Thanks for, well, for everything."

"De nada, señorita."

Closing her door behind Nacho, she leaned against it knowing he was right. She should leave the investigation to the professionals and focus on putting her life back together. Thinking of it brought on a tightness in her head. It squeezed her brain as she raged against the idea. It felt too much like giving up on her parents. Like betrayal.

Going to her closet, she began hurling shoes inside. The board at the back rattled.

"You've got to be kidding me," she wailed.

Lowering down to all fours, she scuttled to the back of the closet. Cold air forced goosebumps to rise on her skin. The sudden change made her queasy. She was certain the air wasn't this cold when she and Nacho were looking for the loose plank.

Reaching forward, pressing against the floor, the board she knew to be the culprit rocked at her slightest touch.

Anger swelled within her. First Marcus put her down. Then Nacho said the same thing, only in a kinder way. Now, a stupid board was taunting her -- loose one minute, secure the next.

She shouted something foul. Pressing down so that the edge of the board rose high enough for her to dig what she had of fingernails into it, Leigh pried the board up.

"No one will wonder which one is loose after I rip the whole floor out," she growled.

She gave a massive tug. Expecting it to go on sticking in stubborn refusal to move, Leigh toppled over as it popped free, banging her head against the sidewall of the closet.

More profanity poured out of her.

Scrabbling back onto her knees she peered into the hole she'd made in the floor. It was a narrow slit, wide enough to slip her open hand through, but not her fist. With a thin thread of light coming from the doorway, allowing her to see, she deftly lowered her hand in and let her fingers feel around until they landed on something wedged inside.

Leigh's heart leapt into her throat as a series of staccato knocks rapped at her door. She pulled her hand out of the hole in the floor so fast she scraped skin off her knuckles.

"Leigh? It's Myra. I'm headed into town to do some shopping. Mom says she wants you to come with me."

"Thanks, but I'm not feeling up to it," Leigh shouted back.

She heard her door open.

"Leigh? Where are you?"

Hastily, Leigh fitted the floorboard back into place.

"In here," she called.

"In where? The closet?"

"Yeah," she said stepping out and into the room. She shut the closet door behind her making sure she heard the latch catch. "Nacho was here. We couldn't find that stupid loose board."

Myra's eyebrows bounced wickedly. "Nacho, huh? He's easy on the eyes, isn't he?"

"Myra! He's at least ten years older than me."

"Oh, sweetie. Just because you don't play an instrument doesn't mean you can't listen to the music."

Myra had a way of making Leigh smile, even if she didn't feel like it.

"You're horrible," she said.

Myra laughed. "Ain't I though?"

"Look. I don't feel like going shopping," Leigh said.

Myra's face turned serious. "I know you don't. But Mom is kind of insisting. She says you've been moping around here for too long and it isn't healthy."

Leigh shot her cousin a cold stare. "She's your mom. Not mine."

"I know that. And Mom does, too, but she is your guardian and she is worried about you. So am I, to be honest."

"I'm fine."

"You're not fine. You spend half your time lying in bed and the other half out wandering the woods in places even I can't find you."

Myra sighed. "Look. I'm leaving in the morning and will be gone for the next three days. I'd like it if you came shopping with me to help me get ready."

"You're leaving?"

With scathing candor Myra retorted, "Yes! You'd know that if you'd spend more time out of your room. I'm taking a campus tour of Columbia University in New York."

Leigh felt the pull of the hidden something beneath her floorboard as if it were a magnet. Myra, on the other hand, was her friend and she was leaving. After Myra was gone, who would she have at Simmons-Pierce Manor to talk to?

Since her parent's murder Leigh tried to pretend her life was still normal. She texted her old friends from school but that was very different from hanging out with someone in person. If she didn't go with Myra she knew she would not only hurt her feelings, but that she would regret it after Myra was gone.

"All right," Leigh sighed, "I'll go."

"Great! Meet you downstairs in five?"

Thirty minutes later, when Myra bounded out the front door, Leigh felt like she'd been kicked in the chest. Self-consciously, she tussled her bangs to tuck her eyes behind them. Myra had changed clothes, applied make-up, as well as brushed and styled her hair. Leigh threw on her hoodie. Leigh was grateful Myra wasn't the type of person to notice things like that or, if she did notice, was kind enough to keep it to herself.

Climbing into a black sedan, driven by a man Myra teased as being named Bodyguard Bob, Leigh hunkered down for an afternoon of boredom. Driving through the estate's gates, it occurred to her that this was the first time she'd left the property since she arrived. Was that weeks ago? Months? Blinking her eyes, she admitted to herself that she'd lost track.

Reaching the shopping center Myra selected, Leigh shuffled along beside her as if she was Myra's personal storm cloud. She knew Myra was humoring her by trying on Leigh's suggestions from the urban-urchin look Leigh favored. The way Myra struck exaggerated tough looking poses was funny and Leigh began to lighten up. She even let Myra pick a few swanky clothes for her to try on. She looked just as ridiculous in a midnight blue cocktail gown, wearing battered Keds, trying to contort her body into alluring poses as Myra did pretending to be her. By the time they were finished, Leigh was having a great time.

When they pulled up to the mansion, Leigh's heart jolted into her throat. Parked beneath a tree close to the house sat Ty's classic Camaro.

All the joy she was feeling drained away. "I don't think this will be anything good," Leigh whispered to herself after Myra climbed out of the car and was out of earshot.

Chapter Seven

Tristin met Leigh at the door and led her into his office. Standing in the middle of the room, Ty wrapped his left hand around the pistol he wore on his hip while hooking his right thumb behind the badge attached to his belt. He didn't waste any time on small talk.

"The department has officially labeled your parents' case *cold*," he said.

Leigh was expecting bad news, but not this. "What! So soon?"

"I know. It hit me hard, too, but there are no more leads to follow, no more witnesses to interview, no more evidence to collect and analyze. Meanwhile, our caseloads are piling up. Cases that are potentially solvable. As things stand, your parents' case isn't. I know that's hard to hear, but you wanted the truth and, well, there it is."

Outside, a mighty gust of wind caused the house to creak.

"So that's it? My parents get forgotten?"

Ty bristled. "Hey, your folks were my friends. Just because the case is considered cold, that in no way means it's closed. You know I'll keep working it."

"You forget," Leigh said in a soulless monotone, "I'm a cop's daughter. I know how this works. You'll do the best you can but your case load will grow. New cases, solvable ones, like you said, will come across your desk demanding your attention. In the end, new leads will have to find you because you won't have time to go out and find them."

"Leigh," Tristin said, "no one is giving up. In fact, Detective Milbank was here to drop off a copy of the investigation file. I will hand it over to

Marcus and we'll see if he can find something that was, maybe, overlooked."

Leigh's eyes darted to the blue folder, embossed with the Baltimore City Police crest, sitting on Tristin's desk. The case file was anorexic, filled with a couple of pages and a few photographs whose corners were poking out beneath the folder cover.

A thickness blocked Leigh's throat as she blinked back tears. She wasn't going to cry. Not here. Not in front of them. Not in front of anyone.

The wind outside howled. A sharp crack rang out followed by the heavy crunch of metal and tinkling of shattered glass. Both Tristin and Ty darted to the window.

"My car!" Ty yelled.

"Oh, for heaven's sake," Tristin groaned. "Come on. Let's go see how bad it is."

The two men ran out of the office leaving Leigh alone. She crossed to the window to see for herself what caused the commotion. Staring in slack-jawed awe at the scene outside the window, she saw Ty standing several feet away from his car, hands on his head, looking at the enormous limb that snapped off the tree and fell across the roof of his car, shattering both the front and back windshields.

She turned, intending to join them, when the draft from the front door, left open by Ty and Tristin, slammed the door to the office shut. In its wake, papers on Tristin's desk, along with the blue folder, fluttered.

Leigh cast another quick look out the window. A crowd was forming around the car. There was much gawking and pointing going on as they discussed how best to get the branch off it.

Leigh knew a handful of seconds was all she had. She whipped her phone out of her back pocket and, like a spy in a war movie, began photographing every page and picture the blue folder contained.

Racing up to her room, she climbed the stairs of the loft and settled onto her bed to read the documents she'd captured on her phone. Her gut clenched when the first to open was a photograph of her parents' bodies.

Leigh sat stupefied. She wanted to hurl the phone away from her but couldn't stop staring. The images were terrible and gruesome and she understood why the photos were never shared with her, but she couldn't stop looking.

"Leigh?" Myra called outside her door.

"I'm here," Leigh said, shutting down her phone with practiced speed.

"Thought you'd be outside with your friend. You know his car is trashed, right?"

"I know. I just didn't want to be out there."

"I knew it," Myra said with genuine concern. "Bad news."

"The worst. They decided Mom and Dad's case is too cold to keep working full time. That means it's no longer an active investigation."

"I'm so sorry," Myra said. "Do you want to talk about it?"

That was the last thing Leigh wanted. "No. Not now. Maybe when you get back?"

"Sure," Myra said cheerily. "Any time you like."

"So, is that all you wanted? To check in on me?"

Leigh realized that sounded like an accusation. "I mean, if it is, it's nice that you did. Thank you."

Myra laughed. "No problem. Actually, I came up to tell you Bob is helping clear the tree limb off Detective Milbank's car so we'll have to lug our loot up to our rooms ourselves. You up to that?"

"Sure," Leigh said with no enthusiasm.

She spent the remainder of the afternoon in Myra's room, under the pretense of helping her cousin pack but, in reality, Leigh knew she was being kept there to prevent her from sitting alone in her room.

"Here's yours," Myra said.

Leigh looked at the new items feeling disgusted. She didn't want the dress or shoes but Myra insisted on buying them for her. Holding the dress at arm's length, she couldn't tell if it looked worse in the better lighting of Myra's room or if her disappointment with Ty was coloring her vision.

"Why don't you try it on?" Myra said, taking the dress out of Leigh's hand and giving it her own inspection.

"I don't know. Maybe later?"

"I don't have much 'later' left. Please? I'd love to see you in it."

Leigh took the dress off Myra's arm and went into the walk-in closet. Despite having complete privacy, she still felt exposed as she dropped her hoodie to the floor and pulled her top off. Slipping the dress over her head she rejoined Myra.

"You always wear jeans under a dress?" Myra teased.

"It's the other way around. I don't wear dresses. Ever."

Myra stepped back and looked Leigh over. "Well, it doesn't matter. You look beautiful. That's a good color for you."

"Thanks," Leigh mumbled as she retreated back into the closet. The sooner she was out of the dress, the better. She didn't belong in it. She didn't belong at Simmons-Pierce Manor. Without her parents, she didn't belong anywhere.

Leigh sniffled.

"You all right in there?" Myra called.

Scrubbing her eyes dry with the cuffs of her sweater Leigh opened the door. "I'm fine. Just dusty in there."

"My closet is not dusty. But there are a few things in there that don't fit me anymore. Tell you what, when I get back, we'll sort through all of them and if there's anything you like, you can keep it, otherwise off to charity they'll go."

"Sounds fun," Leigh lied.

For Myra's sake, Leigh put on a brave face and, for the remainder of the evening, was as pleasant and charming as she could force herself to be. Myra was in rare form -- sassy as ever, making jokes and ribbing everyone equally, to include poking fun at herself. She even got Tristin to laugh when she teased him about the ghosts haunting him.

"I'd hoped," Tristin said in feigned indignation, "that you would be a positive influence on Leigh. A role model even. I can see that is not going to be the case."

Myra and Peg burst into laughter. Tristin struggled to keep a straight face. Leigh pushed the corners of her mouth upwards because she was expected to.

The night should have been a pleasant evening for the family. If things were different, if she were different, it could have been fun. As it was, she had no happiness inside her.

As soon as was possible without making herself appear rude, Leigh said her goodnights and excused herself for the evening. She stood in the middle of her room pinching her lips and arguing with herself. Buried in her phone were the police reports that held no answers, only misery, but she felt drawn to it like a moth to flame. Inside her closet remained the mystery of what, if anything was hidden beneath her floor. Whether it was the lure of the unknown or avoidance of sorrow, Leigh decided to explore beneath her closet floor. If nothing was there, she had the rest of the night to torture herself with the police file.

Armed with her phone for light, she entered her closet and crawled forward on her hands and knees. The board wiggled at her lightest touch, renewing her annoyance that no one else was able to find it. Not wanting to topple over like the last time, she carefully removed it. The plank came loose in her hand with no effort.

A cold draft swept through the closet. She shuddered.

Leaning forward she shone the light from her phone into the crevice. Expecting to see spiderwebs and skeletal mice, she peered in. The little compartment surprised her by being so clean. There were no mouse droppings, no spiders, no layers of dust which, she thought, should have collected over the years. All she found was an old chamois rag.

Afraid that some animal might be lurking just out of sight, she lowered her hand into the hole. Tapping the cloth lightly, she jerked her hand out, watching for the rag to move. There was something solid beneath it, or perhaps wrapped inside the cloth. With more confidence, she lowered her hand again. The chill in the closet increased and she could see her breath coming out of her like puffs of steam.

Leigh let her fingers rest on whatever it was wrapped inside the towel. It wasn't hard like she'd expect a plank of wood to be, but it was solid none the less. Pinching the object on either side, she lifted it out of its hiding place. Looking it over in the light of her phone, she was again surprised to find no signs of dust or age. Whatever it was could have been put in there twenty minutes ago, the object looked so pristine.

The cold started making her fingertips sting. It was making her vision blurry. Holding tight to her newfound treasure, she darted out of the closet and back into her room. Closing the door behind her trapped whatever cold there was inside the closet. Her room was the same comfortable temperature as always. The contrast made goosebumps ripple across her skin.

She struggled to focus her sight. Blinking repeatedly and rubbing her eyes, she moved across the room to the sunken sitting area. Balling up on the couch, she toyed with her find.

She knew before unwrapping the package that she was holding a book. It was thin and rectangular with hard surfaces on three sides and a grove running along three edges. Pulling it from inside the soft leather wrapper, she discovered it was a diary.

Dizziness overwhelmed her the instant her eyes fell on it. Her already blurred vision tinted a pale blue. She felt sick, like she ate something that her body couldn't stand having inside her. Squeezing her eyes tightly shut, she inhaled deeply through her nose and out her mouth. Quick as it came over her, the queasiness evaporated.

Wiping away the thin film of perspiration that beaded on her forehead, she opened the cover and read, "*My name is Ichabod Pierce and I'm ten years old.*"

Leigh gasped. Her first thought was to run and tell Myra, but she was still sitting downstairs with her family. There would be no way to get Myra to notice her without drawing unwanted attention from everyone else.

Settling back onto the couch, she read on. Little Bodie's history was something Myra had little knowledge about. Something dreadful happened to him while his family was visiting Japan. His parents were murdered. Little Bodie returned home alone after having been missing for several years. That was all Myra knew. The boy grew up in this house, became an adult then took over the business. He was, by all accounts, a ruthless businessman. This book told the story of what he was like as a child.

Though he wrote in several places how grateful he was to be living here and how kind and agreeable everyone was, Leigh couldn't help feeling that Bodie wasn't a happy boy. Perhaps it was her own sorrow that tainted her reading, but she got the sense he was grieving. The further she read, the older the boy grew, she came across more entries where Bodie described feelings of intense loss and loneliness. He was loved by the rest of the family, often acknowledging that in his writings but, as he put it, some critical part of him felt as if it were missing. Leigh began forming a picture of the boy and, as much as possible from a book, felt a growing bond with him. Rising, she took his portrait off the wall and carried it back to the couch, alternating between reading and looking at his picture. She tried to put the words and the likeness together as one.

Well past midnight, she fell asleep on the sofa, clutching the journal to her breast. She dreamt of sitting in this room with Bodie, sharing their pain and sorrow.

Myra's voice outside her door jolted her awake. "Come on sleepyhead! You're going to miss breakfast and my taking off."

Leigh's heart thumped in her throat. Moving with frantic speed she wedged the book beneath the couch pillows calling back, "I'll be right down."

In a mad dash, she went to the bathroom and splashed water on her face. Her first impulse was to stay in the clothes she wore yesterday but, realizing that's what she did the day before and the clothes she had on were from two days ago, she shucked them and tossed them into a heap on the floor before pulling fresh ones from her closet.

"Well, there you are," Peg said as Leigh skidded into the dining room and took her customary place across the table from Myra.

"Wouldn't miss it," she said. "It's a big day for Myra."

Myra laughed the comment off. "I've made other campus visits."

"Where?" Leigh asked.

In her mind Leigh pondered what other colleges Myra might be interested in attending. It struck Leigh that she honestly cared. Finding Bodie's journal gave her someone other than Myra to share her sadness with, freeing herself to feel happy for her cousin. Myra was getting on with life, as she should be.

"Swarthmore, in Pennsylvania; Stanford, California; Texas A&M, Texas, duh, and UCLA, again, duh, in L. A."

"Uh-huh," Leigh grunted as she drowned a plate of pancakes in syrup, "and how many of those visits were preceded by shopping sprees?"

Myra's face twisted with pretend indignation. "Shut up."

She cast a furtive glance at her father to make sure he was still oblivious behind this morning's Wall Street Journal. In a hushed voice she said across the table, "You seem to be in a good place this morning."

"Yeah," Leigh said, swiping a lock of hair away from her eyes, "I kinda am."

She and Myra shared a smile. Tristin rattled his paper and drank coffee. Bob-The-Bodyguard entered the dining room.

"Car's all loaded Miss Simmons," he announced.

"Good," said Tristin. "See to it you remember your instructions."

He was talking to Bob, not Myra.

"What instructions?" Myra demanded.

Bob flushed and straightened his tie. "Mr. Simmons said I was to keep you out of trouble."

"Daddy!" Myra cried.

Looking very uncomfortable, Bob added, "Mrs. Simmons told me a little bit of mischief never hurt anyone. Guess that means I'll have to use my best judgement."

"I pay your wages," Tristin reminded him sternly, "not Mrs. Simmons. Don't forget that."

"And he answers to me," Peg said pointedly, "one way or another. Don't you, darling?"

Peg passed behind Tristin and tickled the hairs at the nape of his neck, making him shiver.

"Go, Mom!" Myra cheered.

Tristin retreated behind his paper but, Leigh noted, he was smiling.

After a whirlwind of goodbye hugs and last-minute parental admonishments, the bulk of which came from Tristin, Bob chauffeured

Myra down the long lane. As soon as the car was out of sight, Leigh felt like an ostrich in the peacock pen. Safe, but out of place. Isolated. Alone.

"Leigh?" Nacho called, coming over to her while wiping his brow with a handkerchief.

Leigh turned to meet Nacho halfway across the circular turnaround the driveway made.

"What's up, Nacho?" she asked.

"I wanted to ask if that loose board was still giving you problems."

Leigh felt a guilty flush. She couldn't explain why, but she wanted to keep the journal and the hidden compartment a secret. Maybe when Myra came home she'd share it with her. Maybe.

"No. It's fine, thanks," she lied.

"That's good. I was also wondering when you wanted to go to your old house?"

"My old house?"

"I guess with the tree trashing that man's car Mrs. Simmons forgot to talk to you. The police have finished going through your parents' stuff. She said the two of you were going out there to decide what you want to keep, what you want to bring here, what goes into storage, stuff like that."

Leigh's heart sank. She had, of course, thought about what would happen to all her family's things and the house, but in a distant, some-time-in-the-future sort of way. The future having arrived sooner than she expected, she balked at the idea of dealing with what to do about her family's estate -- her estate, now. It was overwhelming.

"I'll be here to help, whenever it is," Nacho said as if sensing her panic.

"Thanks. I'll let you know what I find out."

"Take your time. I...we...that is, all of us who work here, we understand the hard time you are going through. We're all here to help, if you need it."

Leigh didn't know what else to say so repeated, "Thanks."

Back in her room, she stood in the middle of the floor trying to decide whether she wanted to spend time with Bodie or go back to looking through the documents she'd photographed.

Leigh knew she couldn't dodge the latter chore forever. Those documents had to be gone through. Steeling herself against the horrific task, she climbed up to the loft and sat cross-legged on her bed.

Opening her phone, she flicked her finger up the screen, scrolling past the crime scene photos. If police forensics found anything, it would be detailed in a report. Torturing herself by looking at the pictures served no purpose other than feeding sadistic self-pity.

For two hours, she read every boring word. Opening the picture of the last document, she gasped. The document had nothing to do with the investigation. Instead, Leigh found herself reading Ty's letter of intent to put in for early retirement.

Her heart broke as she hissed, "He's giving up."

Leigh cursed loudly. Fearing Peg might be checking on her, she buried her face in her pillow and screamed out words that would make her ex-Marine father blush.

Leigh spent the remainder of the day hidden. Dinner was an uncomfortable affair, though Peg tried her best to liven things up. In the end they ate in silence.

After dinner, Leigh retreated once again into her room. She tried to go to sleep, but sleep wouldn't come. At three in the morning she crept out of her room. Since her arrival, she paid close attention to every detail she could. Entering the code to disable the house alarm system, she bolted outside.

Dashing shadow to shrub, she avoided the roaming guards and reached the woods. From there, she took the now memorized path leading to the river.

Easing herself down onto the clammy mixture of sand and dirt at the river's edge, Leigh drew her knees up to her chest and hugged her torso against them. Her eyes were scratchy. Her reservoir of tears had been cried dry and all that remained was the grit of evaporated tears.

The last time she felt this shattered inside she gave in to despair and tried to kill herself. She tried not to think about it, but the memory was always there, nagging at the back of her brain, lying to her, telling her she always had a sure and final way out.

"Hey! This place is mine. Go find your own!"

Leigh jolted to her feet. Pulling out her phone, she checked the time: three-thirty-four in the morning. She should be alone.

Staring into the random pools of brightness the moon was casting through the trees she asked, "Who are you? Where are you?"

"I'm right here."

The voice came from the direction of the river.

The moon reflected off the steaming surface like headlights in fog, except this haze was blue. A soft splashing sound reached her ears as the water rippled.

"I don't see you. Just some fish breaking the surface and a blueish sort of mist,"

"I'm not a dumb fish! And what'd you think I'd look like?"

"I don't know, since I don't know who, or where, you are."

"I'm Ichabod Pierce. You and that other girl like to call me Little Bodie."

Leigh's heart thumped one painful throb after another. Each beat was like being kicked in the chest. Her eyes popped wide. With jerky steps she backed away, unable to tear her gaze away from the blue mist that was creeping closer to shore.

"Y-y-you're the ghost of Ichabod Pierce?"

"I am," Little Bodie boomed, his childish voice echoing as if coming from the bottom of a mine, "and I don't want you here."

Leigh gasped in a sharp breath and took another faltering step away. Her heel struck the root of a tree. Losing her balance, she fell flat on her back.

The blue mist shimmered as it swirled and reformed into a translucent boy radiating a pale blue aura, swimming with easy strokes toward the bank.

"What do you want from me?" Leigh managed to stammer through chattering teeth.

"I told you," Little Bodie said as he waded out of the river, blue drops of unreal water glistened on his nearly naked, translucent, body. "I want you to go away."

Leigh scrambled away from his approach. Consumed with fear she stammered out a whispered, "Why?"

Little Bodie's form swirled back into mist. In an instant he returned dressed like a boy from the 1800s.

"Because, you have an ugly glow surrounding you, like you're already dead but still alive at the same time. If you die here, looking like that, your soul will be anchored to this spot, trapped here forever, which would ruin this place for me. So, go away! It's mine!"

Little Bodie's voice rumbled like an earthquake. A stiff wind kicked up around Leigh, blowing sand into her eyes and face. Heavy clouds rolled in to blot out the moon.

Clawing to her feet, her heart pounding in her chest, Leigh stumbled back down the trail toward the manor. The windstorm caused vines and branches to whip against her. After a vicious slap in the face, she stopped and cried out. Looking over her shoulder, a blue ball of light was rushing towards her.

She darted off again and didn't stop running until she reached the forest's edge. The wind stopped as soon as her feet hit the manicured lawn and the night air was still and quiet. Risking another glance over her shoulder, she saw the blue light was gone. Turning her head back she was confronted by two women and a man. All three wore nice suits with handguns bulging beneath them.

Chapter Eight

Leigh stood staring at the rug in Tristin's office while getting chewed out. In front of her, Tristin paced like a caged lion while Peg hovered beside his desk. The three security guards who hauled her in stood off to the side like granite gargoyles.

"What on earth were you thinking?" Tristin demanded, madly gesticulating. "You know full well we have heightened security at the manor right now. So what in heaven's name makes you think it's a good idea to roam around the grounds at this hour?"

Peg spoke up softly. "She can't answer if you keep yelling at her. Leigh, dear, what happened tonight?"

"I...I couldn't sleep no matter what I tried. I thought maybe a walk outside would settle my mind."

"A walk outside I can understand," Tristin said still pacing, throwing his hands over his head. "On the patio, even in the garden. But security found you coming out of the woods. You're lucky a fall and a bruised cheek was all that happened to you."

"I didn't fall," Leigh objected as if that was the point Tristin was trying to make. "That wind just came up out of nowhere. Next thing I know I've got leaves, sand, vines, and tree limbs slapping me from all sides."

Tristin's eyes shot to the security guards who found her. Though she had begged and pleaded, she couldn't persuade them to not snitch to Tristin and Peg. They wore remorseful expressions when glancing at her but gave Tristin silent shakes of the head.

Leigh knew as soon as Tristin's lips jutted to the side that he thought she was lying. "I already told them that was your story. They informed me the night was as calm as could be. No storms. No wind."

Leigh's voice raised in volume and tone. "But there was! I was sitting down by the river and saw..."

Leigh slammed her mouth shut. If she said she saw Little Bodie rise up out of the river, that he was the one chasing her, she would be sent back to the hospital straight away. Worse, Myra would be blamed for it all since she was the one who filled Leigh's head with ghost stories.

"Saw what, Leigh?" Peg pressed. She genuinely seemed to care.

Leigh scrambled to make something up on the fly. "I must have fallen asleep. I have nightmares sometimes. That's why I couldn't sleep in my room. I was afraid of the dreams I would have. When I woke up by the river, I guess I forgot where I was and panicked. I ran back to the house. Thinking back on it, that must be what happened. I'm sorry I caused you trouble."

Her lie worked on Tristin like a soothing balm. In that moment Leigh realized that he was a grouch only when he felt out of control. Supplied with a story that made sense to him, he could take charge and that put him at ease.

"Well, that wasn't so hard to finally say, was it? And I'm glad we were able to get to the bottom of things. Let's do this: I'll tell security to keep an eye out for you in the evenings. If you can't sleep and feel the need to walk outside, they are to note it in their reports but are not to disturb you. However, I insist you go no further than the gardens. Agreed?"

"That's very kind of you," Leigh said and she meant it. "And I am really sorry."

She turned to go.

Tristin cleared his throat. "Just a moment, Leigh. While I can give you some wiggle room in the short term, I can't ignore your insomnia or nightmares in the long run. I think we should bring someone in for you to talk to."

Leigh wheeled around. She wanted to explain -- to plead. Frustration overwhelmed her and instead she shouted angrily, "No! I'm not talking to anyone. I'm sick of talking, talking, talking. All I have to say is what I've been saying. My parents were murdered. They're gone. Not coming back. The police've got nothing, so whoever did it is going to get away with it. Who can possibly have anything to say that will make that any better?"

Tristin and Peg stood with jaws dropped.

Frightened and ashamed over her loss of control, Leigh clamped her hand over her mouth.

"Oh my God! I am so sorry," she said. "I'm not mad at you. Not at all. You have been so good to me. I just want..."

Peg gathered Leigh's hands into her own. "What do you want, sweetheart? Tell us. What can we do?"

Leigh felt like she was thousands of miles away. "Ty was right. He said I've been chucked into the deep end of the pool before learning how to swim."

She straightened her shoulders. "That's all I wanted to say, just not like such a jerk. There's nothing you can do. Nothing anyone can do. What I need is time. Time to learn how to live in a world without Mom and Dad in it. It's like learning how to walk all over again, you know? I take a few steps and suddenly I lose my footing. I just need time. Please?"

Leigh's face burned. She felt exposed and vulnerable. Biting her lip to keep from crying, she turned and ran from the study. She ran up the stairs and into her room. As hard as she could, she slammed the door behind her making Little Bodie's picture rattle on the wall.

"I hate you!" she growled at it.

Spinning around, she shouted all around the room. "Do you hear me? I *hate* you! Myra told me what a mean old man you became but now I know -- you were just as rotten as a boy! All I wanted was someplace quiet and peaceful. To escape feeling sad and lonely just for a little while. I thought you of all people would understand. But you don't, do you? You are selfish, and cruel, and horrible. Now, I'm going to have to start seeing doctors and therapists and God knows who again and it's all your fault."

She glared at Bodie's painting with tears streaming over her cheeks. They made the paint beneath Little Bodie's eyes appear to be running, too.

"I don't care!" Leigh shouted.

She stomped up the stairs and hurled herself onto the loft-bed.

The next morning, a rustling sound in her room roused her from her sleep. She opened her eyes to find Peg arranging an assortment of blue orchids and white lilies in a vase.

The memory of her tantrum last night roared back into her mind and made Leigh's cheeks burn with shame. "Morning," she said in a soft murmur.

Peg turned, a broad forgiving smile on her face. "I think you mean, good afternoon."

"Is it really so late?"

"Afraid so. No surprise, given what time it was when you finally got to bed."

"Yeah," Leigh drawled. "About last night. I'm sorry I blew up like that. Your family has been so kind to me and that was an awful way to say thank you."

Peg stopped arranging flowers. "Leigh, Tristin and I knew before asking you to live with us that there would be ups and downs. Lord knows we've had a few with Myra and, given what you're dealing with -- well. Last night was overwrought nerves and pent-up grief. We'll let that be an end to it. Today starts with a clean slate."

"Clean slate," Leigh agreed.

She watched Peg as she returned to arranging the flowers. "They're beautiful."

"Yes, they are," Peg said, stepping back to admire her work. "You are going to have to show me where you found these orchids."

"Where *I* found them?"

"Didn't you bring them back from the woods? We don't have any like these in the garden."

Leigh climbed down her stairs and stood beside Peg, loving how the rich blue petals played off the white lilies. "I didn't pick them."

"I brought up lilies from our garden and found the orchids on your dresser. Maybe you were too distraught to remember."

"That must be it," Leigh said knowing it wasn't true.

Peg bought it. "In any event, they're here and they do so fill the room with such a wonderful fragrance."

She smiled at Leigh. "Tell you what. Why don't you get cleaned up and dressed and I'll go downstairs and whip up something for you to eat. Then, maybe we can retrace your steps from last night and see if we can find where the flowers came from. I'd love to transplant some into the garden."

Leigh wasn't keen on the idea but the last thing she wanted to do was offend Peg again. After closing her bedroom door behind Peg, she glanced up at Little Bodie's picture. She was curious to know if the running paint was just blur from her own tears, an invention of her imagination, or if it was real.

The first time she looked at the portrait she recognized the garden outside but, like the drumbeats to her favorite song, she knew it was there without really paying attention to it. Leaning in toward the painting, she now noted that behind Bodie was a flowerbed of beautiful blue orchids.

"Clean slate," she whispered.

Pulling a white lily out of the vase and tucking it behind a corner of Bodie's frame she said,

"I'm sorry, too," before moving away to shower.

Water spraying from the shower stung her face where last night's branches flailed across it. The cooler water, the more soothing it felt and, little by little, she twisted the faucet until the water was bitter cold. It hurt. It refreshed. She stood beneath it, face up, and let it stream over her so cold it burned.

A draft outside the shower stall whispered into the bathroom and, almost but not quite in her imagination, heard Little Bodie calling her actions, "Stupid."

Her eyelids fluttered. "I suppose so," she answered aloud.

Leigh shut off the water. "And I suppose I should be mad that a boy is watching me while I shower but, well, you're dead, so we'll call it even."

A spurt of water shot out of the shower head, splashing her face. "Hey!" Leigh cried. "It was a joke!"

She heard the bathroom door click shut.

Softly she said, "Maybe it wasn't such a very nice kind of joke though. Sorry?"

The door squeaked open half an inch. Leigh's lips tugged into an almost smile.

Showered and dressed, she found Peg in the kitchen laying out pastries for her while Jenny was doing the same on a coffee tray. There were three cups and saucers on the tray along with a French press of coffee and a stack of three small plates.

"Do we have company?" Leigh asked.

"Yes," Peg said. "Tristin, Marcus, and Oliver are in the office.

"Oliver?"

"That's right. You don't know Oliver Massy. He's Tristin's personal secretary, though, to be honest, Tristin relies more on Marcus."

"Ready to take these up," Jenny announced.

"Let me," Leigh asked.

"They are in a meeting," Peg said. "I don't think they'd want to be disturbed."

"I won't hang around. I'll just introduce myself to Mr. Massy and," she blushed but kept on, "while there, I can apologize to Tristin."

"Surely there'll be time to do that privately," Peg said.

Leigh straightened, her dad's words coming out of her mouth. "I made a fool out of myself publicly. I can make my apologies publicly."

"That's my girl," Peg said. "Carpe diem!"

"Isn't carp a fish?"

Peg laughed. "Carpe diem is Latin. It means, 'seize the day'. In this case it means I'm proud of you."

Leigh picked up the tray and headed for the office. In her mind, she was rehearsing what she wanted to say to Tristin. Really, there was only one thing to be said. *I acted like a brat and I'm sorry.*

Just before reaching the door she heard Tristin's voice. "I don't see why we need to delay. There is plenty of evidence already. I don't like having this looming over our heads for the next three days."

Marcus's smooth voice answered. "The police have evidence of what's going on but not of who, exactly, is involved. When the shipment arrives Thursday, they will be on hand to scoop up all the guilty parties."

"Well, I don't like it either," a voice Leigh didn't recognize said. "I especially don't like not having all the details."

The smug tones of Marcus cut him off. "It is strictly need to know and you know all you need to."

"Gentlemen," Tristin said. "I will not stand for infighting. Marcus, Oliver is my right-hand man and I won't have you squeezing him out under the pretext of security. Oliver, this operation has been years in the making. Law enforcement is calling the shots, not Marcus. Now, where the devil is that coffee so we can get down to brass tacks."

That was Leigh's cue. She stepped out from behind the doorframe and stood waiting to be invited in. "I asked Jenny if I could bring this up."

"Fine," Tristin said. "Please just set it over there."

Depositing her tray on an end table, she turned back to the group of men. "Uncle Tristin? I want to apologize for how I acted last night. It was unfair of me to treat you and Peg like that."

She caught him off guard. After a few stammered words and uncomfortable looks at his associates, he said, "Well, I suppose I can overlook it this time."

"I'm not trying to get you to do that. Forget about it, I mean. If you think it best I start seeing someone again, then that's what I do. I am sorry. That's all."

"We can talk about it later, I think."

"Sure."

Leigh turned, but not to leave. She extended her hand to Oliver. "You must be Mr. Massy. I'm Leigh."

"Miss Howard," Oliver said taking her hand in his. It was cold and soft.

Oliver Massy was a balding man who reminded her of some of the gamer-geeks she knew at school -- physically soft and in need of several days in the sunshine, preferably breathing ocean or mountain air.

Letting his hand drop Leigh stepped out of the office. Once around the corner, she clung to the wall listening but Marcus poked his head out the doorway and glared at her. He made a sour and suspicious grimace.

"Forget the way to wherever it was you were going, Miss Howard?"

"No," Leigh stammered. "I was just...just...."

He raised an eyebrow at her. "Do tell."

Leighs eyes narrowed into slits of anger. "Just leaving."

She stormed out the front door and let a creative stream of foul words flow from her mouth.

"Everything all right, Miss Howard?"

Leigh spun around to find Nacho at her elbow. "Oh my God! Did you hear me say all that?"

A conspiratorial grin spread across his face. "No."

"I'm fine," she said as she mussed up her long bangs.

Nacho's eyebrows raised in disbelief.

"Well, obviously I'm not fine. I'm furious. Something fishy's going on and, once again, no one is telling me anything. I mean, even bad news would be better than no news at all."

"They are trying to protect you. Give you the space you need to heal."

"Is that what helped you? After your village was wiped out? Did space help you?"

"I didn't get space. Just the opposite. I was an orphan in a very poor country. I had to run, hide, and focus on staying alive. I had no choice but to move on."

He paused, scratching his chin-stubble in thought. "Maybe that's what you need, the opposite of what you're getting. It's possible all this space is giving you room to stay comfortably stuck."

Leigh felt a twist of anger churn inside her. "So I just forget about what happened and move on?"

"You'll never forget. You know that just as well as I do in a way only people like us will ever understand."

Leigh felt hollow. Nacho was trying to help as best he could. "Thanks, Nacho. I appreciate your insight because, well, you've been there, haven't you?"

"Any time, señorita. And if you want to talk, I'm always around but," he shrugged his shoulders as he walked away, "I won't be around for long if I don't finish trimming the hedges."

"Leigh?" Peg called, rounding the corner of the house. "Leigh? You ready to find those blue orchids?"

Leigh groaned.

A wasted hour and a half later, Leigh was curled up on a leather couch in the library flipping through Bodie's journal reading an entry here or there but otherwise turning the pages and admiring the handwriting. All the time she was out with Peg, her thoughts were on Tristin, sealed inside his office with Marcus and Oliver talking about some police operation that may or may not be related to her parents' deaths. The not knowing was maddening. She would have given anything to be a fly on the wall but had to settle for the room next door with Big Bodie scowling down at her from above the fireplace.

The office door opened and Tristin, Marcus, and Oliver emerged. Tristin and Oliver passed by the entry to the library but Marcus slowed, spying her seated inside. He gave her a warning glare, wordlessly telling her to mind her own business. She flashed him the rudest and most defiant smile she could muster. Marcus chuckled at the attempt before moving to join the others.

Once he was out of sight, Leigh shot to her feet. She wanted to make a quick rummage to see if anything useful was left sitting out. Looking over her shoulder, her heart fluttering with clandestine excitement, she pushed the office door open. It began to swing in on well-oiled hinges, then it slammed shut inches from her nose.

She grabbed the doorknob and twisted. It refused to turn. The brass knob was so cold her skin froze to it. She tried to break her hand free and the door rattled from her thrashing.

"What on earth do you think you are doing?" Tristin snapped behind her.

The knob returned to normal warmth again and her hand fell free.

"Oh! Uh...nothing. I was...was...going to take the coffee tray back to the kitchen, but the door's stuck."

Tristin reached around her. Grabbing the knob with half his hand, he twisted and gave a light push. The door opened smooth and wide. "Seems okay to me."

"Yeah," Leigh said. "Guess I wasn't holding my mouth right."

Tristin grumbled. "Guess not. The tray is over there. Thanks for taking it away."

Leigh got the message. *Go away.*

Leigh skulked into the kitchen and, before being seen, left the tray on the counter and beat it back to her room. She threw herself down on the couch and sat staring out the small window, grinding her teeth.

"Why did you do that?" she growled to the empty room.

The blue sky darkened to a rich navy and the temperature of the room plummeted. When the sky's color settled into a consistent Caribbean blue, Leigh squeezed her eyes shut, convinced that, for whatever reason, they are deceiving her. When she opened them, Little Bodie was half sitting, half floating on the windowsill.

"Do what?" the ghost asked.

Leigh's mouth fell open. Her breath made steamy puffs in the chilly air. Just as if she were extending her hand to a large stray dog, part of her was terrified at the prospect of being bitten, but part of her was desperate to make a new, albeit dangerous, friend. Swallowing the lump building in her throat, she forced herself to not run from the room shrieking in terror.

"Do what?" Little Bodie asked again.

Keeping her voice steady took all her strength. "Lock me out of the office."

"I didn't."

Something about the way he said that made Leigh pause. He was afraid, she realized, but what did he have to be scared of other than himself? "But you did. I mean you and Big Bodie are the same person. Or at least you were, right? So, it had to be you."

The temperature in the room dropped even further as the blue light the boy was emitting increased in its intensity to the point it blotted out the light coming in through the windows. Bodie's ghost flew forward, stopping inches away from her. His face distorted into a horrifying and disfigured skeletal grimace of anger.

"I'm not him! I'll never be him!"

Leigh threw herself over and curled into a ball on the couch, covering as much of her head with her arms as she could. "Don't hurt me," she pleaded. "Please! Don't hurt me."

A whoosh of air pulled at her hair and clothing, making her feel like she was being sucked into a vacuum cleaner.

"I'm not going to hurt you," Bodie said in a sneering voice dripping with contempt. "This time. But I warn you, you shouldn't make me angry."

The billowing wind gone, Leigh lifted her neck, looking around to make sure he was nowhere near her. Blinking, she saw the ghost hovering by the window again.

She unfurled into a sitting position. "You scared the crap out of me," she snarled.

"You shouldn't have teased me," Bodie said as he played with a blue-glistening button on his shirt.

"I wasn't teasing you, you little brat. I was trying to figure you out. To understand. To help, if I can."

"You can't, so leave it alone."

"I might, if you explain it to me."

"No." His face curled into a grin of boyhood mischief. "But, if you're determined to get into Tristin's office, I can show you how to do it."

"You can?"

"Sure," he said with Huckleberry charm.

"What do I have to do?"

"Wait until everyone's asleep and go in through the window."

"The windows have security sensors on them."

"Not all of them. I'll show you how to do it." His voice took on a challenging tone. "Tonight, if you like."

"Fine," Leigh agreed. "Tonight."

Bodie twisted in the air, as if rising from some invisible chair. He walked through the window and up, ever higher into the blue sky all the while fading into nothing. Leigh sat in wide-eyed shock watching him go. While talking to Bodie, Leigh found it easy to pretend she was interacting with a real someone and not the ghost of a long dead boy. Now that he was gone, all the terror she was struggling to keep choked down overtook her. Leigh clutched at the pain in her chest which was there all along, but she was too frightened to acknowledge while Little Bodie was there. It was the pang of terror.

She shuffled through the rest of her day in a daze. As night descended, anticipation of what lay ahead of her grew, bringing with it bitter dread. She lay in bed dressed, waiting for Bodie to return as promised. Her stomach knotted and she spent more time on her feet pacing than she did in bed. The strain was more than her body could maintain and, as the massive grandfather clock downstairs bonged out the midnight hour, tension induced exhaustion overcame her.

She awoke curled in a ball clutching for her blankets. The air in the room felt arctic. Pulling her covers up to her neck, she had just dozed off when she found herself trying to pull the blankets up again. They were bunched around her feet just like they had been before pulling them up. With an annoyed yank, she threw them over her but they sailed past her, did an impossible pirouette in the air and sailed over the railing, landing on the floor below. Somewhere in the room but, oddly, not in the room at all, she heard giggling.

"Very funny," she snapped, sitting up, hugging herself for warmth. "Can't you make it any warmer?"

"No more than you can make yourself taller," Bodie's invisible voice said.

"So you, like, know you are a ghost?"

"Don't be stupid. Of course I know."

"Sorry," she said. "I don't have much experience with...people like you. And I have so many questions!"

"They'll have to wait if you're still wanting to break into the office downstairs."

She began pulling on her Keds. "I do, but how are we going to do it?"

Like his earlier fading away, this time in reverse, a pale blue fog appeared and became more and more dense until Bodie showed himself as he walked away from her, through her railing, and off the ledge. His archaic shoes hovered six feet off the floor as he strode through the air towards the small window in the sitting area.

"I did it loads of times when this was my room. All you have to do is crawl out this window and climb down the ivy outside. It's grown thick, with little tendrils carving their way deep into the walls so that it acts as a ladder."

The thought of it frightened her. "I'll fall. Besides, that window is painted shut. I've tried over and over to get it open to let a breeze in."

Bodie looked at her with sad pitying eyes and shook his head. Puffing up his cheeks, he released his ghostly breath in the direction of the window. Not so much as a speck of dust was disturbed anywhere in the room but the sealed window banged open.

"Okay," Leigh drawled in awe of his magic, "but how do I get out? The window is so high."

"How did you get up to try and open it before?"

"I climbed up on one of the chairs."

"I just jumped and pulled myself up," Bodie boasted.

Leigh's lip curled. "You're such a boy."

She climbed down the stairs and stood beneath the high window. She knew she was more than capable of jumping high enough to get her fingers over the windowsill. She knew she could do a pull-up to look out. What concerned her most was the question: would she be able to scrabble up and kneel on the sill without banging her feet against the wall, waking the whole house.

Not willing to risk it, she pushed one of the chairs beneath the window and climbed onto its back. Making awkward kicks with her feet and flailing with her arms, she reached a kneeling position in front of the window. Poking her head out into the night she saw the driveway far below, bathed in moonlight.

"How do I know it's safe? You might be one of those poltergeists that trick people into taking their own lives."

"You want to kill yourself anyway so what does it matter?"

Leigh jerked her head around with such violent disgust she rocked on the sill, nearly toppling out of it. Her fingernails dug into the hard wood as she clutched at the frame.

"That was mean," she snapped once in control of her balance.

"Well it's true, isn't it?"

"Sometimes yes," she had to admit. Before he could feel too good about himself she added, "Sometimes, no. Right now? No. And it was still an ugly thing to say."

Bodie moved through the wall to her left and stood hovering outside the window. "I think you're just afraid to climb out. That's why you're trying to start an argument with me."

Her jaw dropped open. The little brat was daring her to do it.

She clenched her teeth in determination.

Reaching out the window, she grabbed a handful of ivy and gave it a firm tug. To her surprise, the tendrils nearest the wall were big around as screwdriver handles. Repositioning her hand to get more of those and less of the thin vines on the outer edge, she tugged harder. The vines held. Sucking in a deep breath she swung herself up and out the window to stand on its sill while clenching the vines so tight they dug into her flesh.

"There!" she said to Bodie. "Now, where do I need to go?"

"Down, obviously. And keep to the right so you aren't trapped by the next window."

Leigh kicked hard to get her foot deep into the thick tangle of vines. Once her full weight was on them, and not on the windowsill, the growth sagged, making her whimper in fear which, in turn, filled her with shame.

"It'll hold," Bodie reassured her. "I told you, I used to do this all the time."

She began to climb down. "This better not be how you died."

Soon her hands were raw from gripping the rough vines. As her confidence in the ivy ladder grew, she descended faster until she was beside the high window leading into the office. She pressed on it but, like her own window, this one was also painted shut.

"Bodie, help me!"

"Hush," he said as his body faded to fog and seeped into the dense foliage. "Someone's coming."

A man and a woman, part of the night security patrol, passed underneath her. Their voices were loud in the otherwise still night. The pebbles of the drive crunched beneath their boots. Leigh held her breath as if the sound of her own breathing would give her away. The two were walking without a care but to her, it felt as if they were taking forever to leave.

"They're gone," Bodie said, oozing out of the growth as a mist before turning back into boy form. "Try the window again."

She pushed against one of the window panes and to her surprise the window opened making a soft whoosh. Her heart was pounding with a mixture of excitement and fear. She could feel her blood throbbing in the arteries at her neck. Squeezing through the window, she managed to get her feet then hands on the massive bookshelf just inside.

"Now what?" she asked, climbing down the shelves.

Bodie bled through the wall, turning the otherwise black room a blue tint.

"I don't know," he whined. "You're the one who wanted in here."

Leigh snorted in frustration and moved to Tristin's desk where his laptop lay open. As soon as her fingertips brushed the keyboard the screen lit up, filling the room with light. Terrified, Leigh sucked in her breath, swearing on the inhale. Cocking her ear, she listened for the guards' crunching feet. Turning back, she tried a few obvious passwords: 12345, password, OpenSesame, but, as she expected, they didn't work.

"Don't suppose you ghosts have hacking skills that open computers like windows?"

"Don't talk nonsense," Bodie said.

Leigh growled and abandoned the computer. She began rummaging through the items on Tristin's desk. The room was too dark to see, but she was too frightened to turn on a light. Fumbling over the top of the desk, her hand came in contact with the pen holder.

"Bodie?" she asked, picking it up. "Do you know if there is a safe in this room?"

"Sure," he said, floating on his back as if bored. "Push on the bookcase you climbed down."

Leigh set the pen holder back on the desk. Darting back to the shelves, she pushed with all her strength. Nothing happened.

"You push like a girl. C'mon! Push!"

Leigh scowled and made a foul gesture toward the ghost. Leaning all her weight against the bookshelf, it indented half an inch. Leigh heard a click.

"Well, go on," Bodie encouraged, "pull it open."

The bookcase slid on a hidden mechanism across the wooden floor making a sucking sound as it broke its seal with the wall. Behind the bookcase was a massive metal door reflecting Bodie's ghostly blue shade. Reaching out to run her fingers over the smooth cold door Leigh found the handle and a peculiar lock. It had a dial but the numbers were displayed on a tiny screen over it. Like the laptop, the screen lit up when she grazed the dial. She picked up the pen holder.

"Can you burn any brighter?" she asked.

"No," Bodie answered, seemingly indignant over the suggestion he be used as a lamp.

She returned to the safe. "What good are you?"

Bodie snarled. "If it weren't for me, you'd still be stuck in my room."

"I'd have found a way down," she taunted.

In his anger, his dark soft blue turned into the color of the sky on a hot summer's day.

Leigh flipped the pen holder over and read the numbers and turned the dial to each, one by one. "Thanks," she said.

"Hey! You tricked me," Bodie exclaimed.

"Not tricked. Just helped you discover a new skill. And it's my room, by the way. Pretty sure you're done with it."

"Now who's being mean?"

The magnetic seal on the safe clicked off as Bodie's hues darkened again. Leigh pushed the door inward to discover a small room stocked with food, water, a small metal cot and a computer. The walls were lined with shelves upon which sat various stacks of paper, currency from every country, and an assortment of priceless trinkets and knick-knacks.

As she crossed the threshold, an overhead light flicked on. She cringed against its brightness but didn't know how to shut it off. Frightened by the thought of being discovered, she turned her attention to the stack of folders on the shelf nearest the door. Opening the top one she realized she got lucky. The first page summarized the police sting operation. Whipping out her phone, she snapped a photo.

"Wonder how this was done in your day?" Leigh asked absently.

"With a thing called memory. You should try it," Bodie said.

"You aren't still mad, are you?"

"No," he said, "If I was, I wouldn't bother telling you security is coming. So is Tristin."

"What?!"

Leigh shot out of the safe and swung the heavy door shut. She shoved the bookcase back into place and began scaling the shelves. As she pushed off the top of the bookcase and out the window, she felt it slide away from the wall. Stretching her arm back in she scratched at it but couldn't get a decent grip.

The door to the office burst open. Lights blasted on. Leigh saw Tristin standing in the doorway scanning the room. Behind him were two burly men in suits.

"You're certain you saw a light in here?" Tristin demanded.

"Yes, sir," one of the guards answered. "There was a dark blue one then, a second later, a regular one came on."

Leigh swung onto the ivy at the side of the window and clung there, too terrified to move.

"Well, there's no one here now," she heard Tristin say. "Wait," he shouted. "Why is this open?"

Leigh felt the slightest bump and heard the bookcase click.

"Someone's been in here! Search the house and the grounds. I want them found!"

"Climb, you fool," Bodie hissed in her ear.

As fast as she could, Leigh scaled the wall. The crunch of her hands clutching at vines sounded deafening to her. Her fingernails smashed against the rough bricks beneath and shredded what little there was of them. Her feet kicked into the green web but as often as not slid out. She had to pull with all her strength. Biting her lip to keep from shrieking, she climbed on.

Below, lights cracked on all across the lawn and gardens. The grounds were bright as day and anyone looking up would see her as she pulled herself even with her window. She had to get inside! Swinging her weight toward the opening, she used too much force and the vines her hands were clinging to pulled away from the wall.

"What are you doing?" snarled Bodie.

"Falling, you idiot. What does it look like?"

"Reposition yourself and get inside!"

The vines jerked farther away from the wall and Leigh jolted down a few more inches.

"I can't," she cried. "I don't know how! Bodie! Help me!"

Bodie's face hovered even with her own. His eyes were hard and his lips were a thin blue line.

"I can show you how but I can't do it for you."

"Please," she begged. "Anything!"

Bodie became a blue mist. It rushed at her, hitting her between the eyes. A nauseating sense of being violated overwhelmed her. Her insides burned with freezing cold. She wanted to vomit. The urge to swing away from her window then back again, throwing herself off the vines at the last minute so that she could grab onto the ledge overwhelmed her.

"I...I can't," she cried.

Bodie's voice echoed within the icy walls of her brain. He sounded as desperate as she felt. "I can't do it for you!"

Below, Leigh she heard footfalls as the guards began their hunt for her. She had no choice. Kicking hard with her legs while holding as tight as she could with one hand, she rolled away from her window. When her back hit the wall she bounced herself off using all her strength. Just before her face slammed into the rock, the urge to let go consumed her. Giving in to it, she released her hold and skimmed over the surface of the wall, leaves of ivy caressing her cheeks. Flailing her arms in desperation, she managed to throw one inside her open window. Clinging to the windowsill she scratched and clawed her way inside the room where she fell to the floor.

On her hands and knees, she panted for air. The room was spinning. Blue mist seeped out of her and congealed into Bodie. "They're on their way to check on you. Get into bed. Fast!"

She pried herself off the floor. Staggering, she made her way up to her loft and into bed. She rolled onto her side, turning her back to the door, as her bedroom door creaked open. Tristin poked his head in.

She feigned a mumble and a snore.

Tristin entered the room and, standing in the center, gave it a three-hundred-sixty-degree inspection. The longer he lingered, the faster Leigh's heart raced. She heard his shoes rasp against the floor as he searched for anything he could accuse her of. Satisfied there was nothing to see, he left as quietly as he came.

Leigh stayed where she was, too terrified to move. It wasn't the fear of getting caught that made her heart pound, though that added to it. Whatever Bodie did left her feeling wrong inside. She was struggling with her own identity. For a few flashing seconds she owned skills, thoughts, and emotions which were not her own. They were still in there, somewhere inside her head, inside her body, filling her with knowledge about things she'd never done or seen. Strangely, the addition of new memories left her feeling less than she was before instead of more.

"What did you do to me?" she asked the empty darkness.

Chapter Nine

Leigh tossed from side to side under blankets that felt hot and smothering. No matter what position she curled into, she was too terrified to settle. With wide eyes, she stared into the darkness of her room searching for the faintest hint of blue glow.

Giving up on sleep she rolled, then sat with her legs dangling over the side of her mattress. Trembling fingers clamped around her sheets. Her pounding heart and queasy stomach were screaming at her to run as far away from Simmons-Pierce Manor as she could. It took all her willpower to keep her voice silent and her legs still.

She watched the dawn creep in. Rocking like a terrified child on the side of her bed she blinked at the horizon as gray mellowed into orange which, in turn, brightened to rosy pink. Before the full force of dawn's yellow lit the sky, she was in her shoes and out the door. She couldn't escape the room fast enough.

"You're up early," Tristin said as she hopped past him on the stairs.

She shrugged. "Have you seen Nacho?" she called without stopping.

His eyes widened in surprise. "No. Why?"

"I'm feeling a little restless this morning," she lied. "I was curious if he was going into the city on any errands. Thought I might go with him."

"Well, I certainly don't know his schedule," Tristin said with a smug laugh.

Leigh went on bounding down the stairs. "I'll find him."

"You might want to talk to Peg," Tristin called after her. "She may have a chore or two for you, if you're looking to keep busy."

Leigh muttered to herself, "Anything, as long as it gets me out of this place."

Leaping over the last step, she charged to the door, threw it open, and darted outside. The skies were brighter than when she left her room seconds ago. The pastel hues of the gardens, grass, and trees coupled with birdsong to make the morning seem like a fairytale. What should have been a peaceful moment did nothing to soothe Leigh's waking nightmare. She ran across the lawn as if she could outpace the memory of what Bodie did to her last night.

She reached the garage where staff parked their cars and where the Simmons-Pierce vehicles were kept. She spied Nacho's battered yellow truck, so he had to be on the grounds somewhere. Though she'd never seen him working on any of the family's cars she decided to check inside the garage as long as she was here.

Inside she found what she expected from a family as wealthy as the Simmons-Pierces. Ferrari, Aston Martin, Porsche, Rolls Royce -- all the high-end automakers were well represented. Making her way through the rows of cars she admired the sleek beauty of the speeders and the opulence of the sedans. Making her way toward the back of the garage was like walking through time, the further away she made it from the door, the older the cars became until she reached a row of horse-drawn buggies and coaches.

The unmistakable clanking of a dropped socket-wrench made her spin around. A torrent of foul Spanish followed.

"Nacho?" she called out.

"Si...er...yeah, it's me. Who's there?"

Leigh took off in the direction of his voice.

At the far end of the garage was a small door leading into a separate, smaller garage. Inside were numerous motorcycles. Nacho was on his knees working on a dirt bike.

"It's me," she said.

Nacho breathed a sigh of relief. "I thought you were Mrs. Simmons. I don't know how much Spanish she speaks but if it's any at all, she'd not be too happy hearing me talk like that."

He eyed Leigh suspiciously. "How much Spanish do you know?"

Leigh giggled. "Enough."

"Well," he drawled. "I heard you yesterday going off like a sailor. You heard me today. Even?"

"Even," she agreed.

"So what brings you out here?"

"You said I needed to inventory my parents' house. Decide what comes here and what goes away?"

"Yeah. When would you like to do that?"

Leigh shuffled her feet while picking at her fingernails. Her voice timid she asked, "Now?"

"Now? Just like that?"

"Please, Nacho! I've got to get away from here for a little while."

"You asked Mrs. Simmons?"

"No. I wanted to make sure you'd take me, first."

He eyed her again. "More like you didn't want her to know in case I said I couldn't today. That way you could come up with some other way outta here."

"Am I that easy to read?"

"No, but you remind me a lot of myself when I was your age. You ready to go?"

"Yeah, but don't we need to check with Peg?"

Nacho said with a shrug, " Easier to ask for forgiveness than permission. Besides, Mrs. Simmons would want to come along. I get the feeling you'd rather be on your own."

Leigh grinned. "I'll grab my things and meet you out front."

Nacho pushed onto his feet. Looking at his hands he rubbed his thumbs over his greasy fingertips. "Better give me forty-five minutes. It's a long ride with a stinky driver."

"Great!" Leigh beamed, ignoring his jibe. "Outside in forty-five?"

Nacho's lips curled in a half-grin and nodded.

Leigh paced in her room, nibbling on her thumbnail. She had no idea what she intended to do once she and Nacho were out of the manor. She was making it up as she went along. One thing she was sure of, and it made her feel gross. She had to ditch Nacho.

The cruelty of betraying him made her think about confiding in him, but the more she thought about it the more she realized that would never happen. She couldn't imagine Nacho sticking his neck out that far, risking his job, getting in trouble with the police, or his life, for her. Somewhere along the way, she was going to have to desert him. Feeling guilty in no way lessened her resolve.

Grabbing her bag off the dresser, she slung it over her shoulder. It hit her hip with a heavy thud, reminding her that Bodie's journal was inside. She formed the habit of taking it with her everywhere, reading bits and pieces whenever she felt she needed a pick-me-up. That was before last night.

Fear filled Leigh, remembering how she almost fell off the ivy. Confusion also fogged her brain as she thought about how Bodie had taken her over; how he violated her. Even if she did ask for his help, she had no way of knowing he was going to do *that*. That he was going to possess her. The fact that it saved her life didn't seem to matter. She wanted nothing more to do with him.

Taking the book out of her bag she went into her closet. Not giving herself time to think, she dropped to her knees, and crawled as far forward as she could. Prying up the loose floorboards she put the book back in its place.

A jab of sorrow stabbed her heart. At first she thought she was feeling betrayed over what Bodie did, but that didn't feel right. As she closed the closet door behind her, she felt like she was the one betraying him.

A horn tooted outside.

She ran across the room and snatched up her bag. She didn't want to think about Bodie anymore. She wanted out of this place and Nacho was downstairs waiting to take her away. Bounding down the stairs, she bolted out the front door and into Nacho's waiting truck. He started down the drive before her seat belt was fastened. Familiar with his truck, the guards opened the gate and they soared through without Nacho so much as tapping the brakes.

"We're all in now," Nacho said with a grin.

Leigh agreed but kept her silence.

After a few miles, Nacho asked, "So why the sudden urgency to get this done?"

"I told you," Leigh said, her eyes fixed on the passing scenery out the window, "I was feeling cooped up. Like I needed different air, if that makes sense."

"Perfect sense. We all get restless moods from time to time. I just thought you'd have wanted family with you, that's all. This isn't going to be easy, facing so many memories."

"I know, but memories can't be worse than facing him."

Leigh's lips slapped shut. She couldn't believe she said that out loud.

"Who? Leigh, did something happen? Is someone hurting you at the house?"

"No, nothing like that. What I meant was I'm having bad dreams," she lied, "about whoever killed my parents."

Nacho gave her a suspicious look out of the corner of his eye.

She tried to laugh it off but couldn't help telling him the truth. The best she could do was disguise it as a joke. "I'm being a silly little girl who's seeing ghosts."

Nacho smiled. "Ah, the ghosts of Simmons-Pierce Manor."

"You know about them?"

"I know the stories. Myra tells them to anyone willing to listen." He winked at her, "Or to whoever has no choice but to listen."

"So you've never seen them?"

"Can't see what isn't there to see. I don't believe in spooks."

"I thought everyone in South America believed in that stuff."

"Wow! Stereotype much?"

Leigh felt her face drain in embarrassment. "Oh! I didn't mean that the way it sounded."

Nacho laughed at her. "Don't sweat it. Most the old folks do believe in that nonsense, so you're not too far off. The younger generation? We have internet."

Leigh smiled and turned to look back out the window. Nacho had a way of always making her feel better. Then again, so did Bodie, until he...

She shuddered and forced that thought out of her mind.

"You cold?"

"No. Nervous."

Nacho nodded and left her to her thoughts.

Bushes, trees, and buildings flashed past. She cocked her head at the occasional landmarks she recognized. The longer they drove, the more frequently they cropped up until she was in her own neighborhood and everything was a painful memory; her school, her church, and finally, her house.

Nacho eased his truck into the low sloping drive. Turning off the engine, he waited kindly for her to take off her belt and get out. He was giving her all the time she needed.

When ready, she eased out of the truck and walked to the keypad mounted on the garage door. She knew the code by heart but it'd been so long since she typed it in that the last number was pressed with a twinge of doubt tickling her insides.

Electricity hummed. The door creaked and groaned as it lifted. As if nothing had changed, it rattled as the wheels hit that part of the track she clipped with the van's mirror when her dad let her try to back the van out of the garage. Her mom was so angry! Ever since, when Leigh heard that sound, she felt so embarrassed. Now, it made her feel lonely.

"Where's the van?" she asked, staring into the emptiness of the garage.

"Police," was all Nacho said.

Leigh shrugged. "Doesn't matter. Mom wanted to sell it anyway."

Not hesitating, she walked to a tarp draped motorcycle. Gently, she slipped off the cover. Making a sharp gasp she stared at her dad's Ducati Panigale.

Nacho let out a long whistle of admiration. "That is one nice bike."

Leigh circled the bike ignoring Nacho. She let her fingers caress where her dad sat and the raised all too small looking passenger hump behind where she would sit clinging to his torso, thrilled by her dad's expert handling of the powerful machine.

"This. I want this."

"You know how to ride?" Nacho asked opening a notebook.

"Dad taught me. He thought Mom didn't know, but she did. She told me, 'I can no more stop him being the man he is than I can you from being his daughter. Just promise me you'll be careful.'"

Leigh smiled a distant grin. "Mom never told him she knew. I think she wanted it to be our, or at least his, father-daughter secret."

"Sounds like you had one great family."

"I did," Leigh said.

An uncomfortable silence fell between them. Leigh pushed open the door leading inside. She passed through the laundry room, the kitchen, and into the TV room where she froze. Her dad's favorite recliner stood where it always did. Her mom's cross-stitch, her latest craft kick, was left lying on the couch. Dishes, a washer and dryer, tables, chairs, bric-a-brac and knick-knacks -- so much more than she ever consciously thought about, closed in on her from all sides. Her breath caught in her chest. "What's going to happen to it all?"

"Mrs. Simmons says some of it you can put into storage until you are older. A few things can be brought to the manor, like the bike." Nacho studied a wall of pictures. "These family photos."

He turned to face her, gently choosing to tell her the truth. "Most of it will have to be sold off, I guess."

"No," Leigh said firmly.

"Leigh, you can't keep it all."

"That's not what I'm saying. What I mean is, I don't want any of it sold off. I want it donated to families of fallen police officers, women's shelters, that sort of thing. Dad was really big on helping gang kids escape their fate. Can the house be turned into a foster home or something like that?"

"Maybe. You've a big heart, and that's a fact," Nacho said.

"We'll see if you still think so in an hour," Leigh whispered to herself as she wandered off to the bedrooms.

The next step in her plan came to her the instant she laid eyes on her dad's bike. With Nacho out of sight, she rushed into her parents' bedroom. Thrusting her hand into the dish where her dad kept his keys, Leigh picked out the motorcycle's and slipped it into her hoodie pocket. Opening the top drawer, she tossed in her phone.

"Hey, Nacho," she called out, closing the drawer. "There's a suitcase under the bed. I think Mom's wedding dress is in it. Would you mind helping me pull it out to make sure?"

Nacho came into the room. "Sure thing."

He knelt down and peered under the bed.

Leigh ran from the house and into the garage.

"Leigh?" she heard him calling from the bedroom.

With a rough jerk she rammed her head into her helmet, straddled the massive Ducati, and started the engine.

"Leigh," Nacho shouted, racing into the garage.

She left him standing in the driveway, waving his arms and yelling after her as she raced down the street and around the far corner.

For thirty minutes, she drove aimlessly without any destination in mind. All she wanted to do was to put as many miles as she could between Nacho and herself. At first, she was content to just be one with a piece of her father. He loved this bike and she did, too. Her contentment didn't last long. The longer she rode, the more hunched over and sad she became. Frightened, too.

Nacho would have already called, if not the police, then at least Tristin. It was only a matter of time before she was caught. Like a slap in the face, she realized she was on the run and on the clock.

Racking her brain for the next phase of her non-existent plan, she pulled into a secluded cul-de-sac to concentrate. Closing her eyes, she tried to recall all the details from the documents she found in Tristin's safe. To most, the information would appear to be thin at best, but she was a cop's daughter. She knew how fragile leads were. Hunches turned into facts with solid evidence. Until that evidence was discovered, everything was guesswork. She, like her father, was a shrewd guesser.

Her brows knitted as she concentrated. A shipment from overseas was arriving at the docks tomorrow night. What that shipment was and who was supposed to intercept it was still unknown. However, the overseas source of the shipment was suspected to be Russian mafia, driving Leigh's imagination to drugs. Along with the idea of drugs the name Tomika came to her.

She revved the powerful machine purring between her knees and roared off again. It didn't take long before she was standing on Tomika's doorstep, having just rung the bell, with no idea what she was going to say.

"May I help you?" asked the elderly woman who answered the door.

"Um, my name is Leigh. I know Tomika from school?"

Leigh shuffled her feet. Saying she knew Tomika was too strong. She never spoke to Tomika. What little she knew about her was that Tomika was trouble and to stay as far away from her as she could. The truth was, her dad knew Tomika far better than she did. Knew her professionally. He arrested her for dealing. He testified against her in court. He also appealed to the court on her behalf, recommending home incarceration on the conditions of counseling, rehab, and maintaining a B average in school. Leigh hoped that goodwill would buy her the information she needed.

"I'm sorry, but if you know my granddaughter you know she isn't allowed visitors without an appointment."

"Please," Leigh begged. "It's important! I promise it will only take a minute."

"I'm sorry," the woman said as she began closing the door.

A girl's voice called from inside the house. "Leigh? Leigh Howard?"

Leigh slammed her palm against the door, making the old woman's eyes pop. "Yeah, it's me. Look, can I talk to you for a sec?"

Tomika came to stand at her grandmother's shoulder. She was dressed in pajamas and her hair looked like she just got out of bed. Leigh couldn't keep herself from checking out the ankle monitor clamped above the girl's left foot.

Clearly ashamed, Tomika ran her fingers through her wild hair. "Sorry for the look. Day after day with nowhere to go, you kinda give up on some things."

"Tomika, you know you can't have no visitors," her grandmother said.

"It's all good, Gran. This is Detective Howard's girl."

It was Leigh's turn to blush as the old woman's eyes swelled again, this time in sympathy. "Heard what happened. Your daddy was a good man. Didn't deserve what he got. Neither did you."

"Thank you," Leigh whispered, staring at the porch floor, willing herself to not cry.

"I'll give you fifteen minutes, Tomika," her grandmother said, choosing to overlook Leigh's discomfort, "but both you need to know, I'll have to tell your probation officer 'bout this meet."

"That's fine. Last thing I want is for Tomika to get in more trouble."

Tamika's grandmother shook her head. "I'm old, not stupid. I'm thinking it's you looking to find trouble."

To Tomika she said, "Fifteen. And not a minute more."

"Okay, Gran. Okay."

The old woman shuffled inside as Tomika led Leigh to a porch swing. "Afraid this is about as private as it gets."

Leigh sat. "It'll be fine."

"So, I'm guessing this isn't a health and welfare check?"

"No. I'm sorry about coming here, but couldn't think of anywhere else to go."

"Clock's ticking, girlfriend. You better spill it."

"It's about Dad. Everyone's given up trying to find out what happened. I caught word of something going on down at the docks and I think it's drugs and I think it could be related to what happened to Dad, but nobody else is looking at it that way."

Tomika narrowed her eyes and the corners of her mouth drooped. "You think dope and automatically *I* come to mind?"

"No! Yes. Maybe," Leigh said loud and confused. "I don't know! All I want is justice for Mom and Dad. I can't find peace until I know their killer is behind bars. Until I know why my parents had to die."

"All right. All right. Calm down. You trying to give Gran a coronary or something?"

"Sorry," Leigh said picking at the threads around a hole in her jeans. "I'm just so…"

"Desperate? Been there. Your old man saw that and did what he could to help. But you gotta understand, I've been out of the game for a while and plan to stay out when my time is done."

"So you don't know anything that might help?"

"I worked distribution, not procurement. You know? All I have is a name I got off a friend of a friend like, a long while back."

"Anything," Leigh pleaded.

Tomika hesitated, her eyes boring into Leigh's as if looking straight through her. "I'm sitting here thinking to myself it'd be a piss-poor way to repay your daddy for all he done for me by sending his little girl off to get herself killed."

A lump grew in Leigh's throat. She was terrified Tomika wasn't going to help. She balled the cuffs of her hoodie in her hands and clenched her teeth. She knew if she wanted answers she had to be honest with Tomika, but that meant being honest with herself, too.

Relaxing her grip on her cuffs, she slid the right one up and rolled her wrist over. "Not knowing who and why is killing me, too."

Tomika looked down at the tell-tale pink slash across her wrist. "Damn, girl. Just…damn! Didn't know about that."

A tear rolled over Leigh's cheek as she tugged her sleeve back down. "That makes you the only one."

The two sat in silence. Tomika began rocking the swing as if sitting with an upset child. Leigh didn't find that condescending but rather kind and soothing. At some point Tomika took Leigh's hand in hers but Leigh couldn't have said exactly when.

"All right you two," Tomika's grandmother shouted through an open screen. "That's all the time I can give."

Leigh rose and began to leave. If Tomika felt she couldn't or shouldn't help her, she understood. She was asking a lot out of a stranger whose debt was to her father, not her. Tomika was one of the kind ones. She didn't mock her. She didn't pry into her psyche. She let her be and, like Myra, did her best to understand, knowing she never fully could. As Leigh walked, the sidewalk turned blurry with her tears but she refused to make Tomika feel worse by watching her wipe them away.

"Dante Jones. Man at the docks who makes the pick up? His name is Dante Jones. Works nights."

"Thank you," Leigh said, staring at the strip of grass by the curb.

She straddled the Ducati, pulled on her helmet and, like she did Nacho, left another friend to stare at her back as she sped away.

Chapter Ten

As Leigh drove her mind was in a whirl. According to what she read, the police sting would take place tomorrow night. If she was going to confront Dante, it had to be tonight while she had valuable information to trade. In order to do that, she had to find some place to keep out of sight for twelve hours. The Ducati didn't hold enough gas to cruise around town that long. Her jaw tightened as she thought of how many people would be out looking for her by now. She had to hide.

Taking a meandering route, because she didn't know where she was going, Leigh targeted a tall crane on the horizon and, by turning towards it whenever possible, closed in on the Simmons-Pierce freight yard. She drove past the main gate, never slowing down. Burning as much of the layout as she could into her brain without drawing too much attention to herself, she drove on, searching for a hideout. Rounding a corner two blocks away, she found an abandoned, half collapsed gas station and pulled in. Despite it being a warm day, Leigh dismounted and sat on the floor shivering. With her knees hugged to her chest, she settled in for a long wait. As hard as she tried, she struggled to believe she was actually being so foolish and reckless.

The boredom was mind numbing. A crumbling wall's shadow inched across the floor. Fearless and indifferent to her presence, a rat scurried in. The filthy rodent raised up on its hind legs and gave her a furious look before darting away as a feral cat pranced in behind.

When the wall's shadow darkened three quarters of the room, she heard a dog rummaging in the garbage piled outside. It stuck its scared nose through a hole in the wall and growled at her. Her heart leapt into her throat. The beast seemed to lose interest and moved on, leaving her to wipe nervous sweat off her forehead. Though she had been holding it in for hours, the fright pushed her over the limit and, her face burning with embarrassment, she was forced to seek out the deepest part of the building and pee.

The gray shades of dusk started closing in. To Leigh, that meant a good seven hours of more waiting. Her rear end ached from sitting so she paced. Freezing in the middle of the room, she swore loudly.

"You have no idea how you are getting into that place, do you?" she admonished herself.

Leigh thought about driving up and down the outside of the yard's chain-link fence but, the Ducati being such a distinctive bike, that would draw too much attention to herself. Having no other option, she locked the bike and walked back to the fence line.

The sidewalk was sandwiched between a long line of trucks queued at the curb and the silver chain-link fence. On the other side of the barricade, rows of metal shipping containers stood stacked four and five high, one on top of the other, and ran for over a mile until halted by the ocean. Three massive ships were secured to the docks and towering cranes were unloading cargo. As she walked the length of the fence, she noted that it stood twelve feet in height, topped with spiraling concertina wire, and in excellent repair.

She growled, knowing who was to blame for making the yard so impenetrable. "Marcus!"

It didn't take long to decide continuing on the way she was going was pointless. Turning around, she decided to check out the entrance to the yard more closely. When she arrived, she confirmed what she saw as she drove by. There was one four lane passage into and out of the yard. One wide pair of lanes was for trucks to enter and exit and the other, a narrower set, was for employees. Separating the two sets of lanes was a plain white shack with three guards. At all times, two of the security officers worked the line of trucks, checking paperwork and collecting signatures. The third stayed inside answering the phone and monitoring CCTV feeds.

Leigh threaded her fingers through the fence and rested her head against the metal. A sharp spur nicked her forehead, but she didn't care. She had no way in. She'd risked everything, betrayed her family, manipulated Nacho and, despite still being angry with him, felt like she abandoned Little Bodie. Sooner or later she would have to answer for those things, and all for nothing. A heavy sigh of defeat escaped her lungs.

"Hey," a woman shouted, "you can't be hanging around here."

One of the security guards broke away from the line of trucks and was headed in her direction.

"I was...was...I'm writing a paper for school," Leigh lied. School was out for the summer, but she was caught off guard. "On...onnnn...on the importance of shipping to the local community."

"I don't care what you're doing. You can't do it here," the guard said, standing on the other side of the fence from Leigh.

"Please," Leigh pleaded, "I missed a lot of school last year and if I don't make it up over the summer, I'll have to repeat a grade."

The woman dug into her shirt pocket. She poked a business card through the fence. "Call the office number. Set up an appointment. I'm sure someone will talk to you, but you can't stay here."

Someone behind the woman shouted and she turned her head. Another guard was walking toward the shack with a man in handcuffs.

"What's that all about?" Leigh asked.

"Someone trying to sneak into the country, I suspect. We get two or three of those a month. They stow away on the cargo ships then hide until the train pulls out."

"Train?" Leigh asked. "What train?"

"A freight train pulls in every night and gets loaded with containers. Every morning it pulls out before city traffic picks up," the guard explained. "Now, you have to be on your way. Good luck with your paper."

The guard trotted away to join her colleague in detaining the man. Leigh moved away, too, determined to discover where the train entered the shipyard. She had to retrace her steps beyond where she first turned around to inspect the entrance. The coastline curved back toward the city while the fence continued on a rocky wave break well out into the ocean. Following the coastline, she found the network of steel rails leading into and out of the freight yard. Blocking unwanted access, a massive gate stood where the tracks crossed the perimeter of the fence. It was closed and a padlock held a thick length of chain in place. Leigh assumed that the gate was opened on a schedule that coincided with the arrival and departure of the train.

Leigh wanted to move closer and probe the gate for weaknesses but took the precaution of scanning the area for surveillance cameras first. Mounted on tall poles, pointing both in and out of the gated yard, she found several and cursed the name of Marcus Figueroa again. Left with no choice, she followed the tracks away from the yard, keeping her eyes peeled for a secluded spot she could jump onto the arriving train. That was her plan and she knew it was too desperate and too reckless. Her plan sucked.

Back inside the crumbling gas station, having decided on the spot where she'd hop the train, she hunkered down for another long wait. Armed with a plan, time flew by. With every passing second the nervousness of anticipation bloomed like a foul scented weed, making her feel nauseous. The pounding of her heart reminded her of how terrified she felt when she was sure she was going to fall off the manor wall. Bodie, no matter how he left her feeling, saved her. Grudgingly, she wished she'd brought his journal with her. At least then a piece of him would be here with her and she wouldn't feel so alone.

Night was in full swing when she heard the distant tooting of the train's horn. Checking that the bike was secure, despite not seeing another soul all evening, she pelted out of her hideaway and into the darkness. After a brisk run to the tracks, she pressed her back against the wall of a public housing block, ignoring the old men who sat in the shadows drinking wine and beer and who, likewise, ignored her.

The train began to clear the last cross street before making the final stretch to the shipyard. The clanging of the cross-guard put her nerves on edge. Steam, wind, and dust billowed out from beneath the passing railroad cars and the deadly wheels clacked over the rail's seams. Logic told her that the train had to be moving at a modest twenty miles per hour or less, but to Leigh it seemed the train was hurtling along at eighty.

In the streetlight at the crossing she saw an empty, low, flatbed car. Setting her jaw in determination she made that her target. Tiptoeing through the grass, between the building and the tracks, she stepped onto the gravel beside the rails. The cars were whizzing past her. The ground rumbled beneath her tennis shoes. The flatbed was coming up quick. She started to jog. By the time the leading edge of her target car was even with her shoulders, she was sprinting but still, the car was pulling away. Pumping her legs with all her strength, she inched closer and closer to the side of the car. The roaring steel wheels were now less than a foot away. If she fell beneath them she'd be cut to pieces.

Just ahead, both she and the train were closing in on a warning light flashing at the side of the tracks. When she scoped out this spot earlier, she thought she'd be on the train well before she came to the light. Her legs burned and started to falter. Just like when clinging to the ivy, she knew what she had to do, but was afraid to do it.

Letting out a scream that was overpowered by the roaring train, she pushed off with her outside foot. Her hip collided against the hard iron corner of the car and pain rocked through her body. Flailing, nearly hysterical with fear, she held on for dear life. Pulling her knees behind her, ankles to butt, she lifted them as far away from the open gap beneath the car as she could. The floor of the car was made of rough wooden planks. Large splinters wedged into her hands and sliced beneath her nails as she scratched and clawed her way onto the car.

Arms aching, fingers bleeding, she gave a massive heave until her hips cleared the edge and, in a panic, rolled to the center of the car. Her heart throbbed against her ribs with painful thuds. Though she was sucking in air as fast as she could she felt like she was suffocating.

She swore at herself. "Move! You can't stay in the open like this."

Struggling to her feet, the rattling lurching railroad car tossed her back down. Rather than trying that again, she crawled on all fours to the end of the car where the bed rose to allow room for the wheels. A small metal stair led to a raised platform above the wheels. There was no place else to seek cover. She crouched down into the corner of the stairs, making herself as small as possible, and prayed whoever was manning the gate wasn't paying too much attention.

Her eyes raised just above the steps, she watched the fence approach, come even with her, and get left behind. The train rushed past a guard, but he was far to the side and was shielding his eyes from the dirt and debris the big steel wheels were billowing up in a whoosh. Crawling like a baby, she returned to the edge of the car. She didn't know where the train was going to stop but was certain she didn't want to be on it when it did.

Jumping onto the car was terrifying. Jumping off, she knew, was going to hurt when she hit the pavement, but she didn't find that prospect nearly as frightening. Pulling her legs beneath her, she hunkered down into a small ball. Leaping more outwards than upwards, she hit the concrete with a jarring thud and rolled out of control for several feet. When she came to a stop, every bone and muscle ached but she couldn't waste time wondering if she was seriously hurt.

Springing to her feet she sprinted into the concealment provided by two metal shipping containers standing side-by-side. Wedged into their cramped space, she collapsed. Her body heaved as she panted for air. Thoughts refused to solidify in her mind. They were overpowered by both her physical and emotional exhaustion. Huffing like an out of breath dog, she thought about the next part of her non-existent plan -- finding Dante Jones.

Keeping to narrow gaps between containers, she made her way deep inside the yard, all the while hissing at herself to, "Think! Think! Think!"

Wedging herself into another tight gap between two metal boxes, she took a deep breath and sank down to the concrete. "Look," she told herself, speaking aloud, "that train gets loaded every night. Dante works nights. Chances are he spends some of his time working on the train."

She poked her head out past the edge of the containers. The train stood motionless at the far end of the yard and three massive cranes were maneuvering into position to start loading and unloading cargo containers. A crew of men scurried around with orange coned flashlights giving directions and making signals. It reminded Leigh of being at the airport watching ground crews guide planes to the gates. Sticking to shadows, nooks, and crannies, Leigh inched closer to the work crews.

As she closed in, the light and the noise made chaos of her senses. The cranes were loud and rumbling. Massive lights spun in every direction as they moved. Men on the ground were shouting to be heard over the din. A few were in radio contact with the crane operators, who replied in unintelligible static filled squawks.

Leigh's heart shot to her throat when she heard a blonde woman in a sky-blue hard hat scream into the racket, "Hey! Dante! When you want your break?"

Risking being seen, Leigh jabbed her head out into the clear and tried to see who answered.

A young man with a goatee, wearing navy coveralls, shouted back, "You asking me out on a date, boss?"

The woman made an obscene gesture and Dante laughed. "Three," he shouted, returning to his work.

The woman made a note on her clipboard and walked off.

As Leigh watched, Dante received a phone call. Stuffing his phone back into his pocket, he looked over his shoulder and made sure the supervisor was gone. He said something to another man before hustling away. Leigh did her best to stay hidden as she followed Dante into a large building. As far as she could tell, she and Dante were the only two inside, but she had no way of knowing.

Picking up a pry bar off a workbench, Dante went to a collection of wooden crates. He consulted his phone, checking numbers on the crates against what was stored on his cell. Finding the crate he was looking for, he began prying the lid off. Leigh stepped into the light.

"Dante Jones?" she asked.

He spun around raising the pry bar as a weapon. "Who are you?"

"My name is Leigh Howard. I just want to ask you a question. In exchange, I'll tell you something super important."

"I don't know who you are or how you got in here, but you can't be here. I'm gonna get security."

"I'm sure you don't want security poking into whatever is inside that box," Leigh said, forcing more confidence into her voice than she felt.

He raised the bar higher. "You don't want to mess with me.'

"No. I don't," Leigh said. "I just want answers."

"Answers to what?"

"You know a police officer and his wife were killed here a few weeks back?"

"Yeah. So?"

"I'm their daughter. I have to know! Did you do it?"

"You're who? Did I...you asking did I kill them?"

"Please," Leigh pleaded, her voice cracking. The stress of the last several hours was taking its toll. "I have to know why. Why did they have to die? Tell me, and I'll tell you all I know about you getting arrested tomorrow."

"Arrested? Is this some sort of game? Hey! Are you a cop? You trying to finger me for those people's murder?"

"No," Leigh said. "I told you. I'm their daughter. Please, help me if you can. Did you do it or do you know who did?"

"I don't know nothing. And you are going to be in a world of trouble if you don't get outta here. Threatening me like this." He took a menacing step forward. "I ought 'a take care of you right now."

Tires squealed outside. Red and blue lights filtered in through the windows. A swarm of police officers streamed into the warehouse. They all had guns in their hands. Guns which were pointed at Dante and Leigh.

"Drop the weapon," they screamed at Dante. "Hands behind your head! Down on your knees!"

The bar clanged to the floor. Dante's pupils were tiny dots as he spun around to find police officers on all sides. He glared at Leigh. "What have you done to me?"

Rough hands grabbed Leigh from behind and she was half carried, half dragged away from Dante. Ashen faced, Dante dropped to his knees as ordered.

"No! Wait!" Leigh screamed. "Dante! This was supposed to be tomorrow! I didn't know! Tell me! Tell me!"

Her words were wasted. The chaos of the situation drowned them out. Struggling against the hands that held her, she was being pulled away. Outside the building, she was handed off to a tall, powerful, female officer who clamped her hand on Leigh's elbow, her fingers digging down to the bone, and marched her to a police car. Opening the back door, she glared at Leigh.

"I know who you are," the woman officer said, "and that buys you something, but if you make a fool out of yourself in the back of my squad car, I *will* cuff you."

Leigh's head fell. "I'll behave."

Looking out the car's windows she watched the police conduct their operation. Men and women in windbreakers stenciled with the huge letters DEA, indicating they worked for the Drug Enforcement Agency, were in charge and were assigning uniformed officers tasks. Ahead of her, another unmarked car with blue and red lights flashing behind the grill and out the rear window, arrived late on site. A large man climbed out and, putting his hand on his hips, scanned the area.

Leigh scrunched low behind the wire mesh that separated the front and back seats. Pressing her knees against the front seat, she pulled her hood down to cover her face. The back door jerked open. Tyrone Milbank's angry face scowled in at her.

"Never thought I'd see Cal Howard's little girl in the back of one of these," his deep voice scolded.

Leigh looked up at him and hitched a feeble smile onto her face. Raising her hands and pressing her wrists together she said, "I'm not in handcuffs," as if that made the situation any better.

Ty's lips pressed into a thin line and his jaw muscles clenched. "That supposed to be funny?"

Leigh's shoulders sank as she balled her fingers around the cuffs of her hoodie and rolled them into her palms. She stared at the holes in the knees of her jeans. "No, sir."

Ty grunted in approval of her more contrite attitude. "Out."

In obedient silence Leigh slipped out of the car.

"Follow me," Ty commanded.

He led her to another car and yanked its door open. Dante was sulking in the back seat. His hands were cuffed behind him.

"Ask your questions," Ty said.

Leigh peered inside the patrol car. "I'm sorry," was the first thing she said.

Dante nodded but kept his eyes fixed straight ahead.

"I know this is selfish of me. I mean, you obviously have other things to worry about right now, but..."

"They told me who you were," Dante said. "Asked what my business was with you. It really was your folks got shot here, huh?"

Leigh's throat constricted and she was barely able to choke out, "Yes. It really was."

Dante looked at her, his face pale with fear. "I ain't sayin' nothing about tonight so you're free to tell any tale you want. But as far as your folks go? Yeah, I was here that night. Fact is, I was working the place they were killed. Thing is, Jason Small, the night yard-boss, calls me to check out some suspicious cargo just in from Cyprus. Of course I went. Needed to make sure he wasn't looking at my interests, ya know? Turns out it was screwed up paperwork but it took the rest of my shift to sort it out. When done, I went home. See? I was with Small that night. Cops already checked the alibi. Whatever got your parents whacked, wasn't nothin' to do with me."

Leigh looked at him wondering if she could trust his word.

Dante smirked. "Yeah. I know. But it is the truth."

"Time," Ty barked.

"I am sorry," Leigh whispered again.

Dante shrugged. "Bound to happen sooner or later. But hey, I'm sorry, too. For what happened to your family. I hope you find the answers you're looking for."

Ty steered Leigh out of the car door with a firm but gentle hand before slamming the door shut.

"What happens to me now?" she murmured, dragging her sleeves across her eyes to dry them.

Ty jabbed a finger in the direction of a big black car parked well away from the emergency vehicles. "They are going to take you home."

Leigh gulped seeing the tight pressed lips and narrow eyes of a furious Marcus Figueroa glaring at her. Nacho, standing beside him, looked sad and disappointed. She didn't know which made her feel worse.

"I'll come out tomorrow to get your statement," Ty said, still annoyed. "From there? We'll have to wait and see."

"You could take my statement now," Leigh said trying to put off having to face Marcus and Nacho.

"I said tomorrow," Ty snapped. "Maybe by then I'll have gotten over wanting to take you across my knee and paddle your behind."

Leigh kicked the toe of her sneaker into the concrete. "I'd deserve it."

"You would, but that don't make it the right thing to do. Go home."

Left with no choice, Leigh hung her head and walked across the shipping yard to the two men waiting for her. Before either of them could speak she apologized to Nacho. "I did a lot of stupid things today, but it's what I did to you, ditching you and all, that I'm sorry for the most."

She was surprised to see the corner of his mouth twitch. "You did what you felt you had to do. I wish you felt you could trust me, but I know trust is hard to give when you're hurting."

Ashamed, Leigh held out the Ducati's key. "The bike's up two blocks to the right of the shipyard in an abandoned gas station."

"I'll find it," Nacho said.

Marcus cleared his throat in what sounded like a growl. "You two need to hug it out, or are we ready to go?"

Leigh looked at him through narrowed eyes before climbing into the sedan. The drive home was tense and uncomfortable.

Chapter Eleven

Red coals of dawn were glowing in the sky when Leigh and Marcus pulled up to the manor. Peg and Tristin rushed out of the house at the sound of the car's tires rolling through the pea gravel. Leigh could see their faces were gaunt and pale with worry, but only if she looked hard and deep past the red flush and clenched jaws of being ticked off.

"We were out of our minds with worry," Peg howled as soon as Leigh's sneakers touched the gravel.

"I'm sorry," was all Leigh could say, knowing such a weak statement didn't even begin to cover her behavior.

Before she realized what was happening, Peg gathered Leigh into her arms. Leigh felt herself being squeezed as Peg made a soft sob.

"Peg," Tristin said in cold strained tones that told Leigh he was on the verge of a tantrum. "We agreed. Tomorrow is soon enough to deal with this. Leigh is safe. She's home. That's all that matters. We've all had a sleepless night and nothing good will come from trying to sort this out while we're exhausted. Tomorrow."

"That's kinder than I deserve," Leigh muttered as she wriggled as politely as possible out of Peg's hold on her.

Tristin's face became a darker red as he struggled with his anger. "You'll get what you deserve, young lady. Just not now."

Leigh felt the blood drain from her face. What forms of punishment the Simmons family favored was a mystery. She never thought to ask Myra. Weighed down with that uncertainty, she started to shuffle inside.

"A moment, Miss Howard," Marcus sneered after her. "For security reasons I have to ask, how did you get into the office without setting off the alarm? I assume that is where you found the details of the sting operation?"

Leigh stood like a stalagmite. Marcus had the entire drive to ask her that question. The only reason he held on to it until this moment was to shame her in front of Tristin and Peg.

She wheeled around and glared at him, not caring how Tristin and Peg responded to her anger. "That window," she said, pointing back behind her. "The one at the top? By the ceiling? It doesn't have sensors on it."

"Impossible," Marcus scoffed. "There are no sensors on that window because no one could climb up without our noticing. Security patrols or camera surveillance would have caught you. You're lying."

Leigh inched closer to Marcus and jabbed her finger at him. "I am not lying. And I didn't climb up. I climbed down."

Marcus opened his mouth to fire something back but no words came. His lips snapped shut with an audible pop. Leigh's was an avenue of attack he hadn't considered and, judging by the look on his face, he wasn't happy about it.

Gravel crunched under her feet as Leigh did an about face and marched into the manor. Just inside the door she found Myra skulking in the shadows. Still mad at Marcus, her first impulse was to snap at her, too, but seeing the proud smirk plastered on her face and the mischievous admiration burning in her eyes, Leigh surprised herself by engulfing Myra in her arms.

"Hey," Myra soothed as she patted her back, "everything's going to work out."

"What have I done?" Leigh sobbed.

As always, Myra was Myra. "You screwed up. You're sixteen -- that's kinda your job."

Leigh giggled and released Myra. Using her hoodie, she blotted her eyes, asking, "You ever screw up like this?"

"To be honest, no. I think you've won the 'Make The 'Rents Mad' game."

Both girls chuckled as Leigh asked, "Will I face the firing squad at sundown?"

"Don't be ridiculous," Myra said. "We're an aristocratic family. It's the guillotine for you, my dear."

Behind them Tristin's voice boomed, "I have no idea what the two of you can find so funny about all of this. Myra! Take Leigh to her room. Then go to yours."

Tristin walked with a stiff stride past the girls and into his office. Both girls watched him pull open the doors. For a fraction of a second, Leigh saw a hulking figure inside the office scowling at her with a look of malice that made her blood run cold.

"Who's that?" she asked after Tristin snapped the doors shut.

"Who is who?"

"That angry old man in your father's office?"

"There's nobody in there. Lack of sleep is making you see things. C'mon. Let's get you a hot shower. After, you can crawl into bed and tell me all about your adventure."

"I thought you were supposed to go to your room, too."

Myra laughed. "I stopped doing that when I was twelve. I'm certainly not going to start doing it again at nineteen!"

Leigh took her time standing under the warm shower's spray. Initially, the water burned where it struck her fresh cuts and scrapes but soon they soothed into a soft tingling. She scrubbed hard, trying to get the grime from the train and the filthy hovel where she sat hiding, out of her hair and off her skin. Her jeans were so shredded and stained they went straight into the trash. After an emotional struggle, Leigh tossed her beloved hoodie, her armor since her parents died, into the hamper to be washed. Slipping into a fresh set of loose clothes, she scaled the stairs to the loft.

"Feel better?" Myra asked.

"Loads!"

"Good. Now come talk to me. Tell me everything!"

"I will but first, when'd you get back?"

"Headed back soon as Mom told me you were gone."

Leigh hung her head in shame.

Myra patted her arm. "I was due to leave and come back this morning anyway, so don't torture yourself."

"Still," Leigh muttered.

"You can make it up to me by telling me everything and not leaving anything out."

Leigh started with meeting Nacho in the garage and didn't stop talking until she wound her tale up with arriving back at the manor. Myra listened intently, asking only a few questions here and there. When Leigh got to the part where she jumped onto the moving train and her struggle to not fall under the steel wheels, Myra grabbed a pillow from behind her and began pummeling Leigh with it, accentuating every word with a wallop.

"You...could...have...killed...your...self!"

Myra turned rigid. Her face blanched as her hand shot up to cover her mouth. "I am so sorry. I can't believe I said that to you."

Like a jump into icy waters, the reason Myra was embarrassed by what she said jolted Leigh. She turned red as a crayon, but Myra of all people deserved an explanation.

"Myra, you don't have to watch what you say around me. Ever. Besides, it isn't like what I did before I came here never happened. It's just as frustrating to have people pretend I didn't do it as it is to have people walk on eggshells, afraid they'll somehow push me over the edge into trying it again. Besides, before, I was trying to kill myself. This time I was clawing my nails off to stay alive. See?"

She held out her mangled fingernails in evidence.

Myra inspected Leigh's fingers while making a clicking noise with her tongue. "Totally unacceptable,"

Pushing off the bed with a massive thrust, Myra raced down the loft steps and out of the room. Leigh heard her feet thudding as she dashed downstairs. So did Tristin.

"You two are supposed to be in your rooms," he bellowed from far below.

Myra's footfalls were growing louder again. Slamming the door behind her she flew back up the stairs and hopped on the bed.

"What was that all about?" Leigh asked as she bounced on the springy waves Myra's return made.

Myra opened a small bag filled with nail clippers, cuticle scissors, nail polish, brushes, and emery boards. She took Leigh's hand in hers.

"Now, tell me. Did you really climb down from here into Dad's office or was that a fib to spool Marcus up?"

Leigh beamed at her. "I did it!"

Tingling, she wanted to tell Myra all about Little Bodie. How she met him by the lake. How they were becoming friends. About his journal. That it was Little Bodie who showed her how to climb down. Myra deserved to hear the story of how Bodie saved her life. The words were burning on her tongue but a dreadful darkness crept over her, keeping her silent.

Surrendering to Bodie, consenting to letting him enter her body and take it over made her ashamed, like she was somehow less valuable as a person because she agreed to it.

"What's wrong?" Myra asked.

"Nothing. Why?"

"You went all, I don't know. Quiet? You were pretty excited one minute then, whoosh! The lights went out."

"I guess I remembered how much trouble I caused. How much trouble I'm in! All for nothing."

"Not all for nothing," Myra said. "Not if you believe this Dante character's story."

"I do believe him," Leigh said, "but that's just it. If he didn't have anything to do with my parents' murder, who did? I'm no closer to knowing and am a lot worse off for my efforts."

"Yes you are."

Leigh scowled at Myra. "That was harsh, even for you."

"Closer to answers, I mean. If Dante and the people he's mixed up with didn't have a hand in it you can stop looking in that direction, right? Focus elsewhere. Process of elimination."

"You talk as if I'm going to keep pushing this."

"You are. At least I'm pretty sure you are. You're not a quitter and you don't let things that don't add up stay that way. But you have got to be more careful."

Leigh didn't answer. A scratchy discomfort inside her stomach told her Myra was right -- that she'd keep picking at it. And she was going to go at it all or nothing. Looking at the scabby and bruised hand Myra was working to reclaim, she couldn't say that. It would scare Myra.

It scared her.

Not wanting Myra to go into a lecture of how reckless she'd been, Leigh feigned a yawn that turned real in her mouth. She crushed her eyelids shut and reopened them with a small shudder. "I didn't realize how sleepy I was."

"I bet you are exhausted," Myra said. "I'm worn out myself. I can't believe I'm saying this but, I think I am going to my room. You'll be okay on your own, right? You're not going to climb out the window again? Or go busting in on more drug dealers?"

"I promise I won't. Not without letting you know first."

"All right. I'll see you in a couple of hours?"

"Deal."

Leigh turned onto her side to watch Myra go, pulling the door shut behind her. The sun on the rise, its warming rays cascaded in through the massive bay window. To Leigh it felt loving, like playing in the snow all day followed by a long bath and being bundled up in a warm towel.

She blinked weakly, yawned a second time, and fell asleep. While she slept, the heat grew and she began tossing and turning, her sheets clinging to her. It was the worst possible kind of sleep, the kind where she was awake enough to know she was asleep but too deep to fully wake up. No matter how hard she tried, she couldn't force the drowse off of her. She heard herself whimpering as she fought for consciousness and her eyelids fluttered, letting in flashes of light. Straining to lift her eyelids, she could not force herself wake.

Through her delirium she heard a loud click. Her eyes shot open. Gasping in short pants, her heart raced too fast for her to take deeper breaths. She jolted upright in her bed. Beyond the loft rail she saw that her door was half open. Out in the hall a malevolent blue, almost purple light flickered off the walls.

"Bodie? That you?"

The light began to fade.

Leigh slipped out of bed and padded down the loft stairs and across to the door. Peering out, she saw the blue-red reflection of light recede down the spiral staircase. Leigh followed.

"Bodie? If that's you, this isn't funny," she hissed. "If it's not you, but somebody else, it still isn't funny."

The house was bright with afternoon sun streaming in open windows. Lace and muslin curtains swelled and contracted like lungs. The breeze creeping through the house struck Leigh's face like a furnace. The heat was unbearable.

The hideous light moved downstairs. It blazed with purple-blue radiance and had a black outline that sucked all the sunlight into nothingness. The house still and empty, Leigh wondered where the rest of the family had gone.

The light hovered in the doorway of the library and shook, as if beckoning her to follow. She felt a tremor race through the wood of the staircase as she descended. Without understanding, but knowing she had to, she crept behind the glow on tiptoe, silent and secretive, crossing the threshold to the library.

"You wicked girl," a voice screamed, coming from everywhere, yet nowhere.

The library doors slammed shut. Grabbed by an invisible force, Leigh was upended and flipped so that her head hung down towards the floor. Her lungs collapsed as all her air gushed out. Feet in the air, back to the ground, she was floating mid-air. Whatever it was that was holding her let go and she crashed to the floor. Given no time to regain her feet, she began spinning on the floor like a child's toy. Still spinning, she whooshed up, her lips colliding with the ceiling. Pushing with all her might she managed to roll over to find herself staring down at the furniture below.

"How dare you repay the kindness of this family with treachery," the formless voice bellowed.

She was flying through the air again and slammed hard against the wall beside Big Bodie's massive picture. She was held paralyzed against the wall. Turning her head was all she could do. Her eyes landed on the painting of sullen Big Bodie. Terrifying nausea flooded her as the horrific man began to lean out of his portrait, eyes blazing with purple-blue hatred, baring his teeth like an angry wolf.

"Bodie, please," she pleaded, "I thought we were friends!"

Big Bodie threw his head back and laughed. "The little squint isn't here. I am. Oh, but I can hear him. Whimpering. Crying. Always crying! Pleading with me not to hurt you. Begging me to let you down. Should I? Why not!"

The force holding Leigh against the wall vanished and she fell to the floor with a loud crack.

"The brat wants me to let you go, but why? He never listens to me. Oh no! I told him not to open that window for you but did he listen? No! And look at you! Bringing nothing but dishonor to the family!"

A fire poker flew up into the air above her face. Staring in horror, she watched it hurtle down. Leigh tried to jerk her head out of the way but Bodie held her fast. The iron stopped inches from her forehead. It spun away, clattering against a bookshelf.

"Look at the mess you made! The enemies are within the walls! That's down to you, you wretched child."

Leigh struggled to her feet. Something hard smacked the back of her skull and she dropped like a stone in a pond.

Sparks exploded in her eyes. Unable to force them to focus she patted the surrounding space searching for furniture to help pull herself to her feet. Dizziness overwhelmed her. Making a swift swing around the arm of a chair, she flung herself into it.

"Oh, there you are," Peg cooed as she came into the library. "Strangest thing. The air-conditioning went out while you were asleep. We're all out on the garden patio drinking lemonade."

Her voice trailed off. Looking at her with eyes filled with concern, Peg asked, "Leigh, are you all right? You look so pale."

Over Peg's shoulder, Leigh could see the painted image of Bodie scowling down at her. Bile caught in her throat when she saw that there was no book on the floor and the fire-iron was back where it was supposed to be. She wanted to scream but Peg and Tristin were both at the end of their patience with her. Another act of insanity and she'd be back in the asylum before nightfall.

Struggling to keep calm she realized that, yes, Bodie did smack her on the back of the head with a book, but with the flat cover, not a corner. She was dropped from the ceiling but, thinking back on it now, she knew that she had fallen slower than in freefall. As for the fire poker hurtling towards her, he could have killed her with it as easy as swatting a fly. He might be a mean and abusive bully, but he wasn't prepared to kill her. Straightening in her chair she smiled. There wasn't any reason for her to be afraid of him. He either wouldn't or couldn't cause her any serious harm. Understanding that made her feel empowered.

"I'm fine," she told Peg. "Just got a bit woozy from the heat. Lemonade sounds terrific."

"Let's get you a cool glass," Peg said as she led the way.

Leigh spun in the doorway and flung a filthy gesture at the portrait. If war was what he wanted, war he would get.

Outside, she found Tristin and Myra sipping cool beverages, needling each other in that special way only fathers and daughters understand. Seeing Marcus, one leg draped over the other, an exquisite Italian-leather shoe hanging arrogantly in the air, Leigh ground her teeth. She didn't want to be inside alone, not after what Bodie did, but her loathing for Marcus made being outside feel just as bad.

"Here she is," Myra called out before she could slink away.

Left with no choice, Leigh produced a pretend smile and aimed it at the assembled group. "So this is why my ears were burning."

All but Marcus laughed. "Why shouldn't you be the topic of discussion?" he asked.

He took a long sip. Sloshing the cold drink through his teeth, he stared at his glass in meditation before he swallowed. "Of all of us, you do have the most interesting story to tell."

"I doubt that," Leigh said. "I bet Myra had loads of adventures on her campus visit."

Myra winked. "Maybe. But I don't kiss and tell."

Tristin sputtered in his drink.

Leigh recalled Myra confiding about her ongoing experiment on the different ways boys kiss and laughed loudly.

"How nice," Marcus drawled.

Myra smiled at him and patted his forearm in a way Leigh thought strange, given how much Myra claimed to find him annoying.

"You two are going to send your father..." Peg scolded, filling a glass and setting it on the table between Tristin and Marcus, indicating that was where Leigh was expected to sit.

Turning to Leigh she went on, "... your uncle..."

Finishing to both of them, she said, "... to an early grave."

Myra leaned over and gave Tristin a peck on the cheek. "I'd never do that to Daddy."

On one hand, the warmth Myra felt for her father made Leigh feel good. On the other, it hurt. She was happy for Myra but felt sorry for herself. She realized she was growing fond of this new family but missed her own too desperately to surrender into becoming a part of it. Coupled with surviving Bodie's attempt to frighten the life out of her less than ten minutes ago, her emotions were in absolute disarray.

Myra was saying something to Marcus but Leigh couldn't focus on the words. Big Bodie's warning, "The enemies are within the walls," kept bubbling to the top of her attention.

"Was there a stranger visiting here this morning?" she blurted out.

Realizing her question was out of place with whatever the topic of conversation was, she blushed and apologized.

Myra rushed to her rescue. "Leigh thought she saw somebody in your office when she arrived home," she said to Tristin.

Tristin squirmed uncomfortably. "No, there was no one there at that time."

He hesitated for a moment. "I did have a guest later in the morning. A woman named Miss Tree."

Peg spoke up. "Do you think this the best time, dear?"

"As good a time as any," Tristin said with more confidence. Whatever gave him pause a moment ago vanished and his mind was made up.

"Who's Miss Tree?" Myra asked. "Don't think I've ever met her."

"You haven't," Peg said as she ironed nonexistent wrinkles out of her pants using the palms of her hands.

"No," Tristin said. "She's new to the house. Leigh, there is no easy way to say this so I'll be blunt. She's going to be staying here to help you transition into your new life."

Myra let out a derisive snort. "A governess? Honestly, Daddy!"

"I wouldn't say governess," Tristin said. "Miss Tree is a qualified behavioral therapist. And, though we didn't discuss it at length, Leigh knew this was a possibility."

Leigh did know. Tristin brought it up before, but that was in passing. To have it sprung on her like this was a shock. Embarrassed and uncomfortable, she balled her hands, searching for the cuffs of her hoodie, but her security blanket was in the laundry. She covered the underside of each wrist with the opposite hand and let her thumbs caress the raised scars. Looking down, she saw how black and blue her hands were. Their battered and bruised condition was shocking to see.

"I haven't exactly built trust since I arrived, have I?" she said quietly.

"You have with me," announced Myra. She stared at Marcus as if daring him to speak.

"You are sweet. All of you have been." That was a lie. Marcus was a troll, but the others were trying their best to help her feel like she belonged. Leigh felt a sinking feeling in her gut. They were welcoming her with open arms and she was the one blowing it.

Surprised she was saying it aloud, Leigh admitted, "It's just that, I don't see how I can settle in anywhere without knowing what happened to Mom and Dad. I want to but, it's the not knowing. It's like a wall that's keeping me out."

Tristin gave her the same weary yet patient look he so often graced Myra with. "That's why Miss Tree has been put on retainer. No one is blaming you for anything. Given the circumstances you are being a rock."

"Not to mention brave," Peg added. "I never would climb out that top window. Or steal a motorbike."

"Or jump on a moving train," Myra added.

"You did what?" Tristin boomed.

"Um...I haven't filled everyone in on all the details, Myra."

Myra shut her mouth and cast droopy puppy-dog eyes at Leigh.

"Might be best you don't," Peg said as she sat up stiff and prim. "I think we all get the gist and what you did isn't as important as why you did it."

"Quite right," Tristin agreed.

"I disagree," Marcus said.

"Of course you do," Leigh sighed.

Myra snorted and lemonade shot out her nostrils.

As she blew her nose, Marcus asked, "What is that supposed to mean?"

"It means," Leigh seethed, at her wits end with him, "you disagree because you like being disagreeable."

"I disagree," he answered coolly, "because I'm responsible for security. You breached that security. I need to know how in order to make sure it doesn't happen again. I realize you think we are all incapable of doing our jobs and that you are the only one who can do things right, and I'm sorry if taking my job seriously offends you."

"I don't think that," Leigh objected.

Her face burned. She didn't want to believe that about herself but the way she had been acting, ditching Nacho, giving up on Ty, giving Marcus the run-around, all proved that was what she thought. Scowling, she sat for the remainder of the get-together silently sipping her lemonade and wishing she was anywhere but there.

Chapter Twelve

"Good morning," a cheery, sing-song voice chirruped.

Leigh groaned. Rolling over, turning her back to the door, she punched her pillow deeper beneath her head. "It's too early, Myra. Come back in an hour. Two would be better."

Unfamiliar tittering made her eyes burst open.

"Myra is out in the garden. My name is Miss Tree."

Leigh rolled over. "Oh. Sorry. Can you come back in an hour? Perhaps two?"

"No, dear. It's time you were up."

"I thought you were supposed to be my therapist or something, not my alarm clock."

"I am a licensed therapist, but I'm also to be your tutor, your governess, your..."

"Warden?"

"Now, now. Let's not get off on the wrong foot. Shall I draw you a bath?"

Not waiting for Leigh to answer, Miss Tree scurried into the bathroom. Leigh heard the water start to run.

"I agree," Leigh called after her in a firm voice as she rolled out of bed, allowing her legs to dangle over the side. "We shouldn't get off on the wrong foot. So, here's the deal. I admit I could use some help. And I'm glad you are here for that. But otherwise? I look after myself. I take my own baths. I dress myself. I keep my own schedule. And, I get myself up in the morning."

"Of course, dear," Miss Tree said as if Leigh hadn't spoken. "Breakfast will be ready in twenty minutes."

As Miss Tree came out of the bathroom, Leigh glared at her, getting in a good look and making her first impression. Miss Tree was a middle-aged woman who could have been very attractive if not for her frumpiness. Her short-sleeved dress had a floral calico pattern with lace at the cuffs and collar. The hem was even with the bottom of her knees. Pretty streaks of blonde ran through her brown hair but, hanging limp and styled solely with an unimaginative part, they accentuated the frump. Her gum sole, sensible shoes completed the maiden-aunt image and made annoying squeaks as Miss Tree left Leigh's room.

"I can already tell, this is not going to go well," Leigh muttered, getting up to close the door.

Almost two weeks had passed since Tristin announced he'd hired a therapist for her. In that time, Leigh made it a point to keep on her best behavior. Not putting a toe out of line, she began to hope Tristin forgot about it, or reconsidered the decision. He obviously didn't. Leigh shuffled to the bathroom feeling defeated.

She turned off the shower before brushing her teeth. Moving to her wardrobe beneath the stairs, she paid particular attention to making herself look unapproachable, hoping that would keep Miss Tree at arm's length. She selected jeans that weren't too formfitting but weren't overly baggy, either; a dark t-shirt that *was* too big for her; her doodled-on Keds high tops and, of course; her hoodie, fresh from the wash. Outside the closet, she looked at reflection in her mirror with disappointment. She looked the same as she did every day.

Back inside the wardrobe the board covering Little Bodie's hiding place wiggled.

With a playful smirk on her face she snarled, "You better not have been watching me get dressed, you little creep!"

Her playfulness faded remembering how mad she was at him, or at least the older version of him. Bodie had been on her mind ever since the attack in the library. That night, and every night since, she struggled to fall sleep. She jumped at every creak the old house made, fearing Big Bodie would re-appear and assault her again, but days passed and she saw neither Big nor Little Bodie.

Over time, her anger at Little Bodie faded and she started to realize how much she missed him. She still wasn't happy with him for possessing her like he did, but she felt she could forgive him. He was, after all, only trying to help her. Big Bodie, on the other hand, could stay gone till the end of time and she'd be glad.

Uncertain as to what she was going to do, she knelt on the floor. Poking the floorboard with her fingertips, she felt it lift. If Bodie didn't want her to take out his book, she knew the board would be unmovable. So many questions spun through her mind that she rocked back onto her heels and stared at the hiding spot in the dim light trickling in through the door, hesitant to pull the plank away.

Bodie could have materialized any time he wanted. Was he waiting on her? Maybe he was ashamed of what he did to her in the library.

"And you should be," Leigh growled into the darkness of the closet.

Of its own accord, the plank rattled.

Leigh reached out a trembling hand, terrified Little Bodie would somehow take her over again if she touched the journal. That didn't make sense because she didn't have it with her the first time and he never seemed to need it around to reveal himself. In her mind she linked the two together when, thinking it through, Little Bodie's appearance and the book weren't connected at all.

That made up her mind. The book not having anything to do with his presence, one way or the other, she pushed down on the board and took his journal out of its hiding place. Carrying it to her bed, she reread the parts of his story she felt most bonded to; entries where he described feeling like an outsider despite all the kindness the family was showing him. As she read, the pages began to reflect a blue glow that crept in so subtle and slow she didn't immediately notice. Leigh whipped her head around so fast it made her neck hurt.

Sitting cross-legged, hovering behind her shoulder was Little Bodie. Crying out, she fell off the bed and scuttled over the floor until her back was against the wall.

Her voice quavered as she pled more than commanded, "Stay away from me!"

"I will. Promise."

His eyes were downcast. Shoulders hunched, his spine curved so his elbows could rest on his knees, his hands toyed with his shimmering bare toes, sometimes tugging on them, at other times passing his fingers through them like she would pass a finger through a candle's flame. Despite his blue aura, Leigh could see long strands of blond hair hanging down. She recognized it for what it was. It was the same thing she did when she was embarrassed or scared and wanted to hide her face from others.

"You mad at me?" he asked sounding so much like a child Leigh almost forgot he was a ghost.

"Of course I'm mad at you," she snapped. "You tried to kill me!"

His head shot up, surprise written across his face. "Not me! Him!"

"Him. You. For Pete's sake! You're the same person!"

Bodie disappeared and reappeared standing in front of her so fast it stabbed into Leigh's eyes like a strobe light. His color was the darker, more sinister blue Leigh learned to recognize as his being angry.

"I told you," he shouted, "I'm not him. I'll never be him. I hate him!"

"Okay. Okay. Calm down. I can't say I understand, but you seem to believe you two are different people."

"We *are* different. And he hates me just as much as I hate him."

"But he was you. Or you became him. Or, I don't know. It doesn't make any sense."

Bodie's blue haze softened as he once again materialized farther away, sitting cross legged. "Some things never make sense. Anyway, I don't want to talk about him. All right?"

"All right," Leigh said in a testy tone. She had more than enough to complain about. "Let's talk about how you possessed me. Used me like a toy puppet!"

Bodie's blue drained as pale as she'd ever seen. His image faded, becoming so thin he bordered on being invisible. He began to tremble. "Don't say that!"

Blue-white tears, shimmering like moonstones, started dribbling out his eyes. "Please, Leigh. Please! Don't ever say I did such a thing."

The thin line of his lips began to quiver. Looking all around him, he pleaded to someone or something she couldn't see, "I didn't! I swear I didn't!"

Like a blast of frosty wind, Little Bodie was inches away from her face, sobbing. "Oh, please say I didn't!"

"But you did," she said soft and gentle, trying to reason with him like her mother used to when she was out of sorts. "I mean, it saved my life, but still, to be controlled like that!"

Bodie wailed in agony as he soared around the room. Leigh's heart was aching for him as he crumpled to the floor in a heap beside her. Burying his face in his arms, his body jerked as he sobbed. She reached out to touch him, wanting to console him, but her hand passed through his body, leaving him to suffer alone.

Bodie raised his head. He was crying in earnest. "I didn't. I showed you how, that's all. I never forced you -- never took away your freedom to choose. It was your bravery. Your determination. Please, Leigh! It was your decision!"

His pain was overwhelming. Thinking back, his words repeating themselves in her mind, she wasn't as sure that he did force her. He even told her he couldn't do it for her. She had to be the one who decided to let go of the ivy and risk falling to her death to avoid being caught. She tried to pat his back again, her own tears flowing because she couldn't give the comfort he desperately needed.

"Who are you talking to?" Miss Tree asked, standing at the top of the loft stair.

Bodie was gone. Leigh's hand was wafting through empty air.

"I was...was...talking to myself."

In desperation, Leigh pointed to Bodie's book, still on the bed. "It's a very sad story about a lonely boy who had a difficult childhood. He went to live with people who loved him and he wants to fit in but never seems to be able to. Guess it hit a little too close to home."

Miss Tree cocked her head like a confused hound. Her eyes were filled with skepticism. "Maybe you should lay off the heavy emotional reading until you get your own feelings in order," she said.

"Good advice." Leigh picked herself up off the floor and retrieved the book before Miss Tree could make a closer inspection of it. "I'm going to splash some water on my face, then I'll be right down."

Miss Tree gave her another suspicious look, this one colder and harder.

"Promise," Leigh said.

Without saying a word, Miss Tree left, but not before pausing in the door to give Leigh yet another glare that Leigh felt hovered somewhere between worry and malice.

True to her word, Leigh went to the bathroom and splashed cold water over her face. She was more confused than ever by what Bodie told her. He believed he was telling the truth, that much was clear, but nothing else was.

She carried the book back to the closet and moved the floorboard to put it in. Without thinking, she pressed her lips against the cover like she wanted to kiss the anguished boy's forehead. "I believe you. You didn't possess me. I made the choice on my own. Tell whoever it is you're so afraid of that I was wrong."

Leigh dragged her feet as she made her way to the kitchen. When she arrived, she flopped down at a small table. Before her was an assortment of fruits, yogurts, granolas, and bran muffins. A tall glass of slimy green something-or-other she had no intention of drinking stood beside her plate. Across the table, Miss Tree sat reading a magazine with the title Psychology Matters splashed across the cover. Heaving herself to her feet, Leigh went to the refrigerator, carrying her spoon like a dagger.

"Leigh? What are you doing?" Miss Tree asked, noisily flipping a page.

Leigh opened the freezer. "Looking for food."

She pulled out a gallon tub of chocolate ice cream and, hoisting her rear-end up on the counter, yanked the lid open and dug in. As she shoveled ice cream into her mouth, she kept her eyes fixed on Miss Tree, as if daring her to come try to take the bucket from her.

"There's food on the table," Miss Tree said, but didn't move to stop her gulping down her ice cream.

"You eat it," Leigh growled. "I told you. I take care of myself."

"Not very good care, from the look of you." Miss Tree shut her magazine and rose from the table. Leigh, thinking she was going to confiscate her ice cream, hugged the carton to her chest.

"Everyone transitions into being an adult at different times in their lives. I see you are still not ready. Now, if you will excuse me, I must speak with Mr. Simmons before he becomes too busy."

Miss Tree rose to walk out the door leading into the main part of the house as Nacho came in through the outside door. Seeing Miss Tree, he froze, mouth hanging open.

Before he could speak, Miss Tree was across the room, hand extended, a smile on her face. "I'm Miss Tree. I'm here to assess Leigh and determine the appropriate course of action."

"Hey," Leigh yelled, "I'm sitting right here."

Nacho's eyes rounded. "I'm Nacho," he stammered, taking her hand as if picking up a garter snake from behind a bush.

Miss Tree's smile grew wider. "Yes. I know. Now, if you'll pardon me, I do need to speak with Mr. Simmons."

Nacho watched her go, mouth still gaping.

"What was that all about?" Leigh asked.

"I, uh, I came in for a cup of coffee. Wasn't expecting anyone to be in here. Who was that?"

"She told you." Leigh wagged her head disrespectfully. "Miss Tree."

"Yeah, but, I mean, who is she?"

"My new therapist. Tristin hired her a few days ago. She thinks she's going to be bossing me around. She is so wrong."

Nacho smiled.

"What?" Leigh asked.

"You simply can't keep out of trouble, can you? Like a hummingbird to a flower. That's you."

"Hmm," Leigh grunted as she made a playful scowl.

"So," Nacho went on, "we haven't had time to talk. Did you find out anything useful?"

"Like Myra said, it depends on your point of view. I didn't make any progress, but I did learn that I can forget about Dante being involved. He isn't. Or, if he is, he's a good liar."

Nacho frowned and nodded his head. "Bueno. So now what?"

"Why does everyone think I'm going to keep at it?"

"Because we are all getting to know you. Be honest. Did Mr. Simmons bring in Miss Tree to help you cope or was it really to keep an eye on you? Maybe he knows you better than you think."

Leigh's shoulders drooped. "Maybe."

"Still," Nacho continued, "if Dante's out, who's still in?"

Leigh's lips lifted in a smile. "I was thinking about that last night before I fell asleep. Lots of people are still in. I was hoping I could make a case against Marcus but realized that him being a jerk doesn't automatically mean he's a murderer."

"I get you," Nacho said. "I don't care much for Mr. Figueroa either. But, like you said, that isn't evidence, it's just good taste in friends."

Leigh's lip curled farther up her face. "I know. Right? Honestly, though, who else is there? If it's not Marcus, that leaves no one but Jason Small. I mean, he pulled Dante away from the place my parents were killed. Thanks to that, it was deserted. Maybe it's a coincidence. Maybe Small was making sure that part of the dockyard was deserted."

Leigh shrugged. "Anyway, that's all I can come up with, so..."

"No," Nacho said, "that's good thinking. And it fits."

"What do you mean, 'it fits'?"

"I was weeding one of the flowerbeds in the garden when I overheard Mr. Simmons and Mr. Figueroa talking about Small. He isn't well liked and I think they are looking at getting rid of him."

Leigh's heart twitched with excitement. "Do you know why?"

"No. They took their conversation inside, but I think Mr. Figueroa has a file on Small in his office."

"Lot of good that does me," Leigh groaned.

"Maybe you could sneak in there while at the party."

Leigh's eyes opened with surprise. "What party?"

"Simmons-Pierce Shipping is celebrating the anniversary of the merger of the two shipping companies, Simmons and Pierce, way back in eighteen-hundred and something or other. They do it every year. You didn't know?"

Leigh slid off the counter. "No, I didn't."

She moved toward the door leaving the ice cream out.

"Where are you going?" Nacho asked.

"To get myself invited to a party. Then, to figure out how to break into Marcus's office."

"Good luck, little hummingbird!"

When Leigh arrived, Tristin's office door was open and she slid into snoop-mode. Miss Tree was in conference with him, no doubt spelling out how horrible Leigh was. Leigh wanted to linger but knew if they caught sight of her before she made her presence known it would look like she was doing what she was -- spying.

"Leigh, come in," Tristin said in reply to her knock. "Miss Tree was telling me you two are getting off to a bumpy start."

"I don't know," Leigh said, giving Miss Tree a withering look, "I think we understand each other just fine."

Miss Tree turned to Tristin with raised eyebrows, her lips stretched in a long grim line, silently saying, "See what I mean?"

"Give it time," Tristin said. "I'm sure everything will work out in the end. Was there something I can help you with, Leigh?"

"Yes, there is. I overheard a rumor that a party of some kind is coming up soon. I wanted to ask if I could go."

"Well," Tristin stammered, "we were thinking, given recent events, that you may be better off staying home. Miss Tree can supervise."

Leigh felt her face turn roasting red. "I am too old for a babysitter," she growled.

"Miss Howard," Miss Tree scolded, "that'll be quite enough."

Leigh sucked in a deep soothing breath to reign in her anger. "Sorry. All I meant was, no matter what else may be going on, I'm not eight years old."

"Of course you're not," Tristin said, "but..."

Leigh cut him off. "I'd like to go. Remember when I said I want to be a part of this family? That means being part of the business. I promise I'll be on my best behavior and I won't do anything to embarrass you."

Thinking fast she added, "Myra can be my chaperone. I'll stick right by her side all evening. It'll give Miss Tree a night off. I'm sure she'd appreciate that."

Tristin studied her with a cool, calculating gaze. He was sizing up her request as if it were a business proposition. After what felt to Leigh like an hour, he nodded.

"I'll take the matter up with Peg. As for Myra, I'll not put her in the position of being trapped between loyalties to you and to me. If you do attend..."

Leigh beamed a smile at him.

"I said 'if'," he reasserted. "If you do attend, Miss Tree will be your chaperone. That is not negotiable."

Leigh's entire body sagged with impatience tempered with disappointment. "Yes, sir."

A sad half smile hitched itself on her face.

"What's so amusing?" Tristin asked.

"I was remembering, that's how I used to sound when Dad and I reached an agreement I didn't care much for but had to suck up. Maybe we are making more progress than I thought."

Tristin's face brightened. "I think we are because, as long as we are being honest with each other, I can see myself letting you get away with far more than I should, just like I do Myra."

The second half of Leigh's mouth joined the first in its smile. "Please talk it over with Peg and let me know what you decide. I promise, whatever your decision is, I won't be a brat about it."

"I doubt that," Miss Tree said, "but I suppose we have to start trusting you at some point."

"Now, if you would please excuse me," she said as she turned to leave, "if I am to attend a party I have much to prepare."

As she was crossing the threshold of the door, a gust of wind billowed the drapes. The office door swung shut with a fierce slap and struck Miss Tree in the shoulder. She staggered. Tristin shot to her side.

"Are you all right?" he asked. "That was the strangest thing. Must have been a draft or something."

"No. No, I'm fine," Miss Tree said as she rubbed her shoulder. "No harm done."

Leigh snickered, "Maybe the ghosts of Simmons-Pierce Manor don't like you, either."

Tristin whipped around to face her. "That was rude and uncalled for. Apologize to Miss Tree this instant."

Leigh was taken aback by his temper. "It was a joke. I didn't mean it to sound cruel or anything. If it came across that way, I am sorry."

In her mind she was thinking, *but better the ghosts dislike you rather than me.*

Leigh left Tristin's office and walked out of the house to get herself out of harm's way as quickly as she could. Myra came out the door behind her and trotted to catch her up. Together, they ambled toward the stream where the sun trickled through the leaves. Some branches hung over the water; others dipped like paintbrushes into it. Sun and shade mottled the mirrored surface. Without breaking stride, Myra pulled her t-shirt over her head and tossed it onto the sand.

Leigh's eyes darted to the spot where Little Bodie had waded out of the water the day they first met. "Um...what are you doing?"

"Going swimming," Myra said as she popped open the waist button of her jeans. Stopping, she grinned a challenge in Leigh's direction. Fists on her hips she asked, "Don't tell me you still haven't gone skinny-dipping down here?"

Leigh bit her lip, feeling an uncomfortable pink creep up her neck. She hadn't, but that wasn't what kept her still. "Someone might see us."

Myra's chuckle turned into a laugh. "Don't be silly. Who's going to see us? Have you ever seen anyone else down here? I know I haven't!"

Leigh chewed harder on the corner of her lower lip and made a little shrug. "Once?"

She was upset that it came out sounding like a question. Nerves on edge, she knew she was either going to have to explain herself or lie. She liked Myra, trusted her, but wasn't sure how her cousin would take to hearing she'd been hanging out with ghosts the last few weeks.

Nonplussed by her answer, Myra continued to pull off her jeans. "Who?"

The leaves rustled over Leigh's head. The skin on the nape of her neck cringed. She felt the deep freeze that was Bodie. She spun around to find him standing with his back facing her and Myra.

"I won't stick around," he said. "I just came to let you know, it's fine with me if you tell her about me, if you want."

Leigh whispered so Myra couldn't hear, "How do I know you won't, I don't know, turn invisible or something, and watch?"

Bodie's body stiffened. The air turned colder. "In my day boys knew how to act like gentlemen. I said I won't peek and I won't."

"Sorry," Leigh sighed and her shoulders sank. "I should have trusted you. Taken you at your word."

"Come on," Myra called to her, now naked and wading into the water. "Who else have you seen down here?"

The ghostly boy disappeared.

"Little Bodie," Leigh said.

Clenching her jaw, Leigh took off her hoodie, followed by everything else. Moving with high prancing steps, she tiptoed into the water behind Myra. Either she trusted Bodie or she didn't. Either she trusted Myra or she didn't. She was done playing halvesies.

A shower of cold drops pulled her back into the present moment.

"You are such a little liar," Myra teased. "You don't even believe in the ghosts."

"Do you?" Leigh said with such seriousness Myra stopped splashing her.

"You know I do," Myra said.

"No. I'm serious! Do you believe in them? I mean, like, really believe in them?"

Myra's face twisted in surprise over her intensity. "I did. As a kid, I mean. But as I get older, that certainty is fading. I don't know if I still do believe in them or if I want to believe so badly I'm tricking myself into thinking I believe. Does that make sense?"

Leigh's heart fluttered. This was the most open-hearted and honest thing anyone had said to her in months.

"I do understand," Leigh said, "and thank you. See, I had to know where you stood because..."

She paused -- was scared -- was determined. Taking a deep breath she finished, "...because I've seen them. Both of them. Talked to them. And they've talked to me. Little Bodie and I are becoming friends. Big Bodie's a jerk, but I think I can handle him."

Myra stared at her with wide eyes. Leigh gazed back, feeling at peace because she told someone. The shock on Myra's face didn't bother her. She told the truth and, even if Myra didn't believe her, just saying it was enough. For the first time in a long time, being open and honest without being afraid of how what she said was going to be taken, felt good.

Chapter Thirteen

Standing in front of a full-length mirror in Myra's room, the two girls took inventory of themselves. Their gowns were exquisite. Myra lent Leigh some of her jewelry and both their reflections shimmered like moonlit ocean waves. Myra turned to look, as best she could, at herself from behind. Leigh blew out a labored breath.

"What's wrong?" Myra asked, sliding a non-existent wrinkle off her hip.

"You are," Leigh groaned.

Myra spun in a panic to view the other half of her backside. "What? Where?"

"You're all," Leigh bounced her cupped hands in front of her chest. And," she grabbed her butt with both hands and shook it.

"And you're so comfortable with it. And I'm, well, me!"

"What's wrong with you?" Myra asked, laughing at her.

Leigh cast her a weary smile and shrugged.

"Turn," Myra commanded.

Leigh didn't move.

"Come on. Turn."

Leigh heaved a sigh and turned so that her rump was facing the mirror like Myra's. "Look at my calves. Now, look at yours. I'm so jealous of your muscle tone."

Leigh made a skeptical hurumph.

"Turn," Myra commanded.

They both faced forward.

"What do you see?" Myra asked.

"Lots of curvy something sumthin' standing next to next t'nothin'."

"Is that all you see? Look at our middles."

"Your stomach is as flat as mine," Leigh objected.

"Yeah, it is. But yours has more definition. I noticed it when we went swimming. You've got a six pack, you little witch, and it shows through the dress."

"So I'm muscly. Big deal."

"Leigh, you are beautiful! And you're getting pretty..." Myra bounced her cupped hands in front of her chest, imitating what Leigh had done, "yourself."

"I know that. It doesn't have anything to do with how I look. It's, I don't know."

She turned away, frustrated she didn't know how to say what she felt. Turning back she said, "You know how I almost always wear that stupid hoodie? Well, I feel comfortable in it. Safe in it. Like it's a part of me, you know? It's like that. I mean, you're hot. You know it, I know it, and everyone who sees you knows it. That's how you are in you - like I am in my hoodie.

"But I'm not comfortable in my own body like you are. You're probably going to laugh at me, but I feel like a little kid stuffed inside a grown-up woman's body and I don't know how to be me in it. I'm self-conscious all the time. I like the things I wear but sometimes, I wear the baggy so people can't see the curvy. I know. It's crazy, right?"

"It's not crazy," Myra said. "It's normal. It took me a long time to get into my adult stride. I still don't know who I am most of the time. This'll sound ridiculous coming from me, but you are still young. We both are."

"Girls," Tristin growled from below, "either come downstairs or stay home."

"Ready?" Myra asked.

Leigh put her hands on her hips and took one last look at herself in the mirror. Startled by what she saw, she gasped.

Myra began turning in hopeful circles, staring into every corner of the room. "Is it one of the ghosts? Here?"

"In a way," Leigh said softly, putting an end to Myra's search. "For a hot second, I looked like Mom. It's gone, over, but for that one quick glance…" Leigh swallowed hard, unable to finish her sentence.

Myra pushed a wayward hair on Leigh's head back into place. "Let's go break some hearts." She winked at Leigh, "Or into an office."

Pacing at the bottom of the stairs, checking his watch at every turn, Tristin stopped and stared as they descended. His face lit up, all inconveniences forgotten, upon seeing them. Taking Myra's hand, he kissed her cheek.

"You're the reason I'm turning gray," he told her.

"And you, young lady," he said, turning to Leigh and leaning in to kiss her cheek, too.

He hesitated. "May I?"

Leigh smiled awkwardly. "Sure?"

After kissing her cheek he said, "You are going to make me go bald."

He rolled his wrist over to look at his watch again. "Now if we can get my wife down here, we can be on our way."

On cue, Peg appeared at the top of the stairs. She was stunning and exuded a sense of confident power neither girl had yet mastered.

Myra leaned into Leigh's ear and whispered, "What you felt standing beside me? That's how I feel beside Mom."

"Magnificent," Tristin breathed.

The drive to the party was filled with admonitions concerning etiquette, how the press were to be told politely but firmly, "no comment," and paparazzi, who were to be given nothing worth printing.

"Is that a thing? I mean, I thought they hounded Hollywood stars and athletes?" Leigh asked.

"Oh, it's real," Myra groaned. "If there's a chance to make money, the cockroaches come a'crawlin'."

Peg scowled. "Well, let's not get into that tonight. Suffice it to say, keep on your toes and on your best behavior."

Leigh's brow darkened. The last thing she needed was photo-happy sleaze-balls watching every move she made, searching for dirt. She had every intention of misbehaving, but not if it meant giving the family another black eye.

As if reading her mind, Myra leaned in, "Don't worry. They'll be kept outside by Marcus's people. Once inside, you can loosen up."

"Not too loose," Tristin grunted.

"That was two years ago," Myra protested. "Aren't you ever going to get over it?"

Tristin didn't answer, but his lips turned into a frown that was something caught between a tease and a reproach.

The limousine pulled to the curb. Bob climbed out and made a quick scan of the area. As Myra predicted, security forces in uniform were keeping the crowds at bay behind rope cordons. Bob hustled to the sidewalk next to car and opened the door, offering his hand to Peg. The rest of them followed her out and formed a small huddle before moving inside. Miss Tree remained aloof, waiting for Leigh, who was the last to emerge, to join the group.

Leigh's high heels barely hit the concrete before lights began flashing. People were shouting so many different questions at her she couldn't focus on any one in particular person. Myra swooped in and rescued her by threading an arm through Leigh's.

A woman with a weathered face, wearing jeans and a man's sport coat, snapped several photos while shouting, "Ms. Howard? How do you feel about the lack of progress the police are making in finding your parents' killer?"

Leigh clenched her jaw and moved away with Myra.

The woman persisted. "How is the rest of the family coping with having a suicidal teenager in the house?"

Leigh jerked to a halt. The cruelty of that question appalled her. She gave Myra what she hoped was a reassuring smile to show she wasn't going to say anything stupid. She pressed her hand against Myra's, slipping it off of her elbow.

Turning to the journalist she said, "It's no secret I've had a difficult time coping. I still am struggling, if you must know. I mean, who wouldn't be? Right?"

The crowd muttered nervously.

Leigh went on, "But the Simmons family have all been so kind, so open hearted, and so patient, letting me deal with my pain in my own way -- being there for me every second of every day without being pushy. They have shown me respect. They gave me hope. They gave me love when I needed it the most."

Tristin's gentle hand fell onto her shoulder. "It has been our privilege. It's as if Peg and I have been blessed with a second daughter. We couldn't be more proud."

Myra was beside her, linking elbows again. "And I have the sweetest little sister."

Lights flashed in rapid succession. Several people darted off, tapping on their phone screens. Tristin guided Myra and Leigh back to where Peg and Miss Tree stood waiting.

"Well done," Peg said. Her face was lit with a smile of pure pride as she patted Leigh's arm. "You handled that perfectly. I doubt even those vultures would have the nerve to twist what you said into something it wasn't."

"Probably not," Tristin said with less confidence. "Still, I'll tell Marcus to keep an eye on it, just to be safe."

"Hope I didn't do anything wrong," Leigh said. "I just -- grr -- the nerve of that reporter!"

"Told you," Myra said. "They have no soul. Some of them. Others aren't so bad. It'll take time for you to learn who's who."

They passed the uniformed sentries guarding the outer door and a second pair guarding the inner. "Speaking of learning who's who," Myra whispered to Leigh then, in a louder voice, said, "Mom? I'm going to take Leigh and introduce her to some of the other KITs."

"Haven't you outgrown that sort of thing," Tristin grumbled.

"What's a KIT?" Leigh asked.

Not even pretending to make herself unheard, Myra said, "It's a word I invented that gets on Dad's nerves, so I use it whenever I can."

"But what does it mean?"

"Kids In Tow. It refers to all of us who come to these things because our parents are who they are. While our folks mingle and schmooze, we hang out of sight, gossip, play video games, and gripe about how boring these soirees are."

As Leigh followed Myra to a back-corner conference room, she asked, "Are any of these KITs up for a little mischief?"

Myra flashed a perfectly wicked grin at her. "Definitely!"

"It isn't polite to exclude others from your conversations," Miss Tree said as she scuttled along behind them.

"Oh, no!" Myra scolded. "No, no, no, no, no. Everyone above legal drinking age stays out here."

Myra opened the conference room door and ushered Leigh inside. "Strictly minors only."

A baker's dozen of young faces, some no older than eight, others well into their teens, stared at the intruders. Leigh blushed and wobbled on her high heels before realizing they were not glowering at her. Miss Tree was the object of their indignation.

"Oh," Miss Tree breathed out, her hand on her chest, "I see. Well, I'll be right outside the door should you need me."

"We won't," Myra said in a cheery voice as she closed the conference room door on her.

"Who owns the bloodhound?" a curly haired blond boy asked.

Myra scoffed. "Not mine. Leigh, this is Ralph. Ralph? Leigh."

Ralph scanned Leigh top to bottom. "Leigh Howard. Daughter to Calvin and Beth Howard -- tragically murdered last year. You went to live with relatives you never knew you had, the Simmons-Pierces, after, of course, a brief stint in our local version of Arkham Asylum."

Leigh gave an unconscious shake of her head to put her face into hiding behind her hair, but pins and product kept her hair plastered into place on top of her head. She balled her fists and wished she had long sleeves that she could pull over the scars on her wrists.

Ralph smiled genuinely. "Don't sweat it. Been there a time or two myself. Once for stealing a car and, most recently, to dry out."

He pulled a hip flask out of his suit pocket and took a swig. "Didn't take."

A girl stepped up and nudged Ralph out of the way. "You have no sense of compassion, do you?" she snapped at Ralph. "I'm Tessa." She tilted her head towards Ralph. That 'thing' is my half-brother."

"Took my turn inside for an eating disorder," Tessa continued. "Wasn't real. All I wanted to do was to torture Mother for getting married for the fourth time. Never doing that again. Chocolate is too precious!"

Tessa stepped to the side and gestured at the room's conference table. "Speaking of eating, help yourself."

Leigh stared at the table which was strewn with all sorts of snacks and soft drinks, tiny plastic plates and matching plastic cutlery.

Tessa giggled. "Afraid the mice made short work of all the good stuff."

"Mice?" Leigh asked.

Tessa pointed at the group of youngest KITs squatting on the floor, surrounded by candy wrappers and cake remnants, more ground into the carpet than remained on the plates, as they played video games disinterested in what the older KITs were doing. A good-looking boy with jet black hair and porcelain features crawled out of the heap of mice and came over to the conference table. To Leigh's surprise, he helped himself to shrimp and cocktail sauce. He used a plate, fork, napkins, and his manners were impeccable despite the absence of a chaperone to enforce them.

Myra, having finished letting Ralph know he was a jerk for the way he introduced himself to Leigh, joined her and Tessa. "So, how are we going to get you out of here?"

Leigh shot a look of worry toward Tessa.

"Don't worry," Myra said. "We've all got so much dirt on each other that our secrets are safe. Even the mice know better than to squeak. So, how *are* we going to do it with Miss Tree rooted right outside?"

"I don't know," Leigh said. "I was kind of relying on you. You've been to these things before. I haven't."

"True," Myra said, "but never with my own personal jailer."

The boy at the table finished his shrimp and wiped his delicate fingers on a napkin, dabbed at the corners of his mouth, and joined them.

"Something I can help with?" the boy asked.

Ignoring him Tessa said, "Leigh, this is my half-brother, Theo. He's from my mother's third marriage."

Theo held out his hand to Leigh, who looked at it too surprised to take it in hers. When she did, she found his grip was like iron.

Ralph came to stand beside his half-sister. "Theo thinks he's like forty or something. Never acts like a kid." He bent down to peer eye to eye at his half-brother. "Destined for prison, this one. Just like his father."

Theo smiled. "Better than running off with a male secretary, only to be dumped a year later, like your old man."

Tessa smiled at Leigh. "Ralph's from Mom's first marriage. I'm from the second. Theo, the third. We haven't named the fourth marriage-baby yet. She's due in six months."

"Your mom's only been married four months," Myra exclaimed.

"Three," Tessa corrected her.

Myra shook her head in dismay. "Sorry, Tess."

"It is what it is. Actually, us sibs are the silver lining. Despite our issues, we kinda like each other."

"Speak for yourself," Ralph said, but he had a smile on his face.

"So, what's the problem?" Theo asked, all business.

"Leigh wants to have a poke around in Marcus's office," Myra said. "Trouble is there's a governess parked right outside. We need to get past her."

Theo smiled like a crocodile. "I hate governesses."

Over his shoulder he called out, "Hey Charlie! Got a minute?"

A handsome black boy, tall and thin, extracted himself from the pile of mice and sauntered over. "Sup Theo?"

"My sister's friend here needs to break out for a bit," Theo explained. "Remember when Decker slipped that snake into Mrs. Donaldson's desk at school?"

"Yeah," Charlie cooed while nodding, a self-satisfied grin spreading across his face. "I let you bloody my nose then, while we pretended to fight, he did the deed. Sweet little caper!"

"Up for round two?" Theo asked.

"Sure. Only I get to bop you in the nose this time."

Theo shrugged. "It *is* my turn. Go tell the others to crowd around us as we fight. When that lady comes in, get them to stand between her and the door and don't let her see Leigh leave."

Charlie went around the room spreading the plan.

Theo turned to Leigh, digging into his pockets. Pulling out a key, he handed it to her. "You'll need this."

"You swiped Mom's all access key?" Ralph asked.

"Kinda," Theo said with a shrug. "I mean I did, but I made a copy and put it back before she noticed so, borrowed, not swiped."

Tessa clicked her tongue in disapproval. "You're going to wind up in that military school Mom threatened you with."

"Eventually," Theo said, no emotion in his voice. "We both know it's unavoidable. Leigh? Do you know where you're going?"

"She doesn't need to. I'm going with her," Myra said.

"You'll get in trouble," Leigh protested.

"I always get into trouble at these parties. As long as it isn't anything too outrageous Mom and Dad write it off as being bored."

Theo nodded. "You're both going to get caught. Nothing I can do about the cameras so you'll be spotted. It's only a question of how long it takes. Once you get out of here, you'll have to hustle."

Charlie trotted back to them. "All set."

Leigh looked around the room. Each face was shining with conspiratorial glee.

"I don't know if I should be terrified of you people or fall in love," Leigh said to Tessa.

"My advice is to do both," Tessa said. "And one more thing. You got that key from me, not Theo."

"You don't have to do that, Tess," Theo said.

"Military school might be unavoidable but I'm going to do everything I can to put it off as long as possible. Now, shut up."

"Ready?" Charlie asked, saving Theo from having to respond.

Before Leigh knew what was happening, she heard a loud pop. Theo's head jerked backward. Blood flowed out his nostrils like ketchup.

"Nice one, Charlie," Theo said before swinging his fist at his friend.

The room exploded in chaos.

Miss Tree burst into the room, dashing over to separate the two boys. The rest of the KITs pooled between her and the door. Behind their backs, Leigh and Myra scurried out of the room.

The elevator ride to the fourteenth floor felt like it took forever. Leigh fidgeted, balancing first on top of one spiked heel, then the other. Muttering something foul, she leaned against the wall of the elevator and, tearing at the miniature buckles, pulled her shoes off. When the bell dinged and the doors slid open Leigh exited, leaving her shoes behind.

"Either I'll grab them on our way back down or we'll already have been busted and it won't matter," she said. "Which office belongs to Marcus?"

"To the left," Myra whispered. "Last one on the right."

They trotted down the hall and to their astonishment, found Marcus' door unlocked. Myra hesitated. "This is wrong. Marcus would never leave his door unlocked. Never."

"Well, it's unlocked now," Leigh said. "Maybe a cleaner left it open. Doesn't matter at this point. We've got to get in and get out before the cavalry arrives."

They moved inside and, throwing caution to the wind, turned on the lights. "If we're already caught, we might as well make things easy on ourselves," Myra said.

Leigh nodded in agreement and began rifling through Marcus's desk. "Do your best to memorize anything interesting you find. Any copies or notes we make will be taken away from us."

"True," Myra agreed.

Finding nothing in or on Marcus's desk, Leigh moved to the lateral file cabinet standing behind it and pulled the long drawer open. Pasted to the back of the drawer, almost invisible behind the tops of folders, was a white label reading "Disciplinary Files."

"Jackpot," Leigh exclaimed, working her way through the alphabetized folders.

"Leigh, we should get out of here. This is all wrong as wrong can be," Myra said as she crept in beside Leigh. "It's so unlike Marcus to leave things open like this."

Leigh pulled out Jason Small's file and slapped it down on top of the desk. "Can't worry about that now."

She was no speed reader but did the best she could, turning pages and skimming the contents. The lights of the office flashed on and off rapidly. Looking up Leigh saw Marcus standing in the doorway, a trio of security guards behind him. Dangling off his fingers by their straps were Leigh's shoes.

"I'll have the access key, please," he said.

Myra pulled it out of a hidden pocket in the sash of her dress, pinching it between her fingers and sliding them over the key's surface. Marcus grimaced at her.

"So much for prints," he grumbled. "Whose key is it?"

"We found it," Myra lied as she handed the key over. "That's where we got the idea to go snooping around."

Marcus studied the key. "Liar."

"I beg your pardon," Myra said, standing tall and indignant.

Marcus continued to inspect the key. He spoke impassively, "That is what we call people who tell lies. There's no serial number on this key. All our keys are numbered. You wouldn't have found this. You either had it made or you know who did."

"Fine! I had it made from Dad's copy."

One of Marcus' eyebrows arched. "More lies? Mr. Simmons, along with the other board members, use a private elevator. Different looking key."

He moved to a bookshelf that had an ornate set of grills covering each shelf's contents. Giving it a small tug, the grate lifted. "How did you manage to unlock this?"

"We didn't. Everything in here was unlocked when we arrived," Myra said.

Marcus sighed. "Lie after lie after lie."

"It's true," Leigh said. "Everything was open. Even the door."

"I will check, but for now..."

He pulled a thick book from the shelf. Carrying it to his desk he glared at Leigh and Myra until the girls moved out of his way.

"Thank you," he said, his voice dripping with scorn.

He flipped open the book and began comparing the key to images inside. "As I was about to say, every key has a notch that is unnecessary in any of our locks but which does uniquely identify the owner of the key. Ah! Here we go. This key, or rather its parent, belongs to Sarah McCain. I'll be talking to her in the morning."

"Tessa," Myra blurted out. "I got the key off Tessa."

"Tessa?"

"Yes."

"No."

"What?"

"Ralph, maybe," Marcus said. "Theodore? More likely. Tessa? No."

"I'm telling you the truth," Myra pleaded. "It was Tessa. Marcus! Please!"

He studied her. "I see. Commendable, but misguided. Still, if that's how you want it, so be it. Which delinquent copied the key is far less important than whatever it is you were looking for."

Closing the key book, Marcus turned his attention to the folder beneath it. "Remarkably logical, Ms. Howard. Yes, very well-reasoned. If, I assume you believe as I do, Dante Jones is as innocent as he claims, the next question would naturally be..."

He looked at her with brows raised waiting for her to fill in the blank.

Leigh locked her eyes onto his. "Why did Jason Small pull Dante away from the very spot Mom and Dad were murdered?"

A hint of a smile flashed over Marcus's face and he nodded with amused admiration. "And why did he?"

"I don't know, " Leigh was loath to admit. "I couldn't read the file fast enough."

Chapter Fourteen

Leigh sat in one of the library's deep leather chairs with her arms wrapped in a hug around her ribs. The cuffs of her hoodie sleeves were clenched in her fists. The fabric stretched at the elbows making it look like she was wearing a mustard yellow, powder blue, tied-dyed, straight jacket. Her hips were thrust out to the edge of the seat cushion so that her shoulder blades dug in mid seat-back and her chin pressed against her chest. Knees together, shins angled out, toes pointed inward, she pouted, locked in a battle of wills against Miss Tree who sat across from her in a matching chesterfield doodling in a notepad, content to wait her out.

Leigh broke first. "So, we done or what?"

"Done?" Miss Tree smirked. "We haven't even started."

She looked at her pad. "All I have from this session is..."

She flipped the pad around allowing Leigh to see a well-drawn likeness of her sullenness sketched across the top sheet of yellow legal pad.

"Burn that," Leigh ordered.

"It's all I have to show that I at least attempted to conduct a session with you."

"But you haven't! You want to talk about what happened at the party. I don't. What I need are skills to help me not fall apart whenever I think about my parents, which is every minute of every day."

Miss Tree let out a great sigh. "And I tried to explain that it is all connected. Your feelings, your loss, your past behavior, your motivations for future behavior -- it's all tied together. Your obsession with solving your parents murder is a symptom of the very thing you say you want to work on, but won't."

"What a load of bull..."

"You finish that sentence, young lady, and I'll see to it you regret it," Miss Tree snapped.

Leigh glared. "I'd like to see you try."

Miss Tree got to her feet. "I can see this is going nowhere. My opinion is that talking to you isn't ever going to be productive."

Leigh's face brightened. "You mean you're giving up?"

"Not at all," Miss Tree said, "but a different approach is in order. I'll give it some thought."

"You do that," Leigh snarled at her back as she left the library.

Her gaze fell on the portrait of Big Bodie. "What are you staring at?"

"A little girl in sore need of a spanking," a hollow voice echoed at her side.

Turning her head, Leigh found the old man's ghost sitting on the arm of her chair.

She leapt out of her seat. "You wouldn't dare!"

"We both know that I would," the ghost said, " even with that little brat doing his best to keep me from it."

Leigh grimaced at him. "That 'little brat' is you. You know that, right.?"

"Bah! He was me once. Pathetic! I outgrew him. Would get rid of him all together, if I could, but I can't, so I'm stuck with him."

Leigh took a step forward. "You do anything to hurt him and I swear you'll pay for it!"

"And, supposing you could do anything about it, why would you?"

"He's..." Leigh balked. Why would she? The answer shone clear and bright in her mind. "He's my friend," she said.

A look of surprise overtook the old man's face, his angry purple aura fading slightly. "Is he now? Oh, sweet irony! A wants-to-be-dead girl has made friends with an already-dead boy. Charming!"

"Say what you want, but I mean it. You hurt him and I'll find some way to hurt you back."

Bodie's laughter sounded like cannon fire. "I've already hurt the little runt in the worst way imaginable."

Worry and fear tore through Leigh. "What have you done?"

"Calm down, you little yipping mutt. I did it long before you were even born. I became me!"

The ghost roared in laughter at his joke.

"Why are you such a jerk?" Leigh asked.

Bodie flew off the arm of the chair and soared around the room, rattling the paintings on the walls. "Because I have to be. Nobody else was ever willing to be."

No longer laughing, he roared in rage. The entire house shook with it. In some far-off room something fell to the floor and Leigh heard it shatter.

She ran from the library, knowing better than to hang around when Big Bodie was throwing a tantrum. Outside, she forced herself to slow to a walk. She couldn't think of anywhere she wanted to go, only places she didn't, like her room or the river. She turned her steps toward the garage. She spent a lot of her time there since her escapade at the shipyard, sitting beside her dad's bike and missing him and her mom. It was the place she felt closest to them. Nacho was typically there, too, tinkering with something and, unlike Big Bodie, she enjoyed his company.

"You back?" he asked as she entered the garage.

"No," Leigh said.

Nacho raised his eyebrows and smirked.

"Better disappear yourself," she said.

"Uh-oh. What you got cookin' in that head of yours?"

Leigh pulled the cover off the Ducati. "I'm going for a ride."

"Leigh, you know I can't let you do that."

"That's why I told you to get lost."

Nacho hung his head and shook it. "Can't do that either."

"I promise I'll only go to the gate and back."

"No offence, señorita, but honesty isn't your thing lately."

Leigh's eyebrows knotted in anger.

"I don't mean it like that. You aren't *dishonest*. It's just, you start out one way, but then you see something shiny, like an opportunity to dig deeper into what happened to your parents and, well, you sorta get distracted. Verdad?"

"You're right. But this is me promising you. As a friend."

"A friend you ditched first chance you got." Nacho shrugged. "I'm not holding no grudges or anything, but I gotta think of my position here. You know?"

"Yeah," Leigh said, her face burning with the memory of how she did run off and leave him. "I get that."

"So, knowing better than to try to talk you out of it," Nacho said grinning, "the only thing left for me to do is to come with you."

"No, that's okay," Leigh said with not enthusiasm. "You're too heavy for me to take for a ride."

"That's not what I meant," he said. "See, I knew it was only a matter of time before sitting beside that bike wasn't going to cut it. Follow me."

He left the lawnmower he was repairing and, wiping his greasy fingers on a shop rag, led Leigh out the back door of the garage. Parked in a narrow strip of shade at the back end of the cement drive sat Nacho's own Harley-Davidson. It was a low riding Fat Boy painted silver and electric blue.

Leigh's eyes bugged wide. "Why didn't you tell me you brought a bike out here!"

"As I said, I knew you'd get to this point, but I didn't want to be the one who drove you there."

Leigh jammed her fists onto her hips and scowled. "Chicken."

Nacho made a sad puppy face and said, "Pollo? Yeah, that's me."

He winked at her.

"Well, you better get over it," Leigh said, "if you plan on keeping up with me."

She raced back inside the garage, leaving him to start his bike and meet her around the front. Snatching her helmet off a shelf she rammed her head inside, pulling her hair and not caring. The Ducati's engine roared to life and she took off with such force that the front wheel kicked off the ground. Thankfully, Nacho hadn't made it from the rear lot to the front drive yet and wasn't there to see her wobble on the back tire, her flailing legs coming so close to the garage door track her jeans grazed it at the knee. As the front wheel touched down, she took off toward the front gate. Nacho's loud rumbling bike roared in behind her.

Beneath her tires, the snaking drive leading to the guard shack felt like smooth glass. The pathway twisted like a "Curvy Road Ahead" warning sign. Leigh leaned deep into those curves like her dad had shown her. Nacho's lumbering machine was no match for the agile Ducati and she easily left him behind. Reaching the guard shack, she braked so hard it was the rear tire that lifted off the ground.

The guard shack emptied in a flash. One guard held a rifle across her chest and her two colleagues stood in profile, hiding handguns with stiff arms scarcely behind their back legs. As the bike halted and she pulled off her helmet, relieved recognition deflated their tension. The woman holding the rifle re-entered the guard shack and swapped that weapon for a phone. Leigh didn't need anyone to tell her she was being ratted out to the family.

Shoving her head back into her helmet, she cranked the throttle, sending the bike into a smoking half-doughnut. On her way back up the drive she passed Nacho finishing his way down. He shook his head in silent scolding of the risks she was taking by pushing the bike so hard.

Leigh laughed inside her helmet. She felt free. Her knee inches above the pavement, she threw the bike into the curves. Up past the manor she flew. Tristin, Peg, and Myra, along with a few staff members, stood like an audience. Finishing her lap back at the garage, she decided to take one more. The look on Peg and Tristin's faces told her it might be a very long time before she would be allowed to ride again.

Pausing for a moment to make sure Nacho wasn't in the way of her second run, she watched as he reached the group of onlookers. His helmet hadn't cleared his ears before Tristin began gesticulating in her direction. Tristin's face was tomato red as he yelled at Nacho.

She ground her teeth in frustration. The last thing she wanted was Tristin giving Nacho a hard time because of her. If he did, she'd let him know loud and clear that no one controlled her. Not him. Not Nacho. Certainly not Miss Tree.

As she glowered at the group a blue haze spread across her visor, adding to the windscreen's tint, turning the world a deep evening shade. In that mist, Little Bodie's face appeared, opaque enough to be seen like a movie projected onto a glass screen. Leigh fought against crying out or showing any other signs of fright. She didn't want to be afraid of the boy-ghost but couldn't help herself.

"Want to race?" the spectral boy asked, his voice quivering with excitement.

"You can disappear and reappear wherever you want. That's hardly fair!"

"I promise I'll run the whole way."

"Still not fair, but you're on!"

The blue tint faded and she saw him beside her, crouched in preparation to run.

Leigh started the count. "Ready. Set. Go!"

She twisted hard on the throttle and the bike hurtled forward. The gears soon began whining, begging for a shift. Leigh waited until she was roaring past her audience before obliging, making the bike lurch forward with even greater speed. Taking a risk, she took her eyes off the road and looked into the bike's rearview mirror. Myra was cheering her on. Peg looked horrified. Tristan was scowling. Nacho tried to hide his smile by turning his head away and covering his lips with his hand. Miss Tree stood behind the family. She was standing with arms folded across her chest, smiling with what, to Leigh, looked like admiration.

The look on Miss Tree's face unsettled Leigh, breaking her concentration. The first curve came up so fast she wasn't prepared for it. Swearing, she heaved the bike over into a drastic lean, struggling to keep the tires on the road. Regaining control, she slid over to the other side of the seat to take the second curve, her knee so close to the pavement she thought she could feel it passing beneath. Beside her, Little Bodie was keeping pace, running faster than any living person could. His face glowed with unbridled joy as the trees and pavement blew by.

Another set of twists and turns was coming up. She could see Bodie laughing beside her, but the sound of his mirth was inside her helmet and kept her company all the way to the guard shack. As she roared toward it, he began falling back. He was going to let her win.

"Guess you are a gentleman," she said.

"Of course I am," his voice, ringing with glee, said inside her helmet.

The guards came out of their post again but in a far less intense way. They were smiling, watching her enjoy herself. No guns were drawn this time. Leigh waved a playful hand at them.

Grabbing the handlebars with both hands, she leaned hard and revved the engine, cutting circular doughnuts into the road. Acrid smoke rose into the air. Pulling the bike up, she turned back toward the garage.

"Time to pay the piper," Leigh said.

"How's that?" Bodie asked.

"I have to face Tristin and Peg. Did you see the look on their faces? They're furious. I don't know what they plan on doing to punish me, but I know it'll be something. And Miss Tree! Did you see her smiling? Bet she was picturing me falling and breaking my neck."

A breeze blew down the length of the drive and with it came a prickling chill. "I don't like her," Bodie said.

"You and me both, but I'm stuck with her."

The breeze picked up and the temperature dropped even lower. Bodie's voice dripping with mischief he asked, "Want me to drive her off?"

"Yes," Leigh said, "but no. I have to deal with her or else Tristin will find a replacement and, who knows? They might be worse. Besides, I don't want you to do anything mean. If I ever do, I'll ask the other you, not *you*."

Hearing that said aloud sounded so strange it made her giggle. Bodie began snickering, too. By the time she ground the bike to a halt back in the garage and killed the engine, Nacho had rumbled up on his big Harley. They shared a high-five and laughed at each other.

"Enjoy it while you can, señorita," he said.

"Are they off-the-scale pissed?"

His head pulled back in surprise that she needed to ask. "What do you think?"

"Give me a ride down to the house?"

"No way. Remember? I'm un pollo grande. A big chicken? Besides, this might be your last walk outdoors for a long time. I will say this, you'll want to go to them before they have to come up here to get you."

Leigh took in a deep breath and let is out slowly. "I get it. I'm going."

She started down the drive between the garage and the manor.

"Hey, Leigh," Nacho called out from behind. "You got skills on that bike."

A dark cloud of sadness gathered around her. "I had a good teacher."

Nodding his head and smiling wide he said, "The best. You made your dad proud. I'm sure of it."

His words stopped the sense of emptiness from consuming her. She still felt it, that all too familiar cold and empty pit, but she wasn't being sucked in. She stood at its edge knowing it was her choice to either take the plunge or walk away.

"You're scared," Bodie said softly, his blue outlined form floating by her side.

Leigh eyed the family standing at the front of the house. "Yeah, but not of them," she said more to herself than to him.

Turning to look at Bodie she asked, "Can they see you?"

"Not if I don't want them to. And I don't."

"Will you walk with me?"

"Sure, but you don't have anything to worry about."

Everyone was facing her, waiting. "I think you're wrong."

"Tell that Miss Tree hag you were tired of stewing in the depths of your sadness. Tell her you want to live, not die, and riding like your dad taught you makes you feel alive. They'll forget this stunt with the motorcycle ever happened."

Leigh began walking, looking at her shoes as they swayed one in front of the other. "How do you know I'm feeling all that?"

"Because I'm dead. Remember when we first met and I said I could tell you wanted to be dead? Well, now I can tell that you don't. At least not all of you. It's just a little spark," he said in a distant, almost sad tone, "but a little spark is all life needs."

Leigh sniffled. "It must be hard for you, having a living friend."

"Better than dead ones."

Half of Leigh's lips hitched into a smile. "You'll have to explain that one to me later."

"Not allowed," Bodie said.

"That makes no sense."

"Why? The living have their rules. Is it so hard to believe the dead have rules, too?"

Though intrigued, Leigh didn't have time to press further.

"Have you lost your mind?" Tristin demanded as soon as she stood in front of them.

Bodie swirled around him, sticking out his tongue. Leigh had to bite hers to keep from laughing.

"I thought you were awesome," Myra declared. "Don't let anyone tell you differently."

Bodie had the audacity to kiss her cheek. Myra swatted the air as if being pestered by a mosquito.

"Myra," Peg scolded, "now is not the time for you to put your defiance on display."

Peg turned to Leigh. "I was terrified you would crash or something. What got into you? Why would you do a thing like that?"

Leigh thought about how she nearly lost control of the bike after seeing Miss Tree in the mirror but lied, "Dad taught me how to ride. I was in complete control the whole time."

Tristin held out his hand. "Keys."

Leigh hesitated.

"Either give me the keys or I'll have that machine removed from the property."

Leigh slapped the keys into his hand and ran into the house.

Behind her she heard Myra howl, "Daddy! That was cruel."

Myra's feet made angry crunching sounds as she stormed in behind her. She followed Leigh up the stairs. She kept silent until they reached the threshold of Leigh's room. "I can go away, if you want," she said.

Leigh squirmed. All her emotions were fighting inside her like a professional wrestling battle royal, trying to decide which would win. She felt angry, sad, and at the same time oddly hopeful, even proud of herself. She wanted to be alone, wanted company, wanted to run away, wanted to stay. Above all she wanted to be any person in the world other than herself.

"I don't know what I want," she said, barging through the door and standing in the middle of the room. She didn't even know which part of her room she wanted to retreat to.

Behind her she felt Myra's presence waiting patiently.

"Come or go," Leigh sighed with impatience. "You pick because I can't."

As soon as she heard her door click shut, she realized she wanted Myra to still be there.

A thousand pounds fell off her shoulders when she heard Myra say, "I'd like to stay."

Relieved, Leigh knew what she had to do. Running forward, Leigh hurled herself off the ledge separating the sitting area from the rest of the room. With intentional force she slammed her feet against the floor when she landed.

"I hope the whole freaking house heard that," she said.

Myra smiled before taking a running leap off the ledge as well.

"Me, too," she said after banging her feet as hard as Leigh's.

They stood cocking their ears, listening for reproach. None came.

"They had to have heard that," Leigh whispered.

"I'm sure they did. They must know better than to complain at this point."

Leigh walked to the armchair and sat, curling her feet beneath her like a cat. "I wasn't trying to be bad."

"I know you weren't. Mom and Dad know it, too. You frightened them. That's all."

"Bet Miss Tree is down there telling them a different story. One about what a naughty little girl I am. Or how that was another suicide attempt."

Realizing what she said, Leigh sucked in her breath. She avoided that word, "suicide", at all costs. Giving a name to what she'd done gave her ownership of it and she didn't want to be saddled with that stigma.

As she was always able to, Myra changed her shattering fall into despair into a soft parachute landing. "You've moved past that," she said with finality. "At least I think you have. As for Miss Tree? Whatever you might think of her, she knows her game. I don't think she'll see it the way you described."

"Maybe you're right. Probably are. It's still so frustrating, though. I got into trouble at the party and dragged you down with me. Peg and Tristin are furious at us both. I haven't had the courage to check out the newspapers to see what, if anything, those reporters wrote. And all of it was for nothing. Marcus showed up before we found out anything that was helpful."

"That's not entirely true," Myra said. "You did find a file on Jason Small."

"Big whoop! I didn't have time to read it. And, besides, remember how Marcus was toying with me? Like a cat playing with a mouse before eating it?"

"Morbid much?"

"You know what I mean. He had already thought of Small and must have checked him out. If there was anything there, Marcus would have found it a long time ago. Which I'd have known, if anyone would tell me what is going on!"

"Leigh, they're only..."

Leigh shot her a daring glare. "If you say protecting me, I swear I'll scream!"

Myra stared back. Both girls got the giggles.

"Well, here's something I did notice," Myra said after settling down.

Leigh's eyes rounded with eager anticipation. "What?"

"Inside that disciplinary drawer was a file on Oliver Massy of all people."

"Tristin's personal assistant? I missed it!"

Chapter Fifteen

Leigh burned with curiosity, wanting to know why her escapade with her dad's motorcycle went unremarked. It had been twenty-four hours and no one, aside from Myra, who thought the whole thing was a crazy kind of cool, so much as mentioned it. Leigh was astounded that no punishments were issued. She wasn't called into Tristin's office for a chewing-out. The Ducati keys, to her greatest surprise, were returned to the garage's key cabinet. She hadn't the nerve to touch them, but they were there. As much as she hated doing it, she had to agree with Myra that Miss Tree had something to do with the leniency she was being given. When Miss Tree showed up wearing a track suit the following morning to start their new method of therapy, Leigh felt she owed her something and, biting her lip, went along without a fuss.

They walked across the manicured lawns and into the woods. Leigh, at first, thought they were headed to the river but Miss Tree turned down a trail Leigh had not as yet explored. Dusty and overgrown, the path was a long, meandering thread that reached the far edge of the Simmons-Pierce acreage. A sinking feeling in her guts told Leigh that, whatever Miss Tree had in mind, it wasn't going to be pleasant.

"Ready?" Miss Tree asked when she brought them to a halt.

"For what?" Leigh countered, doing her best to keep notes of derision out of her voice.

"For the run back."

"Run?'

"Yes. Run."

Leigh scowled. "And how is this therapy?"

"Since you don't respond to talk-therapy, that leaves physical therapy. See, when we exercise, our brains get tricked into believing we are either fighting or running for our lives. You may have noticed, if you weren't too busy feeling ashamed of your behavior, which you should be..."

Leigh glowered at her but Miss Tree kept right on talking. "...that after your little adventures you felt better about yourself and that your thinking was clearer, whatever that means to someone like you. Moreover, while you were out making a fool of yourself, you may have noticed pain and discomfort that should have been intense in the moment didn't register until after.

"So," Miss tree concluded, "if you won't let yourself feel better by talking through your issues, we can try to force you to feel better by getting your body moving."

Leigh folded her arms and jut out her hip. "My body moves just fine."

"We'll see," Miss Tree sang at her as she jogged off at a slow pace. "Try to keep up."

Leigh, having no intention of running, began walking back to the house. Miss Tree turned and trotted back to her.

"I can see why you haven't made any progress in finding your parents' killer," she said.

Leigh froze. "What did you say?"

"You heard me. I mean look at you. Out of shape. Lazy. Did you think catching killers would be easy?"

"Hey," Leigh yelled, "chasing down a moving train, hopping on, jumping back off wasn't easy."

"Then a short run to the house should be no trouble at all."

"No trouble," Leigh snarled, "aside from the fact I don't want to."

"Of course you don't," Miss Tree said. "Just like you don't want to catch your parents' killers. Oh, you talk a good game but, in the end," Miss tree shrugged, "too much effort."

Leigh shouted and lunged at Miss Tree, but she was no longer there. She had darted off down the trail taunting her, "You'll never catch your parent's killers if you can't catch me!"

Leigh put everything she had into chasing down Miss Tree. For the next several minutes they ran like an accordion, Leigh catching up and, when she was closing in, Miss Tree pulling ahead, increasing their pace. When the house came into view Miss Tree didn't stop.

"You angry?" she shouted over her shoulder.

"Yes," Leigh shouted back.

"At me?"

Leigh screamed something filthy.

"At your parents' killers?"

Leigh ran harder. "Yes!"

"At yourself?" Miss Tree asked.

Leigh was panting in earnest. So desperate for air she had difficulty speaking.

"You know I am," she wheezed.

Leigh's sides were burning. Her legs trembled every time her foot hit the ground. She was pushing herself harder than ever before. Miss Tree let Leigh almost catch her, but Leigh was too spent to make the most of it.

Running beside her, Miss Tree asked, "Why are you angry at yourself?"

Leigh struck out her hand to grab Miss Tree by the back of her neck, but the woman darted away, remaining just beyond Leigh's fingertips.

"Because I'm still alive! Because I have to keep on going alone!" Leigh shouted.

Miss Tree stopped running. Leigh, bawling and gasping for air, fell to her knees.

"If you are all alone," Miss Tree asked, "who are you chasing?"

Miss Tree turned and walked back toward the mansion. Looking over her shoulder she called out, "You're pretty fast, by the way. For a child."

Leigh rolled off her knees and onto her rump. Wrapping her arms around her shins she sucked in air and sulked.

"Who am I chasing?" she sneered aloud, adding on a horrible string of words to describe Miss Tree.

The worst part was, as her breathing calmed, she realized it was true, as foolish as it sounded. She had been chasing someone. Someone who cared enough to risk making her enraged. She growled at the idea. The last thing she wanted to believe was that Miss Tree cared.

Scraping herself off the drive, Leigh made her way back to the house. When she arrived, she found Myra standing by the door. Miss Tree had to be lying in wait because, as soon as Leigh came within hearing, she passed behind Myra, sipping orange juice and saying, "Oh look. Another person who isn't really here. This place must be filled with ghosts."

Leigh's face burned so hot with anger her eyes watered. "Did she put you up to this?" she demanded from Myra.

The shock of Leigh's accusation stretched Myra's face with surprise. "Who? Tree? That was the first I've seen of her this morning. Well, aside from you chasing after her like you wanted to kill her."

"I did. And I still might."

"Come on," Myra said, tugging on Leigh's arm. "Let's get you cooled off with a shower then you can tell me what happened."

Later, after drying off and getting dressed, Leigh explained what had transpired.

"That witch!" Myra exclaimed.

The forced chuckle Leigh added to her, "I know! Right?" was too obviously phony for Myra to ignore.

"What gives?" Myra asked.

Leigh dropped onto the sofa. "Look, I know Tree is a bit of a, you know... but she has a point. I wasn't being very cooperative in therapy."

Myra flashed a sarcastic grin at her. "You? Uncooperative? Get out!"

Leigh raised her eyebrows and waited.

"Sorry," Myra said, "but you lobbed that one to me. I had to swing at it."

"And are you done swinging?"

Myra grinned wickedly. "For now. Go on."

"All I'm saying," Leigh continued, "is that Miss Tree was right. And, mean as it was, it worked. I was too worn out to be defensive. I don't know about all that brain-chemical-trash she was yapping about, but I said some things I'd never have said otherwise and, now they are said, I can't unsay them."

"What kind of things?" Myra asked.

Leigh tugged at the sleeves of her hoodie. "About how mad I am at myself for still being alive when Mom and Dad aren't. And about how the idea of living my life on my own is so overwhelming I can't bear thinking about it."

"But you're not alone," Myra said. "Not anymore."

"That's the point Miss Tree was trying to make. And I know it's true. But knowing something and feeling it can be two different things."

Myra's shoulders drooped.

"Now don't be like that," Leigh groaned.

"I thought you felt, I don't know, *something* for us."

Leigh picked at her sleeves. "I can tell you; you don't feel like my cousin."

Myra sniffled, but nodded.

"You feel more like a sister. It's like that. I know we're cousins. But you *feel* like a sister."

Myra looked at the floor -- at the wall -- anywhere but at Leigh.

"Oh, come on," Leigh groaned. "Why do you think I'm telling you all this and not Tree, or your mom and dad? It's because I trust you. I..."

Leigh let that sentence hang unfinished. She wasn't ready.

Myra smiled and wiped her eyes. "I love you, too. But where does that leave you and Miss Tree?"

"I'm not sure."

Before Leigh could speculate, the sound of crunching tires outside stole her attention. From the noise, she knew not just one vehicle, but several, were pulling up to the manor. Voices began shouting -- loud -- commanding -- threatening.

"Get inside and don't let anyone go anywhere near papers of any kind. I don't care if it's today's edition of *The Wall Street Journal*. No one but us handles documents, computers, cell phones. Nothing!"

Leigh shot out of her seat and bounced up at the window, hooking her fingers over the ledge and doing a pull-up to see outside.

Tristin's voice rang out, "What the devil is going on? Who are you people? Where's my security team? I want answers and I want them now!"

"Just calm down, Mr. Simmons," an older man, thin as a whip, wearing a ball cap embroidered with SEC, called out. "We have a warrant to search the premises."

"This isn't a premise," Tristin shouted back. "It's my home. Let me see that."

Leigh watched as Tristin scanned the document. "This thing better be water tight because if I find so much as a pinhole your entire agency is toast."

Leigh lowered herself onto her toes. "We'd better get down there. Something's up and it's not good."

"What?" Myra asked. "What'd you see?"

"Agents from the Securities and Exchange Commission, the SEC, they're swarming the house. Myra, I think Simmons-Pierce Shipping is being raided."

Myra shot out of her seat. "What? We've got to do something."

Leigh didn't share in her cousin's sense of urgency. Her dad's voice echoed in her mind; "When it comes to the police, keep calm, do everything you are told to do, go overboard on the politeness and respect, and sort out any grievances you have on the back end when you get your day in court. The last thing you want to do is give a judge any reason to hold a grudge or a cop any reason to shoot."

Tristin's voice drowned out her father's. "No you may not have my cell phone. As you can see, I am using it to call my attorneys and my head of security, Marcus Figueroa."

Myra gasped. "Cell phones! Marcus!"

"What about them?" Leigh asked.

Myra pulled hers out of her back pocket. "I've got to hide this."

"Myra! We can't hide evidence from these people. That is the one sure way to look guilty!"

Myra's eyes darted around the room, searching for some place to stash her phone. "There's nothing on it that has anything to do with the company. But there are personal things on here that, well, let's just say Dad's head would explode."

Leigh looked hard at Myra. "You promise? There's nothing on your phone in any way connected to whatever the SEC is looking for?"

Myra looked at her with eyes filled with both sincerity and fear. "I promise."

"Give it here," Leigh said in a rush.

Taking Myra's phone, Leigh ran into her closet. Pulling out the loose plank in the floor, she placed Myra's phone on top of Bodie's journal. Replacing the board, she darted back out into the room and stood in front of Little Bodie's picture.

"Don't let anyone find it," she said to Bodie's likeness.

A draft wafted through the room, making Leigh's bangs gently flutter.

Myra's eyes darted left and right. "You have got to be kidding me!"

"It's my house and I'll go in if I bloody well want to!" Tristin roared.

"Mr. Simmons," a stern voice answered, "if you can't calm down and let my agents do their jobs, I'll have you removed."

"We'd better get down there," Leigh said. "Your dad is making things worse."

As she swung the door open, Leigh was surprised to find a female officer on the other side. Startled, the agent blurted out, "Who are you and what are you doing up here?"

"We're criminal masterminds plotting the overthrow of western civilization," Myra said. "This is our evil lair."

The agent glared at Myra.

Leigh growled softly and admonished Myra. "That's not helpful."

To the agent she said, "Sorry about that. My sister's a bit out of sorts given everything that's happening. This is my bedroom."

The agent, responding to Leigh's gentle and polite attitude, regained her composure. "Sisters? Our briefing said you were cousins."

Myra was about to make another nasty comment when Leigh nudged her with her elbow. "Technically we are cousins, ma'am. We've grown very close since I arrived."

"I see," the agent said. Leigh was glad the agent was a female officer. She probably did understand in a way most men wouldn't.

"Miss Simmons," the agent continued, "you are nineteen, is that correct?"

"It is. What difference does that make?"

"Miss Howard is a minor. I have to make a search of this room. Normally, I'd ask both of you to leave but, if you agree to be a responsible guardian on Miss Howard's behalf, I can allow you to stay, given Miss Howard's..."

The agent's voice died away.

"My history? That's very kind of you," Leigh said before Myra could shoot her mouth off again, "and please, call me Leigh."

Not responding, the agent began her search. She put in a half-hearted effort, which told Leigh the officer didn't expect to find anything.

Myra gasped when the agent entered the closet.

"Calm down," Leigh whispered in perfect confidence. "Everything's going to be all right."

The agent called out from inside, "Miss Howard? There's a board here that looks more worn than the others. I know young people sometimes like to squirrel things away. Is that what is going on here?"

"No," Leigh lied confidently. "It was a loose board that was getting banged around. I had the handyman, Nacho, glue and nail it down. He did a good job, didn't he?"

Thumping sounds came from inside. "He did. That board isn't giving an inch."

"Do you need anything out of this room?" the agent asked as she exited the closet.

"No, thank you," Leigh said. "Why?"

"I'll need the both of you to join the rest of the family downstairs. We want everybody in one place while we conduct our search."

Myra spoke up rudely. "Will I be shot for asking what you are searching for?"

"You won't be shot," the agent fired back. "Further explanations will be provided in due course by the lead investigator."

"That'll be fine," Leigh said before Myra could say anything else. "Thank you."

The agent led the way out of the room. Myra followed while Leigh brought up the rear. As she passed Bodie's picture Leigh whispered, "Thank you."

The room sighed as a breeze blew in through the open window.

Leigh and Myra were escorted to the library. When they arrived, Peg dashed over and hugged both of them.

"Are you two all right?" she asked.

"We're fine," Myra said.

"Yeah," Leigh added, grinning at the agent who searched her room, "they were professional and even kind to us."

The agent's face cracked into the smallest of a reciprocating smile before she left them in the custody of two agents guarding the library door.

"Where's Tree?" Myra demanded of her mother. "There are a few things I'd like to say to that woman."

Peg looked startled. "She had a family emergency she had to go deal with. Why?"

"Now's not the time to worry about Miss Tree," Leigh said, crossing the room to where Tristin stood brooding.

"Uncle Tristin," she said in a hush, one of the rare moments she addressed him as Uncle, "you have got to be nicer to these people."

Tristin was shocked and incensed. "Mind your own business, young lady," he snapped.

"I am. I care about all of you and about this company!"

She took a deep breath to regain her composure. "Look, I'm a policeman's daughter. I know how these people think and how to deal with them. The more you resist, the harder they dig. Even if you do have something you're trying to hide..."

"I beg your pardon," Tristin roared.

The two guards twisted their necks to look in. "Is there a problem?" one asked.

"None what so ever," Tristin replied curtly.

Leigh returned to whispering, "I don't believe you have anything to hide but, listen! You are acting like you do. At least that's how they'll see things. You've got to be more cooperative. They have to see you as someone on their side. Someone willing to help."

The rail thin agent Leigh saw outside came to the door and spoke in low tones to the two agents standing guard.

As he entered he said to the family, "My name is Davies and I'm heading up this rodeo. I want to thank you all for waiting so patiently. My people tell me there was a bit of tension a moment ago. I'm sorry if we were the cause."

Tristin laid a gentle hand on Leigh's shoulder. "Not at all. The problem was mine. My niece pointed that out and gave me some excellent advice. I was, well, a bit shocked, to put it lightly, and I'm afraid I behaved rather foolishly."

Davies placed his thumb and forefinger under his nose and smoothed his mustache by spreading his fingers. "Perfectly understandable. I'm sure you have thousands of questions. Now that our preliminary search is finished, I hope to give you some answers."

Peg slid her fingers across the back of a large chesterfield couch. "Won't you please sit down?" she offered before seating herself at the far end.

The man grumbled his thanks as he sat with a groan. "I'm getting too old for this job."

"Since when is twenty-five too old for anything?" Leigh asked as she plopped to the floor beside the chair Myra was seated in.

"Oh, I like you, sweetheart," Davies chortled. "Remind me a lot of my granddaughter."

He turned to Tristin. "Better get down to it. Insider trading. That's the issue. Someone, or a group of someones, has been dumping a lot of Simmons-Pierce shares lately. Enough for us to notice. Your figures look stronger than ever. Quarterlies are either right on or above target. There's absolutely no reason for such a sell-off. As you know, the SEC does not have any criminal authority. We can, however, refer matters to state and federal prosecutors. Somewhere up the line the decision was made to act proactively on this one to decide if such a referral is warranted."

"Can you tell me who, or which group, was doing the selling?" Tristin asked. "It would help if I knew. There are a few share-holders who are looking to move out of the old-world of shipping and to break into the new world of automation -- self-sailing boats -- like the self-driving cars that are starting to emerge."

"I appreciate your willingness to help," Davies said. "Truth is, it's your man Oliver Massy we've got our eye on. I can tell you that because, as we were poking around here, other agents were rounding him up."

"Massy?" Tristin scoffed. "Absurd."

"Your loyalty is admirable, but there are some discrepancies in his taxes, things he failed to report, that sort of thing."

"I'm sure that isn't uncommon for people as wealthy and diversified as Oliver," Tristin said. "Cash flows, assets, and so forth are always in a state of flux. That usually warrants a nasty letter from the IRS, not a raid from the SEC."

"You're right about that, but there's the massive sell-off of Simmons-Pierce stocks. There also seems to be some connection with the drug smuggling that was going on. I'm sure you have been kept abreast of the recent arrest?"

"I am very aware of the events of that evening, I assure you."

Leigh saw Tristin's eyes shift in her direction but paid no attention to it. As she sat, listening to Davies paint a very black picture of Oliver Massy, all she could think about was how any of it might be connected to her parents' murder. If Massy was in league with drug smugglers, who knows what else he was into. The answer had to be in his folder, but that was safely tucked away in Marcus' naughty drawer.

Her heart began to flutter. What if the file was overlooked, or it had been moved, or destroyed? No one would ever know about it.

Leigh swallowed hard. She had to decide if she was going to side with loyalty to the family or seek justice. Closing her eyes, the horrific images she stole from Ty's folder flashed through her mind's eye.

"Uncle Tristin," she said, trying to sound like an innocent and naive child, "when I was in Mr. Figueroa's office the night of the party, I saw a folder with Mr. Massy's name on it. Do you think that has anything to do with this? Mr. Figueroa is head of security."

"Oh, Leigh," Myra rasped, disappointment oozing out of her voice.

Tristin stared at her with frozen eyes. "That," he said, "is a purely internal affair. A personnel issue, if you must know."

Davies looked back and forth between Leigh and Tristin as if watching a tennis match. "I'll follow up on that with Mr. Figueroa, but I'm sure it is just as you say. Nothing at all to concern us."

He pushed himself to his feet. "We are done here, you'll be happy to know. Didn't find anything. Then again, can't say I expected to. There are one or two documents we are holding on to, more to prove we were here than anything else."

Davies smiled at his own joke. No one else did.

He cleared his throat, "I'll show myself out."

"Nonsense," Peg said rising.

Myra shot a withering look at Leigh. "I'll go with you, Mother."

Leigh remained seated on the floor as Peg, Davies, and Myra left. Tristin rose to his feet and followed without saying a word to her. With a heavy sigh, Leigh heaved herself up and went to look out one of the big windows facing the drive. The SEC troops packed and loaded their vans, then started a single-file procession down the drive. Leigh watched them go just as she knew Peg and Myra were doing from the front of the house; as Tristin was doing from his office. After the last van pulled away she heard the front door close. No one came to the library.

Her shoulders fell and she hung her head in loneliness and shame. A hollow feeling grew within her chest. She believed she had done the right thing but felt nasty all the same.

Throwing herself down on the chesterfield, the flat of her back on the seat cushions, her battered sneakers hanging over the arm, she muttered to herself, "Well, I screwed that up. And, I don't even know what *insider trading* is!"

"That's because you are a stupid little girl," a voice echoed as if it came from the depths of a well.

Leigh crossed her arms over her chest. "Go away, Bodie. I'm not in the mood."

The ghost rattled the windowpanes with his laughter. "Like I care about *your* mood."

She rolled her head to the side and looked at his painting. An acid purple mist swirled inside it then spiraled outward as Big Bodie appeared. He was coming toward her using his walking stick as if descending invisible stairs between the floor and the painting. Remembering the last time they were alone together, she twisted into a sitting position. She wasn't altogether frightened, but felt it best to be on her guard.

"For your information," he said while stepping down, "insider trading is the using of or sharing of information known only to a few within a company, that is, insiders; information that is not known to the larger trading community."

"Used for what?" Leigh asked.

"Idiot child! To make money. What else?"

"I don't understand," Leigh said.

With a loud rush of wind Big Bodie's nose was inches from her own. "That's why females have no business meddling in business!"

"You are such a dick! I know you died soon after the Suffragette Movement. And a lot's happened since! Guess you ghosts don't keep up with the times?"

Big Bodie's laughter cackled again as his head, trailed by a hideous purple plume of smoke, soared in crazy circles around the room.

"When you're done showing off, maybe you could explain it to me," she groaned.

"Ooh, we are in a snit today," he said, disappearing from the air and reappearing in a chair across from her. "You do know what stocks and shares are?"

"Partial ownership or investments in companies?"

The ghost shook his head. "Close enough. Those are bought and sold every day. Money is made when they are bought cheap and the company does well. Later, those commodities can be sold at a higher price."

"I get that," Leigh said, "but how does insider trading play into it?"

"Let's say you know some juicy news that is going to make a company much more profitable. You could buy more stocks in that company at today's rate knowing its value is going to increase. Alternatively, if you knew something terrible was coming you could sell your investments at today's value before the disaster struck, making your investments worthless."

"I get it," Leigh said, "but what was Oliver Massy's insider knowledge? Was it good news or bad?"

Bodie's haze darkened and the room smelled of rotten egg. "I'm a ghost, not a clairvoyant!"

Calm again he continued, "I suspect Simmons-Pierce is being pressured by outside, criminal forces. If that's the case, and I do believe it is, Mr. Massy could have been selling his shares before blowing the whistle, driving prices down, down, down. He'd make a quick fortune. Then, he could buy them all back, and more, at the new lower price."

Leigh eyed him suspiciously. "Why do you think it's some crime organization? Do you have any proof, or are you lying to me?"

Bodie smiled an evil grin. "Why would I lie?"

"Because you like to be mean."

"How little you understand. Nevertheless, I think that's the case because things feel like they did when it happened before."

Leigh took a chance. "To you?"

Big Bodie nodded. "A young hooligan named Al Capone wanted to use my shipping yard for his illegal trade. I refused."

"He had you killed?"

"Yes. And left me stranded here with that damnable brat!"

Frustrated, Leigh shook her head. "I don't understand that bit, the two of you, either."

"What's there to understand? He won't go and without him I can't. Funny thing is, I'm the reason he won't go."

He smiled at her and his face looked rotten, dead, and decayed. "It's a deliciously nasty cycle of torment that's been repeating itself for over one hundred years."

Leigh rubbed her temples with her fingertips to ease her nausea, not wanting to give the ghost the satisfaction of seeing her gag. "I still don't understand."

"Then ask him," Bodie bellowed as his ghostly body exploded in bright purple light, wisps of acrid mist billowing away. In a distant and fading echo he said, "I've grown tired of your stupidity."

"I'm pretty sick of you, too," Leigh said as she stood and left the library.

From a side room that was converted into a mini theater, she heard the sound of the local news. Shuffling over to the room, her heart wrenched at seeing the rest of the family watching the big screen. Oliver Massy was being escorted out of the courthouse. No one thought to invite her to join or, if they did think of it, they decided they'd rather not have her around.

Hovering in the doorway Leigh watched the screen where reporters were pressing in on Oliver, their cameras and microphones jabbed into his face. Their voices squawking out questions reminded Leigh of the bird house at the zoo. A loud crack, like a firecracker, echoed from somewhere behind the crowd. People dove to the ground. Shouts and screams and chaos filled the airwaves.

Eyes glued to the TV, Leigh watched as Oliver Massy's eyes rolled back in his head. A red dot between his eyes grew larger and larger. The camera that was on him fell to the ground capturing Oliver's own collapse, shot dead in the midst of so many.

Chapter Sixteen

Myra, Peg, and Tristin bounced to the front of their seats, petrified by what they witnessed. Leigh stood as motionless as if the television were the cursed eye of Medusa and she had turned to stone. Tristin was the first to break the spell and bolt out of his chair.

"I've got to call Marcus, get out in front of this," he said.

In Tristin's haste to leave he collided with Leigh. Standing in the doorway, mouth agape, lips trembling, unable to speak, unable to move out of his way, Leigh could not take her eyes off the blacked-out screen of the TV.

"Leigh?" he asked softly. When she didn't respond he spoke louder, taking her by the shoulders. "Leigh! How long have you been standing there?"

The TV blared out, "We're back live in the studio trying to make sense out of what we just witnessed."

"Turn that damn thing off!" Tristin roared.

Myra scooped up the remote and shut the system down.

"I...I saw it all," Leigh said as if far, far away. "I saw the bullet hit my parents. I mean, Oliver. Mr. Massy. I saw them...*him*...I saw him fall to the ground. It was..." tears began roiling out of her eyes.

She looked up at Tristin. "It didn't look like it hurt at all. Do you think Mom felt anything?"

"No, sweetheart, I don't," he replied gently. "Let's get you sitting down."

She felt him pull her into the room and steer her toward a chair. Her feet felt too heavy to lift and she stumbled along beside him.

"Peg," Tristin ordered, "bring Leigh a glass of chocolate milk. The sugar will do her good."

As her mother ran for the kitchen Myra knelt beside Leigh and took her hand.

Leigh looked at her, glassy-eyed and unfocused. "Oliver was shot. It was Mr. Massy, not my parents."

"That's right," Myra said, her voice trembling with concern.

Peg returned and pressed the cold milk into her hand. "Drink that."

To Myra she said, "Call Miss Tree. Her number is in my phone. You know the password."

Myra dashed out of the room. She was only gone a moment before she was back at Leigh's side. "Couldn't reach her, but I left a message."

Myra laid a soft hand on Leigh's shoulder. "She'll be here as soon as she gets it."

"I'm better now," Leigh said. She straightened out of her slouch. "Seeing that happen! It looked like the photos of my parents. I mean, I was already thinking about them, you know? Wondering if Mr. Massy had anything to do with their deaths? That's why I said what I did. I mean, I wasn't going to until I thought about those pictures."

"What pictures are you talking about?" Peg asked.

Realizing she'd said too much, Leigh's eyes rounded. "I…er…I copied some photos from out of Ty's case file. Crime scene photos before the bodies were moved."

Myra's heart broke as she let out a sigh. "Why didn't you share that with me?"

"It was, I don't know. Too personal? I couldn't bear anyone else seeing my parents looking like that." Leigh shuddered. "Not like that."

Tristin pressed his fingertips against his lips as if caging an angry reproach. "I see," was all he said.

Peg laid the back of her hand against Leigh's forehead and caressed it down to her cheek. "I think the best thing at the moment is for Leigh to have a lie down. We can decide what needs be done about these pictures, and anything else, later."

"Myra," she said, the issue being decided, "take Leigh up to either your room or hers, whichever she feels most comfortable being."

Myra stood and offered both hands to Leigh.

"Really," Leigh insisted, "I'm all right."

Myra smiled down at her. "Did your mom have a special tone that let you know arguing was pointless?"

"Sure. Why?"

"That was Mom's special tone. You're either going to do what she says now or after a big fight but, trust me, you are going to do it."

Leigh let Myra pull her to her feet. Consumed by a sudden impulse, she reached out and hugged Peg. Without hesitation, Peg cradled Leigh's head against her breast and rocked her for as long as Leigh wanted to stay there. Breaking the embrace, Leigh looked at Peg with eyes filled with gratitude.

Retaking Myra's hand, she allowed herself to be led off to bed like a four-year-old.

"You good up here?" Myra asked as she pulled Leigh's sheet up to her chin.

She nodded. As much as she was loath to admit it, being babied was what she needed.

"Maybe Little Bodie will come to keep me company," she breathed out as she snuggled into her mattress.

"I can stay, if you want," Myra said.

"Would you?" Leigh murmured. "I hate to be a bother and I know Bodie'll look after me, but if you'd please stay? Just until I fall asleep?"

"Of course I will," Myra said as she brushed a stray lock off Leigh's face. "And you're not a bother. Maybe a brat sometimes, but never a bother."

Leigh gave a weary sigh as she burrowed deeper still into her sheets. Within seconds, she drifted into a deep, much-needed sleep.

When she woke, Myra was gone and her room was graveyard quiet. She climbed down from her loft and made her way downstairs. Consumed with drowsiness, she shuffled to the first floor. Wonderful smells tickled her nose and her stomach rumbled. Walking as if still asleep, she made her way to the dining room on her way to the kitchen. The family, along with Marcus, who sat beside Myra, were seated around the table which was leaden with eggs, bacon, waffles and assorted fruit juices and syrups.

They all stared at her as she entered. Miss Tree, who was serving herself from a coffee urn at a sideboard, turned and gasped, "Good God!"

Ignoring her, Leigh dropped into an empty seat and zoned in on the silver taurine of eggs. Something was wrong about them but her mind was unable to pick out what.

Eggs? Eggs were for...

"Breakfast?" she asked in a dry scratchy voice.

"You've been asleep almost twenty hours," Myra said.

In her confusion, Leigh reached up to scratch her head. Her hair was sticking out in wild confusion. Embarrassment jolted her fully awake as she realized she was a barefoot mess.

"I'm so sorry," she said as she lunged out of her chair. "For a second I forgot where I was. I'll go change. Clean up."

"Nonsense," Peg said as she briskly walked over and, with a firm hand, pressed Leigh back into her seat. She went to the sideboard and retrieved a plate for her. "You are home. I, for one, am glad you decided to join us looking just as you are, that is to say, as you would have in your old home. I think it's a sign of good progress."

She slid the plate in front of Leigh and pulled the serving bowls and platters closer to her. "Don't you agree, Miss Tree?"

Still not recovered from the sight of the disheveled Leigh, Miss Tree stammered, "Of course it is. Especially when it was such an unconscious act and not deliberate defiance."

Looking insightful she said, "It reflects a growing acceptance of a reality that, hitherto, was being suppressed."

"I can't believe," Myra said, her voice dripping with scorn, "you used the word 'hitherto' in a sentence."

Miss Tree sat at the table prim and straight backed. "Just because my vocabulary has progressed beyond the confines of *Dick And Jane* is no reason to taunt."

"Yes it is," Leigh muttered into a glass of orange juice.

Tristin spanked the table with his hand. "Girls! Miss Tree is our guest and you will treat her as such."

Thinking she was already on thin ice for what she told the SEC, Leigh shot a worried glance at him. Catching her eyeing him, he winked.

The remainder of breakfast was spent either in silence or strained conversation. The murder of Oliver Massy tainted the atmosphere. Tristin and Marcus began talking business but Peg put a stop to it saying, "Not at the table."

The two men politely finished their coffees before excusing themselves to Tristin's office. Peg left soon after, mumbling vague excuses about having arrangements to make. To Leigh's surprise, Myra said she promised to help her mother and followed her out. Miss Tree rose and took Leigh's plate away.

"Hey," Leigh yelped. "I hadn't finished that!"

"You can reheat it when you get back."

"Back from where?" Leigh asked, her grim questioning eyes focused on Miss Tree.

"Our morning therapy session," Miss Tree said in a sing-song tone as if talking to a toddler.

"You're joking, right?" Leigh asked. "I mean, after what happened yesterday, you think we should keep carrying on like it didn't happen?"

Miss Tree turned and crossed her arms. "You haven't listened to a word I've said, have you?"

Leigh snapped back, "About how exercise makes you feel better? Yes! I listened!"

"No child. About how you quit so easily. Any little hiccup and you're willing to stop moving forward."

"A man was murdered!" Leigh shouted.

"People die, dear. It's a fact of life. You can't stop them from it and you can't stop yourself from carrying on. You tried that once and, well, it was a disaster, wasn't it?"

"You are horrible," Leigh growled on the verge of tears.

"And you are weak. My job is to toughen you up so those facts of life don't snuff yours out. Now, if my being invested in keeping you alive makes me a horrible person," she paused to shrug, "I guess I am."

The two glared at each other before Miss Tree shrugged. "I'll meet you outside or you can go to your room and give up...again."

Miss Tree turned her back on Leigh and walked off.

Leigh sat for a moment then, muttering words that would have made her mom wash her mouth out with soap, then stormed off to her room to get dressed for morning exercise therapy. True to her word, Miss Tree was waiting for her outside the front door.

"You see," Miss Tree cooed, "we're making great progress. Follow me."

She moved down the path that led to the gardens and, ultimately, to the wood. Leigh followed, making an obscene gesture behind her back.

"When you are brave enough to do that to my face," Miss Tree said, "and not because you feel I'm daring you to, that's when we'll know we're done with each other."

Leigh ground her teeth. Whether the woman had eyes in the back of her head or managed to see their reflection in the house windows, Leigh didn't care. She found herself feeling envious of Miss Tree's ability to know everything that was going on around her. Admiring something about a woman she otherwise loathed made Leigh feel sick.

"Here we are," Miss Tree announced when they reached the same place they started their run the first day.

Leigh asked, "How do you plan on making me feel like crap this time? Another run?"

"No running today. You ate too much and I don't relish watching you puke."

"You didn't give me the chance to eat that much," Leigh objected.

Miss Tree ignored her. "I want you to go over to that tree. The big one standing by itself."

Leigh marched to where Miss Tree wanted her and wheeled around. "Now what?"

"I want you to put your hands on the ground and walk your feet up the trunk until they are about knee high," Miss Tree commanded. "Move your hands forward as you go up until your legs and back are straight."

Leigh put her hands on her hips and rocked all of her weight onto one leg, pushing her hip to the side. "Do what?"

"Which part didn't you understand?" Miss Tree asked. "I did use small words."

"This is ridiculous. I'm leaving."

"Of course you are. Giving up is what you do. So, the answer to both our problems is perfectly simple. The sooner you give up your obsession with finding your parents' killer, the sooner I can be done with you."

Leigh wanted to say something horrible, but her throat was so pinched with anger she couldn't speak. Leaning over, she put her hands on the ground and, inching them forward as she walked her feet up the trunk, achieved a triangular position with her head tucked down and her butt pointing up at the sky.

"You call that flat?"

Leigh growled at her and inched her hands forward so that her butt, back, and head were in line. "There," she puffed out, struggling to hold herself up, feeling her face turning purple from the strain.

"Not good," Miss Tree said, "but good enough. Now, do a push-up."

Leigh growled with fury.

She bent her elbows slightly, making her nose lower a half inch before straightening out her arms.

"I'm waiting," Miss Tree said.

"I just did one!"

"Did you? I must have missed it. Do another."

Leigh screamed in frustration. She bent her elbows, dipping her head even less than before but couldn't straighten out her arms and crashed into the ground.

"Did I miss that one, too?"

Leigh lifted her face out of the dirt. "Let's see you do it."

Miss Tree walked toward the tree. Bending at the waist while keeping her knees straight, she placed both hands flat on the ground just in front of her toes. Miss Tree's legs lifted, straight as arrows, until she was in a handstand. Lifting one hand she pirouetted so that she was facing the tree. Lowering her legs in the same smooth motion she lifted them, she rested her toes against the trunk. Back straight as a ruler, she lowered herself until her nose brushed the tips of the grass blades. She pressed herself back up and, lest Leigh think that was a one-off, did another perfect inclined pushup before returning to her handstand and then to her feet.

"You need to be as strong as, if not stronger than I am, if you plan on catching your parents' killer. Are you willing to put in that much effort? That much time?"

Tears started to flow from Leigh's eyes. "Why are you being so mean to me?"

"Do you think your parents' killer will be any kinder?"

Leigh twisted to sit cross-legged on the ground. "No. But can't you teach me these things without being so cruel?"

"I tried, remember? You chose this for your path."

As if talking to herself, Miss Tree went on, "I'm beginning to see that I may not be able to dissuade you from your silly obsession."

"It's not silly. What if it were your parents?"

Miss Tree looked at her as if she'd forgotten she was there. "It is silly because you're not ready. So, if I can't change your thinking, the best I can do is prepare you as much as possible. You're not dealing with nice people, Leigh, and you have to be as mean and cold as they are if you plan to survive."

Leigh's shoulders sank as she sulked.

"That's not going to get you anywhere, either. Not with murderers and certainly not with me."

"What do you want me to do?" Leigh asked without enthusiasm.

"Push-ups. That's why we are here. Start on your knees, if you must."

Leigh's fingers curled, searching for the hoodie she wasn't wearing, trying to ease her embarrassment.

Leigh and Miss Tree spent the next hour and a half doing push-ups. Breaks came only when Leigh couldn't do any more, at which point Miss Tree ordered her to roll onto her back and do V-ups, lifting her arms and feet at the same time, meeting in the middle over her belly-button. Miss Tree matched her exercise for exercise, never losing perfect form. Leigh looked ridiculous, flopping around more than exercising, with knees bent, arms quivering, and tears of rage and humiliation pouring out of her.

"That's enough for today," Miss Tree said after Leigh fell flat onto her stomach for the third time in a row trying to do push-ups. "Let's see how dedicated you are. I want you to do as many push-ups and V-ups as you can every morning, every midday, and every night. We'll know soon enough if you aren't doing them or if you are lying to yourself about how many you are capable of doing."

Miss Tree got up off the ground and began to walk back to the manor. Leigh rose also, but didn't move to follow her.

"Aren't you coming, dear?"

Leigh's body ached too much to walk, but she refused to let Miss Tree know that. "I want to stay here for a bit. Think about what you said."

"Suit yourself," Miss Tree said turning her back on Leigh, "but don't be long. Lunch will be served soon and you didn't eat a thing for breakfast. That's not healthy, you know."

Rage washed over Leigh, but she was too sore to do or say anything. Once Miss Tree was out of sight, Leigh did the one thing she wanted to do for the last twenty minutes. She stumbled into the bushes and was sick. Staggering back to the clearing she collapsed into a ball, her stomach too cramped to straighten and her arms too spent to do anything more than cross over her chest. Sobs of pain, both physical and emotional, wailed out of her.

"What's the matter with you?" Little Bodie asked, fading into being and floating on his back a foot off the grass.

"Go away," Leigh said through her sobs.

Bodie shrugged. "Okay."

Leigh forced herself up into a sitting position and searched the clearing for him, but he was gone. "No," she moaned. "That isn't what I want! Please come back!"

"Why can't girls ever make up their minds?" he said. In a blue flash, he rematerialized beside her.

She gasped and scooted away. "Can you not do that!"

Ignoring her reaction he asked again, "So? What's wrong?"

"Miss Tree," was all she said.

Bodie growled. "I know. I've been watching."

He grinned wickedly as the temperature plummeted. "Want me to kick her down the stairs?"

Leigh smiled at the idea. "I'd love to see that, but no."

She paused and thought for a moment. "The thing is, I can't tell if she's right about me or not. Maybe I am weak and a quitter."

Bodie scoffed. "You aren't. You've been reading my journal so you know how long it took me to get used to my new life here. You're adjusting better than I did."

Leigh picked at blades of grass nervously. "Bodie, I've been meaning to ask you something but I don't want to upset you."

"I won't get upset. Ask me."

"Well, your journal starts after you arrived here. You never wrote about what happened or where you were before. I know it was something terrible and I know it happened in Japan, but I don't know what."

The air turned so cold it made Leigh shiver. Her breath steamed out of her as if she were standing in an open field in the middle of winter. The grass surrounding Bodie frosted over as the pale blue aura surrounding him turned as dark a navy as she'd ever seen it. Occasionally it sparked with angry purples matching Big Bodie's aura when he was on a rampage.

"It's fine," Leigh said, fear welling up inside her. "You don't have to tell me."

Somewhere in the distance thunder boomed. "I never told that story to anyone," Bodie said, "and part of me doesn't want to."

"Bet I know which part," Leigh said.

Bodie smiled a weak smile and nodded.

Serious again, he said, "But I'll tell you anyway."

"Really, you don't have to."

"I want to. It's been so long since I've had a friend to share anything with." He sat quietly thinking then nodded, his color returning to a more pleasant blue. "I *want* to."

Leigh didn't say anything. If Bodie was determined, she would let him tell the story in his own way and time.

"My dad, Bradford, was a great man," he began. "At least that is what I was told. I never had the chance to know him.

"He was a captain on one of our boats when Japan opened a few of their ports to American traders. Dad was there when the samurai ruling class, the Shogunate, signed the treaty.

"When the Civil War broke out here in the U. S., Father left the company for a time and served as a captain in the Union Navy. Because of all that, he married very late in life, at the age of thirty-four."

"That's not all that old," Leigh said.

"It is when most people died in their fifties. Remember, I was born in 1867. Things were very different then."

Leigh fell silent, embarrassed that she hadn't thought of that.

Bodie returned to his story. "After the Civil War ended, Father resigned his commission and returned to the company. A few years later, in 1869, Japan was ending its own civil war. The Imperial Court took control away from the Shogunate and Father, with his military background and his prior experience with Japan, went there personally to make sure the bargains that were struck between Simmons-Pierce Shipping and the Shogun would be honored by the new Emperor, Meiji. He took his wife and three-year-old son -- me -- with him.

"There's really not much to tell after that. The samurai were defeated, but they didn't simply disappear. There was a lot of resentment against westerners for the aid they gave to the Meiji government. My parents were murdered, much like yours. I was taken prisoner in the hope I could be useful as a bargaining chip or for ransom. It didn't work out like that."

"What did happen?" Leigh asked.

"The Imperial Government grew in power and so did restrictions against the samurai class. In the end, they couldn't let me go for fear of what I might tell the authorities about them. They couldn't kill me because that would bring harsh vengeance. I became an unwanted anchor around their necks. I was fed little and used as a slave. When they were teaching their own children the arts of combat, I was used as a punching bag."

Bodie grinned mischievously at Leigh. "I actually got pretty good at fighting."

Leigh's eyes bugged in her head. "Hold on. Hold on. Are you telling me you were taught how to fight by real samurai?"

"No. Their children were taught how to fight. I picked up what I could in order to stay alive. I was never taught anything. It didn't matter because I learned to never make it look like I won a fight. I couldn't make it look like I lost too easy either. Every time I did either, I was beaten by my adult masters. I was never allowed to forget I was Gaijin -- a non-Japanese -- inferior to dogs, cows, pigs. Inferior to mud."

Little Bodie sat brooding for a long while. Since she couldn't reach out and touch him, or hug him, or console him, Leigh did all she could for him, which was sit beside him and respect his silence.

"Miss Tree is right about one thing," he said at last. "The way she is treating you will make you stronger."

"I don't want to grow stronger. At least, not like that."

Bodie's eyes swelled and gleamed, shimmering diamond blue. "I can always bash her in the head with a thick book?"

Leigh giggled at his tone because it sounded as if he were asking permission. "No, Bodie."

He hugged his legs to his chest and rested his chin on his knees, deep in thought.

"Hey," he cried, his head floating off his shoulders and gliding to hover in front of her, "I've got an idea."

Leigh clamped her eyes shut as a shiver of revulsion rattled down her spine. "Put your head back where it belongs! Now!"

Bodie's body swooped over to join his head. "I don't know if it'll work but..."

Leigh opened one eye and squinted at him, ignoring what he was saying. "Are you back in one piece?"

"Yes," he groaned in that uniquely sarcastic way only an eleven-year-old boy can manage.

She opened both eyes. "Don't ever do that again. At least not where I can see you. Now, what's this idea of yours?"

"Well, I don't even know if this will work but, remember when I showed you how to climb back inside the window?"

"I remember," Leigh said cautiously. Merging with Bodie wasn't one of her favorite memories.

"What if," the boy said enthusiastically, "what if I share my memories of when I was a prisoner? You might be able to cope with that Miss Tree witch better if you had more experience facing cruelty. You know, make you stronger without having to go through all that abuse to achieve it."

Leigh's heart raced. Having him inside her mind, body, and soul was too weird. Too gross. She never wanted to experience those feelings again, but she didn't understand the first time. She hadn't been taken over. Possessed. Bodie was sharing with her, not taking control of her.

Pinching her bottom lip she asked, "How do you do it?"

Bodie shrugged. "I don't know how I do it. I know that I can and that's it."

"Can I do it?"

"Of course not. You can't put your spirit into somebody else. You're still alive. You're still using yours."

"What I mean is, while you're inside me, can I give you something, too?"

"I...I don't know. Never thought about it. Now that I am thinking about it, I don't think I'm supposed to know."

Leigh pulled a weary face, fed up with his cryptic answers. "Is that one of those rules only dead people get to know about?"

"Honestly," Bodie said, "I don't know that, either."

Leigh tried to straighten her spine and rolled her shoulders back. The pain in her muscles was so great she couldn't keep from wincing. The pain made up her mind.

"Let's try, and see what happens. When you are done, hang around inside my head and I'll try to give you something."

Bodie turned into a ball of pure blue light. At first he was the size of a truck tire, then a basketball, a baseball, a bee. He came at her forehead like a bullet and before she was ready, she felt him sharing her identity. The essence of her being, everything that made her who she was, began to ice over.

Locking her throat against the urge to puke, she closed her eyes and concentrated as hard as she could. "Are you in here?"

A thought in her brain said, "Yes," but the voice wasn't hers.

"Now what?" she asked.

"Now I can give you my memories. If you want them."

"Do you not want to give them to me?"

"I do, but I've never done this before. I don't know what it'll do to you, that's all."

"Will it....kill me?"

"No. I'm sure it won't, but this isn't like before. I'm not giving you one memory about how I did one thing. I'm giving you years of memories. Bad memories."

Leigh squirmed and tightened her jaw. "Let's do this."

Her brain exploded with images roaring through like a white-water river; shivering in cold nights with no shelter, blistering hot days working in fields, constant yearning for food, brutal fight after fight after fight with boys much older and bigger than Bodie was. Experiencing the memories in her own mind, seeing them from her perspective, she saw the abusers as being so much older and bigger than *she* was.

Anger welled inside her as she watched herself in Bodies memories grow older. The boys weren't winning their fights as easily. She learned what to do, how to move, but also knew that, in the end, she had to lose every time. She had to allow a final punch or kick from her opponent to slip past, ending the fight.

Even worse were the beatings by adults. They were brutal and constant, often daily. With no way to protect herself against them, the only way to stop suffering was to tuck herself into a ball and turn her mind off, to stop thinking completely, until the beatings were over.

Consistent through it all was an agonizing loneliness. She felt the heartbreaking longing for a friend. In these tragic memories any kind word would have meant so much, but it never came. She never thought about the future because it looked too horribly like the past. Day after day she was told she was worthless and she was starting to believe it. She was in so much pain, physically and emotionally, that she screamed over and over, unsure if her shouts were in her head or if she was screaming out loud.

"Hey?" Bodie asked inside her skull. "Are you all right?"

The memories faded and settled alongside her own, distant but always there, like shrapnel that could never be removed. She felt the same but, at the same time, like a very different person.

"I'm...I'm fine," she stammered aloud.

"I'll go," Bodie said. "You can give me whatever you wanted to give me some other time."

"No. I'm not sure I'll ever agree to this again. It's so personal. It hurts too much."

Pressing her eyelids closed she imagined herself standing in her room. "Can you see me?"

Bodie materialized in front of her. He wasn't bathed in blue but looked like an alive boy.

"I see you," he said. "And you are making yourself see me as I was before I died. Weird!"

She held out her hands, palms up.

He looked at them frightened. "I haven't touched anyone in over a hundred years."

A sob broke from her lips and she grabbed him by the shoulders and pulled him to her, wrapping her arms around his small body. "I'm sorry for every crappy thing that's ever happened to you. I'm sorry I can't hold you when you need to be held. I'm sorry for how your life and your death turned out. You don't deserve it. You are my best friend and I love you like a little brother."

Like any true boy he squirmed out of her arms. His eyes were wide with wonder as he put his hands on his cheeks.

"Warm," he gasped. "My face feels hot."

Leigh giggled at him. "You're blushing. I feel the heat, too."

Bodie dropped his hands.

"Can you feel what I feel?" she asked.

Bodie nodded.

"How much I care about you?"

Fiddling sheepishly with a button on his jacket, he nodded again.

"Can you take it with you when you go? Can you keep it?"

A chill rose up inside her. Bodie returned to having his blue halo and was gone.

Opening her eyes, she blinked against the morning sun. With slow stiff movements, she pushed her aching body up until she was standing. She hurt but, compared to a small boy lying curled on the floor of a filthy barn, exhausted, bloodied and bruised, huddling against a cow for warmth, her suffering was nothing.

Tilting her face to catch the breeze she whispered, "Bodie? You still here?"

The leaves rustled but they were doing that before. "Guess that was as creepy for you as it was for me. Come back whenever you're ready."

Chapter Seventeen

"Give them back," Leigh demanded, standing in front of Big Bodie's portrait.

Big Bodie's painted likeness turned its balding, white-bearded head to scowl in disapproval at her. Leigh stood barefoot in front of the painting in a knee length black dress not caring what the cranky old ghost thought of how she looked.

Unable to get a rise out of her with his derisive glare Bodie asked, "What is it you young people say to each other nowadays? Bite me? What an odd expression."

"Give them back," Leigh repeated, refusing to be distracted.

"Without them, she can't leave," the Big Bodie's painting said haughtily.

"That's the whole point. I want her to leave."

"I don't. There's something peculiar about that woman and I want to know what it is."

"She's just going to borrow one of the family cars. In case you haven't noticed, the garage is full of them."

"Oh, have them then," the painted old man said.

He began hacking and coughing. Making a vile retching sound Big Bodie vomited Miss Tree's car keys onto the floor below his painting. They were covered in slimy ooze.

Bile struck the back of Leigh's throat. Watching the old man wipe ick off his chin with sadistic glee, she thought she was going to be ill herself.

Closing her eyes, she remembered mucking out a horse stall with her bare hands only, it wasn't her memory. It belonged to Little Bodie, but the way he gave it to her made it as much hers as his. Snot-covered keys weren't all that gross after all. Leigh picked them up and, carrying them to the tissue box on the secretary desk, wiped them clean.

"Is that why you are picking on her so much?" Leigh asked as she worked. "You think there's something fishy about her?"

"Yes," the painting said.

"And Marcus? Something odd about him, too?"

"No. I don't like him, that's all."

"Why's that?"

"It's not my secret to tell."

"Whose is it?" Leigh asked.

As soon as the words left her mouth she regretted their tone. They sounded too hopeful. Too interested. A book flew off one of the shelves and whizzed inches over her head.

"Stupid little cow," Bodie bellowed. "If I won't say what the secret is, what makes you think I'll tell you whose it is?"

Knowing Bodie could have hit her if he wanted, Leigh ignored his words and sighed at his childish behavior. Picking the book up off the floor she put it back where it came from.

"What about the rest of us?" she asked. "What'd we do to deserve rugs being pulled out from under us while we're walking on them, or glasses getting moved to the edge of the table where they're certain to be knocked off?"

The painted man let out a cackling laugh. "You lot didn't *do* anything. I'm bored!"

"What you are is horrible," Leigh said.

A book on the shelf twitched and banged.

"You better go," Bodie said. "I sense my aim is improving."

Leigh pursed her lips at the painting and, lifting her hand, made an obscene gesture. On her way out she heard more cackling laughter. From across the foyer, she also heard the sound of Miss Tree complaining loudly to Tristin.

"I know the girl took them."

Leigh was pleased to hear Tristin defend her. "What evidence do you have of that? What evidence do you have that anyone took them? Keys get misplaced all the time."

"Not mine," Miss Tree said.

"You can quit worrying," Leigh said as she entered the sitting room, "I found them."

"Where were they?" Myra asked without any real interest in her voice.

"On the floor of the library."

"Ridiculous," Miss Tree said. "I haven't been in there for days."

"I didn't say you lost them there," Leigh said. "I said that's where I found them."

"Because you put them there."

"No, I didn't."

"Liar," Miss Tree snapped.

Tristin slapped the copy of *The Financial Times* down beside him, "I will not have people in this house speaking to each other like that. Especially not right after Oliver's funeral."

Leigh's back straightened and her eyes narrowed as she stared back at Miss Tree. "It's okay, Uncle Tristin. That's where I found them and I didn't take them. I don't care whether she believes me or not."

Miss Tree's eyebrows unknotted and rose as her face shifted from an expression of anger to one of puzzlement.

"You've changed recently," she said as she eyed Leigh with suspicion. "More confident. Less concerned over what others think of you. I may need to change my tactics."

Myra sneered. "Again? Because your latest trick of belittling and cruelty isn't harsh enough?"

Miss Tree turned to Myra as if not having noticed her presence before now. "Not at all. In fact, I think our relationship may have reached its end. You have to admit, my methods seem to have done the job."

Leigh was stunned. "You don't think I need more therapy?"

"There is one more thing we need to sort out. A sort of graduation."

Miss Tree grinned. "I'll arrange it and let you know the details."

Leigh's lips pulled to the side as she said flatly, "You don't have to."

Miss Tree threw a chummy arm around her. "But I want to, dear. One last session, a special session, and I promise, we'll be done with each other. I know you are looking forward to that."

Leigh shrugged the arm off her shoulders and stepped away. "Fine. Whatever."

Miss Tree smiled like a cartoon cat stalking a mouse as she walked out of the room. The look made Leigh shudder.

"That woman's creepy as they come," Myra said.

"Creepier," Leigh agreed.

"That's enough, both of you," Tristin said.

Myra pushed to her feet, exhaling loudly. "I'm going to change into something less gloomy."

After she left, Tristin returned to his paper. Leigh dropped into a chair and began plucking at the piping stitched into its arm. In a soft murmur she asked, "Are you still mad at me?"

"Mad at you? I was never mad at you."

Leigh smiled at him. "Nice try, but I know you were. When I told that SEC investigator about Mr. Massy having a file in Mr. Figueroa's security drawer? You were mad and you had every right to be."

Tristin set his paper down again. "All right. I was very angry at you. What you told the SEC had nothing to do with insider trading and therefore was none of their business. After a few days, after what happened to Oliver and what we found on your phone, I understood why you -- there is no nice way to put this -- why you betrayed us. So, yes, I was angry to start with, but I'm not now. Do you believe me?"

"I do. Thank you. At the time, I was so confused." Leigh laughed. "What's that Miss Tree always says about me? That I'm 'discombobulated'?"

Tristin chuckled and picked up his paper again.

Leigh took a moment to work up her courage. "I still am confused. I mean, if you guys weren't investigating Mr. Massy for his trading, why was he being investigated?"

Tristin's face darkened and the paper was slapped back down. "You really do beat all, don't you? We, Marcus and I, we both told you it has no ties to what happened to your parents. It couldn't possibly. I wish you trusted us more and believed that."

"I want to. Badly! But you don't understand. Mom and Dad are dead. They aren't coming back. I know that. But why did they have to die? What was so stinking important to whoever did it? What was their reason? Those questions are like gaping holes in my life and the longer they go unfilled with answers, the bigger they get. I can't forget about them. I don't know how."

Tristin's face softened. "No one is asking you to give up. Certainly not to forget. It's a huge part of your life and always will be. Leigh, what happened is going to define you to a large degree but it is up to you how. It can make you stronger or destroy you and we, none of us, want to see your life consumed by the empty promises of unanswered questions."

"Empty promises?" Leigh asked.

Tristin nodded. "Yes, empty because no answer is ever going to be good enough. It will never make sense when measured by the suffering it caused."

Tristin groaned, shut his eyes, and pressed his fingertips over his eyelids. Pulling his hands away he said, "Look, Oliver Massy's accounting didn't add up. His departments showed small losses where there should have been gains. The gains he did record were smaller than actual gains reflected in related business units. We began looking at some of his personal financials," he looked at her with a grave face, "strictly off the record. So, you can imagine why we didn't want it broadcast to the SEC."

Leigh nodded and Tristin continued. "While there are still some unanswered questions, taking into account his personal expenditures and recent investment history and, yes, in that sense it is loosely related to the SEC's investigation, the money began to be accounted for."

"I don't understand," Leigh said.

"Of course you don't. It took a special team from accounting and a big chunk of Marcus's time to make sense out of the shell game Oliver was playing with corporate money. In the simplest terms, he was embezzling. You know what that means?"

"Stealing."

"Yes. And let that be an end to it. Please. There was no way your father could ever have known about what Oliver was doing. Even if he did, it wouldn't have mattered much. Your dad worked organized crime and murder investigations. Oliver never killed anyone and his crimes were all for himself, not as part of any larger organization."

"That you know of," Leigh said.

"Oh, for Heaven's sake, Leigh! We traced the money. It was all tied to him and him alone. There were no payments to others. It was personal greed, nothing more."

"It was something more to whoever shot him," Leigh said.

Tristin sighed. "I suspect that is linked to his insider trading activity but we may never know with certainty in the same way we may never know why your parents were killed. Leigh, it is time you considered that possibility. I can't pretend that'll be easy for you. In fact, I know it won't be, but that may be the way things turn out. I admire your loyalty and your courage, but you have to be prepared for whatever comes your way, good or bad. I hope that doesn't sound too hardhearted of me."

Leigh sat in quiet thought.

"I've talked to so many people since what happened," she said at length. "They generally fall into two groups, those who tell you what you want to hear and those who risk telling you what you need to hear. I'm beginning to realize that the second group are the ones who care."

Tristin hitched a feeble smile onto his face. "I'm glad to see you understand or, at least, are trying to understand."

"I understand that you'd be saying the same thing to Myra if she were in my situation. You are doing the best you can to be a father to me. It may look like I'm making that difficult, but you've no idea how much your trying means to me."

Tristin cleared his throat.

Leigh stood to leave. "I think I'll go change too, before I make both of us cry."

Tristin stood as well. "Miss Tree is right. You are very different from when you first arrived. For what it's worth, I'm very proud of the progress you've made."

Inside her room, Leigh traded her dress for her standard uniform of jeans, t-shirt, and hoodie. Moving to the sunken sitting area, she nestled into a chair and thought about what Tristin told her regarding Oliver Massy being suspected of embezzling. Competing thoughts of happiness and guilt over how she felt about Tristin doing his best to step in where her dad once stood kept interrupting, confusing her.

She wondered if Tristin, or Marcus, shared what they knew about Mr. Massy's embezzling with the police. She questioned whether or not she would tell them, if the chance presented itself.

"Leigh," Myra's voice called from below, "it's time for dinner."

"Be right down," Leigh hollered back.

She looked at herself in the mirror. Red-rimmed eyes stared back.

"You cry too much," she told herself, but wondered if she was saying it or if this new person Tristin and Miss Tree both say she has become was the one making the observation. The new person Little Bodie changed her into.

Her fingers pressed against her forehead and she pulled her bangs tight back, away from her face. "What did you do to me?" she asked the empty room, exhaling loudly.

"Leigh? You coming?"

Leigh tore her eyes away from the mirror. "Yes!"

She met up with Myra one floor down and together they went on to dinner with Tristin and Peg. The meal was a quiet, somber affair that spilled over into the evening. The family sat through an unmemorable movie which both Peg and Leigh opted out of finishing. Once in bed, Leigh lay awake, staring out her big window at the trees swaying with hypnotic movement in the night breeze. She drifted into slumber still wondering if she was still herself or someone else.

A freezing chill woke her. The bedposts were coated in frost. She knew something was wrong. This wasn't Little Bodie. She'd felt the chill of his anger before. This was worse, more malevolent. Wicked and deadly. She knew in her heart Big Bodie was going to do something terrible. Rolling out of bed she tiptoed down the frost covered stairs and across the icy floor to her door. Refusing to yield to her pulling, the door was frozen shut.

"You can't keep me locked in here," she growled as she pulled relentlessly on the door.

Yanking with all her might, the door made a loud cracking noise as it swung open causing her to topple onto her butt.

"Stay out of my way or else," Big Bodie said with so much violence in his voice it made the walls rumble.

Leigh scrambled to her feet and leaned out past the doorjamb to peer into the darkness below. Her ears strained to catch any sound, but silence reigned and all she heard was her own heartbeat. Slow as dripping honey, she climbed down the stairs to the second floor. Repeating her movements from above, she edged her head out just enough for one eye to clear the hallway wall.

A plumb-purple glow, so dark the light was scarcely visible in the black, hovered near the top of the stairs. On the stairway, a pinprick of green tinted flashlight made a silhouette out of the intruder creeping his way up.

Bodie's glow brightened as the intruder moved toward the top stair. Growing long and thin, Bodie shifted into the shape she knew all too well -- that of Big Bodie himself, glowing with more malice and hatred than she'd ever seen from him.

The approaching figure froze on the stairs. "Who are you?"

Big Bodie chuckled. "I'm death."

"I'll be the one doing the killing tonight, old man. First you, then the girl, then the rest."

The man's hand swished up and a blinding flash, accompanied by a muffled noise filled the manor. The bullets passed straight through Bodie and lodged into the wall behind him, leaving a swirling mist where they struck his body. Bodie let loose a terrible shriek that made Leigh throw her hands over her ears.

In the rooms along this floor, other voices screamed and demanded to know what was going on.

Leigh watched in terror as Bodie transformed from human form to something that looked like it came straight from Hell. He was more skeleton than flesh, his clothes tattered from long years spent in the grave.

"What are you?" the intruder shouted. "Stay...stay away from me!"

The gun fired again and again.

Trapped behind a mystically locked door, Peg screamed.

Bodie flew down the stairs and went into the body of the man with the gun. The intruder's booted feet left the steps and he slammed against the wall beside the staircase. Moving so fast Leigh's neck strained trying to keep up, the man flew high into the air until his face smashed against the ceiling high above.

"No! Don't," Leigh cried out but her pleading was wasted breath.

Bedroom doors rattled but refused to open. "What the devil's going on?" Tristin shouted. "Leigh? Is that you out there? Someone tell me what is happening!"

The evil purple glow held the man pinned to the ceiling. When it disappeared, the man's body plummeted down, making a sickening crunch at the bottom of the stairs. Like wicked lightning, Bodie's purple aura engulfed the body at the bottom of the stairs, rose to the ceiling and again let the man fall. The intruder made no movement. No sound. That didn't keep Bodie from hauling him to the ceiling and dropping a third time. The purple mist drifted upwards until it was absorbed into the plaster of the ceiling and was gone.

Tristin burst from his room in his pajamas, a revolver in his hand. "What is going on out here?"

Catching sight of Leigh, he whipped the gun around and pointed it at her. She screamed.

Tristin lowered the gun as Peg crept out of the room to stand beside him.

Myra's door slammed open and she dashed to the end of the hall where she slapped in a frenzy at the light switch. The first thing catching her eye was the bloody pulp of a body at the foot of the staircase and, making gagging noises, covered her mouth.

Peg ran to her daughter and gathered her into her arms, shielding her face from the gruesome sight below. "Leigh," she cried, "what have you done?"

In shock Leigh stammered, "I...No...Not...He had a gun and...and..."

"A gun?" Tristin asked in a panic.

He darted down the stairs pointing his own pistol at the lifeless body. "There is a gun here, behind this potted plant. Who is this man? What did he want?"

Turning his face up to his family he shouted, "Peg! Take the girls into our bedroom and call the police. I'm going to my office to call security. Where the Hell are they?"

Peg steered Myra toward the bedroom, scooping Leigh into her embrace on the way. Leigh turned her head to look down at the terrible scene below and saw a faint purple glow in the library before the door shut with impossible silence.

Tristin's security team arrived within seconds and, sequestered in the master bedroom, Leigh heard the tantrum Tristin was throwing over their absence in the moment of need. The guards tried to make a few stammered apologies but couldn't get a word in. The police showed up not long after, sirens and lights ripping into the night. Straining her ears to hear, a calmer Tristin explained what took place. Someone said her name and he burst out louder, refusing to allow anyone to speak to her until the morning.

Muffled and diminished, she heard Ty's voice. She slid off the bed and moved to the door.

"Leigh," Peg said, "you don't have to. Whatever they need to know it can wait until the morning. You need time to recover."

"It's okay, Aunt Peg. Ty's a friend. I'd rather talk to him than to some stranger."

"Want me to come with you?" Myra asked.

"No, you stay with your mom. Tristin's down there and, well," Leigh shrugged, "it's Ty."

"If you need us," Myra said, "we're here."

"I know. You have been since the day I arrived."

Myra and Peg's feeble smiles told her they understood.

With all the courage she could muster she descended the stairs and passed the sheet-covered lump of flesh that was once a person. It flashed in her mind that she was barefoot and wearing nothing but a sleeping shirt while surrounded by so many strangers, but as quick as it came, so did the feeling that how she looked in front of these people wasn't important. Not near as vital as doing her part to find out who this person was and what they were after.

"Leigh," Tristin said, catching sight of her, "go back upstairs. There's nothing you can do tonight that can't wait until the morning."

Everyone was trying their best not to stare at her. Some of the sidelong glances were filled with sympathy. Others were of what looked to be fear. A few reflected disgust and revulsion. The shocking truth struck her like a sledgehammer. They thought she killed this man. Self-defense or premeditated, they all were convinced she was a sixteen-year-old killer.

"I want to get this out of the way," Leigh told Tristin. "While it's Ty I'm talking to. Not one of them."

Ty emerged from Tristin's office. Without waiting to be acknowledged he said, "It will always be me, sweetheart. Whenever you're ready, I'll be there."

"I'm ready now. No point putting it off."

"Let's go in there," Ty said, gesturing to the library.

"No," Leigh gasped gulping down her fear. "Not there."

She looked at Tristin. "Can we use your office?"

"Is that all right?" Tristin asked Ty, looking confused over her reluctance.

"Fine," Ty said. "It doesn't look like the intruder was ever in there. Whatever he was looking for, it was upstairs."

Tristin's face drained of color. "There's nothing upstairs but the family bedrooms."

"Me," Leigh said.

"What was that, baby-girl?"

"Me. What he said before he fell. He was going to kill me, then the rest, as if I was the target and everyone else was simply in the way."

Ty's breath hissed out in a loud whoosh. "All right. Come in. Sit down and tell me what happened."

Leigh started her explanation with how she woke up feeling cold.

"The front door was wide open," Tristin explained. "The alarm was manually turned off. Whoever that man was, he knew the key code."

Ty nodded and returned his attention to Leigh. She told them what she saw and heard. When she came to the part about Bodie being at the top of the stairs, the lies had to start.

"It must have been my shadow he saw," she said with as much confidence she could throw behind it.

"And he fell down the stairs? That's what you are saying?" Ty asked.

"She already said that's what happened, Detective," Tristin said, shielding her from questioning.

"I heard," Ty said in a tone of voice much harder than she was accustomed to hearing from him. "Thing is, preliminary examination of the body indicates he'd had to have fallen down those stairs a dozen times to get those kinds of injuries."

He fixed a cold stare onto Leigh, "And where was the light coming from to cast your shadow on the wall at the top of the stairs? If the light was behind you, your shadow would have been farther up the hallway. If light was coming from the intruder's flashlight, your shadow would have been behind you or, at least, beside you."

"I...I don't know. All I know is what I told you."

"I think we are done," Tristin said.

"We're not done," Ty growled. "We're just getting started and we will keep going until we get answers that make sense."

"Leigh?" Ty asked, "Are you wearing what you wore when you first came downstairs?"

"Yeah. Why?"

"Somebody beat this man to death. Beat him terribly. If you did do this, you would be soaked in blood. We are going to have to search your room."

Leigh's eyes flared open. "You don't believe me?"

"I don't know what to believe. You said he fell down the stairs, but that can't be true. It doesn't explain the extent of his injuries. It certainly doesn't explain why there are blood stains on the ceiling directly above where the body was found on the floor."

"Splatter, perhaps?" Tristin suggested, trying to offer a reasonable explanation.

"No. Splatter looks different. These were smudges. Same as you'd see if you pressed a paint-soaked sponge against a wall."

Leigh closed her eyes. The memory of the body bouncing off the ceiling before dropping to the floor, over and over, was nauseating.

She knew if she so much as mentioned Big Bodie she'd be admitting she killed him and, what's more, that she was crazy. "I don't know what to tell you. He came up the stairs and saw, I don't know. I thought it was my shadow, but you say it couldn't have been. He fired his gun at nothing. Fired it over and over. After, he just sort of fell."

Leigh was quiet as her mind swirled, replaying the scene, struggling to come up with believable lies. "His gun," she said in an effort to stall. "I saw it fire but only heard a puff of air."

"The gun had a silencer on it. We can be pretty confident he was sent here to kill someone."

"Me," Leigh gasped. "He was here to kill me. Remember what he said. 'First the girl.' Someone knows I've been snooping and maybe thinks I found out something. Or that Dad told me something. I don't know."

"Did he," Ty pressed. "Did your dad say anything about what he was investigating?"

"I already told you no."

"I think that's enough for tonight," Tristin said.

Ty looked at her for a long time. He was studying her. "Yeah," he said, "that's enough. For now."

The tone of doubt and mistrust in Ty's voice hit her like a slap. Leigh's cheeks burned. She opened her mouth to make a nasty response, caught herself and tucked her lower lip between her teeth.

"Screw this," she said, pushing herself off the couch.

She marched out of the library and past the working forensic teams who eyed her suspiciously. Straightening her back, Leigh bit her lip again and breezed past them. A woman in a navy suit with a large purse, who had a badge and a gun attached to her belt, fell in behind. Leigh ignored the fact she was being followed and made her way to the entrance to her room. Making a derisive snort, she found the way blocked by yellow police tape and a female police officer standing guard.

Leigh spun around. "I want to go to my room."

"I'm sorry," the woman officer behind her said. "We need to go through your room. We've spoken to your cousin Myra and you'll be staying with her tonight."

"Is that so? You just decided what I'm going to do and where I'm going to do it?"

"Not me," the woman said. "We. I talked it over with Mrs. Pierce, who is your legal guardian, and she agreed that was the best option."

"Is that a fact?" Leigh said, raising her voice. "And what was the alternative? Maybe I'd like that one better."

"Doubt it," the police officer said. "You can either cooperate or spend the night in juvie. Maybe the next few nights." The officer leaned in close. "Save us the trouble of moving you when we find out whatever it is you're lying to us about."

"So you think I did this?" Leigh said, still shouting.

"Don't know. All I know is that your story and the physical evidence don't jive. You're lying about something. My experience? That's what the guilty do. They lie."

"Okay," Leigh said, "Here's the truth."

Leigh looked at the woman with impatient eyes. "I woke up because of the cold. I came down to this floor, like I said. That man was creeping up the stairs. One of the ghosts that haunts this place was standing at the top landing. The man fired at the ghost, who lifted him up off his feet and threw him down to the ground. The ghost did it over and over and over."

Leigh shut her eyes and shuddered, but the memory was relentless. "It was horrible."

The police woman crossed her arms over her chest. "If I were you, I'd stick with your first cockamamie story. Otherwise, we'll be taking you to County General and, trust me, juvie is better than that place."

"I know. I've been there," Leigh said softly.

The police woman nodded. "Right," she said in a gentle way. "If you'd care to join your cousin?"

Leigh turned to find Myra leaning against her doorframe, the door standing open. "How long have you been there?" Leigh asked.

Myra smiled. "Long enough to hear you be, well, you."

Leigh returned Myra's smile. "No matter how much trouble I get into, you always make me feel better."

"That's what sisters are for," Myra said. "C'mon. I've got an old nightgown for you."

Leigh's brow furrowed as she tugged at her nightshirt. "I was sleeping in this before all the excitement."

"I need to bag that and take it with me," the police woman said.

Leigh's face turns to granite in her anger. With a harsh jerk she pulled the shirt up and over her head. Holding it out to the police woman she snarled, "Want my underwear, too?"

The woman's lips pressed into a thin line of impatience, clearly not impressed with Leigh's bravado. Leigh could see the woman's tongue running over her teeth beneath her cheeks making a bulge in them. Digging into her purse she pulled out a large plastic evidence bag.

Holding the bag open she said, "That won't be necessary."

Leigh dropped the shirt into the bag and stormed past Myra, who followed, shutting the door behind her.

"I don't know if I'm appalled or impressed," Myra said.

Leigh ignored her. "You got something for me to put on?"

"On the corner of the bed."

Filled with a sudden rush of modesty, Leigh pulled the nightgown over her head. It looked like something out of an old western movie. "This yours or your grandma's?"

"That is the last piece of clothing Dad ever bought me. I think Mom had a quiet word with him about being clueless. Anyway, there is one thing you can be certain of."

"What's that?"

"It's clean, because I never wear it," Myra said as she pulled back the covers. "Think you're going to be able to sleep?"

"I don't know," Leigh said climbing into bed. "I'm still pretty freaked out but, the more I calm down, the more sleepy I feel."

Myra turned off the light. "I bet."

Lying still and silent, Leigh tried to fall asleep, but the soft scrapings and movements in her room above them pressed on her nerves like an itchy sweater on her skin. "Myra? If I told you that story about Big Bodie killing that man was true, you'd believe me, wouldn't you?"

Leigh felt Myra roll over to face her. In what little moonlight was trickling into the room she saw Myra's silhouette prop itself up on an elbow. "No, Leigh, I wouldn't. But I wouldn't be as quick to not believe you as everyone else is going to be. So, even if that is what you think happened, you're better off keeping it to yourself."

Leigh snuggled down beneath the blankets. "I love you always being honest with me. Don't ever stop."

"I promise," Myra said, lying back down, "but will you do something for me?"

"What?"

"Start thinking about what you're doing and saying before you get yourself into trouble, not after as you pick up the broken pieces."

Leigh giggled. "I can try."

Within minutes she was asleep.

Chapter Eighteen

"Why is it so cold in here?" Miss Tree asked in a waspish tone.

Leigh jerked her head up, startled to find Miss Tree standing next to Myra's bed. Myra was gone.

"What the flipping firetruck are you doing in Myra's room?" Leigh snapped.

"Getting you out of bed for morning therapy."

Leigh snarled, rolling her back to Miss Tree. "Exercise torture? I thought we were done with each other."

"We were. But that was before a man got killed and you were the only one around to see it. Most likely, you are the one who did it."

Leigh flung her blankets aside and vaulted out of bed. Jabbing her finger at Miss Tree she shouted, "That's a lie! I told Ty and Tristin and now I'm telling you; it wasn't me!"

Miss Tree smiled. "Actually, I believe you. You don't have what it takes to kill."

"And I don't want to," Leigh snapped.

"Even if it's the people who murdered your parents?"

A cold chill rushed up Leigh's spine. "You're horrible. And no, not even them. I want them arrested. I want them to face a court. I want them locked away. I want to see their faces when that sentence is handed down."

Miss Tree snickered at a private joke. "Well you'll never see that day if you can't keep up with me. But, it's up to you. You can try or you can quit. Again."

Miss Tree left Leigh seething with rage. Leigh stormed out of Myra's bedroom and up to her own. Flinging open her closet door she went in to change. The air was bitterly cold and Leigh wrapped her hands tightly around her upper arms.

Rubbing her arms for warmth she said, "Couldn't you have done something more useful than turning the place into a refrigerator?"

"Like what?" Bodie's voice said from outside her closet.

Leigh poked her head out from behind the door. Little Bodie was standing with his back to the closet. She didn't know where he went when she couldn't see him and, not for the first time, questioned if he was secretly watching her when he shouldn't be. The idea made her uncomfortable but, for some reason, not as much as it would if he were a living breathing person. All she knew was that he wasn't peeping now and, because of that, she felt she could trust him even when she couldn't see him.

"I don't know," she said less intensely. "How about you not let her into any room I'm in alone. Ever. Unless I open the door for her."

"I can do that," Bodie said, "but it would be easier to drop a bookcase on her."

The vision of the killer bouncing floor to ceiling flashed through her brain. "No," she whispered. "Don't hurt her just, don't let her in."

Bodie shrugged. Leigh didn't know what to say if he wasn't going to talk.

"I've got to go," she said when the pause became embarrassing. "We can talk later?"

Bodie snickered. "Not like I'm going anywhere."

Dressed in shorts and one of her dad's police t-shirts that had shrunk in the wash, she moved downstairs to face Miss Tree. Stepping out the front door she found her across the lawn in a heated argument with Nacho. They were too far away to hear what they were saying but from the look on Nacho's face, Miss Tree had the upper hand.

Leigh moved to where they were standing, intending to stop whatever Miss Tree was torturing Nacho over. "Hey! What's going on?"

Miss Tree raised her eyebrows. "If you don't know it's because you're not supposed to know. Mind your own business, please."

"It *is* my business," Leigh declared. "Nacho works for the family and I'm part of the family. And while I'm at it, let me remind you that you work for the family, too."

Miss Tree's lips curled in a patronizing smile. "Aren't you cute, trying to be all grown-up. A failure, of course, but cute."

"No need to be like that," Nacho said.

Miss Tree turned a scathing look onto him. "I don't tell you how to prune a hedge. Don't tell me how to conduct my therapy sessions. I assume you've lots to do so go get busy."

Leigh watched Nacho's jaw muscles quiver as he ground his teeth together to keep from answering back. She heard the turf rip under his boots as he turned and walked away. As she watched his tension stiffened frame retreat to the garage, her eyes bloomed with a sudden revelation.

"You're nothing," she said to Miss Tree.

"I beg your pardon?"

"I said you are nothing. Nothing, that is, but a bully. Maybe that was what you were trying to teach me. That you are nothing but a cruel and pathetic bully and that I don't have to take it."

"Oh," Miss Tree hissed, "but you do. See, your Uncle Tristin pays me, not you. I work for him, not you."

"You won't work for him very long after I tell him what you've been doing. To me. To other staff members. And besides, I don't have to take it. I get to choose. I can walk away and that's that. Not you, not Tristin, nobody can force me."

Miss Tree folded her arms across her chest. "Well, well, well. Look who decided to grow a spine. I didn't think you were ever going to stand up for yourself."

"I don't care what you think. You aren't important enough to me to give you that kind of power. I think you are horrible and we are done."

Like Nacho, she spun on the balls of her feet and left Miss Tree standing alone. Behind her, she could hear the woman laughing.

"You are tougher than I thought," Miss Tree called to her back. "Not near tough enough. Certainly not tough enough to catch your parents' murderer, but tougher than I gave you credit for."

Furious, Leigh rushed into the house so flustered and reckless she bumped into Myra, who was on her way out.

"I saw something was going on," Myra said, "and I was coming out to help."

"I'm fine," Leigh said. Looking over her shoulder, she added, "I'm better than fine. I'm done with that woman."

Myra's face lit up with pride. "Good for you. I told you she was evil."

"I don't know what she is. Don't know if she was honestly trying to help me or something else. Either way, I don't need it anymore."

Myra hooked her arm through Leigh's elbow and tugged her toward the kitchen. "How about we nab some food, pack a few drinks, and spend the day getting sunburnt in the river?"

"Can't think of anything more perfect."

When she and Myra returned late in the evening, Tristin was waiting for her. "I'd like a word," was all he said as he turned toward his office expecting her to follow.

"Close the door, please," he said.

Leigh's stomach fluttered. She felt she was in trouble because of her argument with Miss Tree but was determined not to let Tristin bully her into apologizing or worse, to continue with Miss Tree's sadistic therapy.

"Miss Tree has left us," Tristin said without preamble.

Leigh's eyes swelled and her face drained in worry over what was coming next. "Did she, um, say anything?"

"She said she was convinced there was nothing more she could do for you. I couldn't get more out of her so I don't know if she feels you are ready to cope on your own or if you're being too stubborn to continue with. I do know you had an argument with her this morning. Tell me about it."

Tristin wasn't asking. The cold dread of being in trouble washed over Leigh.

"She was chewing Nacho out for something," Leigh explained. "I told her to leave the rest of the staff alone. She was hired to make me miserable, not everyone else."

Tristin's body stiffened with anger. "She wasn't here to make you miserable. She was here to, and I think did, help you learn how to cope. You have to admit, you are not the same as you were that first day you arrived."

Though Tristin was talking about Miss Tree, his words made Leigh's mind latch onto Little Bodie and his gift of memories. "I don't know how much she had to do with that."

Tristin shook his head, his eyes narrowing in impatience. "That's a pretty selfish attitude. Frankly, I'm disappointed."

Leigh sucked in a gasp. "Dad said that to me once," she said in a soft voice. "I never thought anything could hurt so bad. Saying I'm sorry isn't enough. Not about Miss Tree. I never liked her and never will. I'm sorry for letting you down. If you replace Miss Tree I promise, I'll try harder."

Tristin cleared his throat. "Miss Tree doesn't think you need another therapist. She recommended giving it a couple of months to see how you do on your own."

Leigh's eyebrows rose in surprise.

"Why don't you go to your room and collect yourself," Tristin said. "Dinner will be served in thirty minutes."

Leigh turned to leave. Opening the door Tristin's voice stopped her in her tracks.

"Leigh? Just because I'm not happy about how you handled yourself in this particular situation doesn't mean that's how I feel about you overall. On the whole, I think you are a wonderful young woman."

Leigh looked over her shoulder at Tristin and smiled. "That's pretty much the same thing my dad said. I..."

She paused, unsure if she was ready to express what she felt. Deciding she was she said, "I love you, too."

They stood blinking at one another, neither sure where to go or what to do, when the phone rang. "Tristin Simmons," Tristin said answering it.

"Nacho? Slow down. What do you mean we have to get out of the house? The police ordered us moved to a safe-house? Twenty minutes. We'll meet you out front, but we're not going anywhere without a better explanation."

Chapter Nineteen

Nacho pulled the big limousine past the mansion's gates and into the ochre hues of dusk. At the house, as she and the rest of the family were piling in, Leigh wanted to say something -- an apology, a pep-talk, a tirade of frustration, anything -- but she saw everyone else was struggling with their own interpretations of what was happening. Now, Myra was staring into the fading light outside while Tristin and Peg held hands with eyes locked straight ahead.

"Leigh, none of this is your fault," Peg surprised her by saying.

"What? Oh! No, I wasn't thinking that. I..."

Leigh looked down and discovered she was running her thumb across one of the scars on her wrist. Forcing herself not to hide her scars she said, "I guess I've gotten into the bad habit of doing that when I'm nervous. And I am nervous. But I know none of this is my fault. That's on whoever is doing this to us, not me."

Tristin did his best to reassure her with a weary smile. "You've come a long way in a very short time. I'm sure Myra's told you I can be a bit tight lipped when it comes to praise, but I'm proud of you."

He turned his head toward Myra. "Of both of you. You are amazing young women."

Not giving either of them the chance to reply, Tristin turned his attention to Nacho. "Tell me again why we're supposed to be going with you?"

"It's like I said before," Nacho explained, "I get this call at home and it was that detective who's been out to the manor a couple of times. The big one."

"Ty?" Leigh asked. "Detective Tyrone Millbanks?"

"Yeah, that's him. Anyway, he calls me and says he wants the whole family moved to a safe house. He says sending police to the manor would raise suspicions. After what happened the other night, there's too many reporters and paparazzi hanging around. I was told to load you all up and drive you to this one road, somewhere out in the middle of nowhere, where we are supposed to hook-up with an armed escort."

"Sounds a bit fishy to me," Myra said.

"Me too," said Leigh. "You sure it was Ty?"

"Sounded like him. Talked like a cop, too. Said they found out a few things about the guy who came to shoot everybody? That he was part of some team and that they were going to keep trying. I am supposed to pick you up so it looks like a normal night out, then we meet the cops and they do the rest. That's all I know."

Nacho flashed a wide smile into the rearview mirror.

"What do you think, Peg?" Tristin asked.

"I agree with the girls. It doesn't sound right. Maybe we should turn around and go straight to the police station. We can sort all this out there."

"Look," Nacho said, "the place we're supposed to meet is just ahead. No harm in keeping on going. If it looks funny, I swear, I'll keep on driving. Ram through if I have to, but I don't think it will come to that. I mean, who else knows you were going to a safe house soon? Only you guys and the cops. I didn't even know until that Ty-cop called me."

"All right," Tristin said. "We'll drive on, but you're not to stop unless I say so."

"Sure," Nacho said in a tone a little too upbeat for Leigh's ear. "And here..."

Nacho twisted around in the driver's seat and handed a revolver to Tristin. "...you can take this, just in case."

"What in the blazes are you doing with that?" Tristin roared.

Nacho made a nervous chuckle as Leigh watched crimson creep up the back of his neck as if he were a thermometer. "Strange phone calls from the police. Meetings in the middle of nowhere. A team of killers on your trail. Yeah! I brought a gun."

Tristin hefted the heavy pistol in his hand. "Yes," he said in a quiet and unsure voice. "Well, thank you, Nacho."

"De nada," Nacho said.

Tristin pressed the catch that allowed the revolver's cylinder to fall open. Watching closely, Leigh saw that the gun was fully loaded. Tristin returned the cylinder to its proper position and slipped the gun into his sport coat pocket. He leaned back against the limo's leather, the darkness making his face look grim and hard.

Peg nestled against him and whispered, "It'll be all right."

They drove on as the orange dusk continued to fade into the long shadows of night. Leigh, like Myra, stared out the window. With the growing darkness, her sense of jittery panic increased. She had no idea where they were or where they were going. That wasn't new, since she didn't know those things before the light died, but the collecting black made her worries worse.

"Here we go," Nacho said. "We got something going on up ahead."

"What is it?" asked Peg with a tremor in her voice.

"Looks like a pair of eighteen wheelers pulled to the side of the road," Nacho said as he squinted into the dark distance.

"Go around them," Tristin ordered. "You are not to stop for any reason. Understand?"

"I'll do my best," Nacho said, "But this road is pretty narrow for such big rigs."

Nacho slowed the car to a crawl as he passed the first rig. Leigh twisted around to look out the back window. "Four men walking behind us. They're following the car!" she cried out.

"Speed up!" Tristin shouted.

"Can't," Nacho said. "This other truck is taking up too much room. There's not enough shoulder and there's a huge ditch on this side."

"I don't care," Tristin shouted.

"For God's sake," Myra yelled. "You've got to get past them."

"Oh no! No! No! No!" Leigh shouted. "Those men behind us! They have rifles!"

"Damn it, man," Tristin said, slapping the back of Nacho's headrest. "Move it! I don't care if you smash the car. You've got to get us out of here."

Nacho stopped the car. A group of men rushed out from in front of the second rig and stood in a line blocking the car from going forward with rifles raised.

"What are you doing?" Tristin yelled. "Run them down!"

"I can't do that," Nacho said, turning around and throwing his arm over the seat back. "These are the people we came to meet."

Myra ducked her head and peered out the front windshield. "They don't look like cops."

Leigh's mouth dropped open. Her eyes rounded like dinner plates as she stared in stunned realization at Nacho. A single tear rolled out of one. "They aren't cops. There were never going to be any cops. This was you. It was all you."

Nacho shrugged but didn't answer.

Tristin jerked the revolver out of his pocket and pointed it at Nacho using some of the foulest language Leigh ever heard. "Drive us out of this mess or so help me, I will shoot you."

"Did you check that thing was loaded?" Nacho asked.

"Of course I did."

Nacho smirked. "Did you check what it was loaded with?"

Tristin's face fell. He opened the cylinder again. Removing one of the rounds he turned the case over. No bullet was crimped into the top. Instead, a green covering sealed in the gunpowder. "Blanks," he said.

"Now that's settled," Nacho said, "get out and do as you are told and no harm will come to you."

Leigh's eyebrows shot upwards. "Really?" she asked. "No harm will come to all of us? Even me?"

Nacho squirmed. "You and I need to talk."

Myra lurched over, shielding Leigh. "Leave her alone."

"Not my call, chicita," Nacho said. "Get out."

Tristin turned rigid. "No."

"All right," Nacho said, nodding. "In that case, we will pull you out and I can't make the same guarantee for your safety."

One of the men at the front of the car brought the butt of his rifle down on the hood of the car. "What's the hold up, Nacho? We have to get moving."

Nacho waved at the man to be patient. He turned back to face his passengers. "Your call, but think of the girls. These men will hurt them if they struggle. If you do what I tell you, I promise no one gets hurt."

"Except me," Leigh pointed out again.

"Maybe not. Like I said, we need to talk."

Leigh looked Nacho square in the eyes. "Fine. For now, we have no choice."

She turned to Myra, "We need to do what he says."

"No," Myra said. "I won't let anything happen to you."

Leigh's heart was thundering in her chest but, for Myra's sake, she forced her lips to bend into a phony smile. "Nacho said nothing is going to happen to me. At least not right away. But if we don't do as he says, bad things are going to happen to all of us now. Not later. Don't you get that?"

"Leigh's right," Tristin said. "I wish she wasn't, but she is. All we can do is hope for something better down the road. As things are, we've no choice."

Leigh reached across Myra and pulled the door lever. She was about to climb over Myra to lead the way when Tristin pushed her back down. "Me first."

"Then me," Myra said, "and heaven help anyone who tries to lay a finger on you."

One by one, they each climbed out, forcing Leigh to exit last. When she did, the others had formed a semi-circle around the door, protecting her.

"Good choice," Nacho said, getting out himself.

He turned to the men in front of the car. "Load them up. Gently. The organization doesn't want any of them damaged in any way. If anything goes wrong, no matter whose fault it is, you are all dead men. Got that?"

The man who slammed his rifle butt down on the hood of the car moved forward. "We are loading you into the back of this truck," he said tilting his head toward the leading truck. "You are going to be bound and gagged with duct tape. Not pleasant, but that don't mean it has to be *un*pleasant. Up to you."

Myra sneered at him. "Get a load of this. A kidnapper who thinks he's got manners."

"This is my first kidnapping," the man said as he stared at Myra with dead, shark eyes, "I'm usually hired to kill people. So, if you would be so kind as to move into the truck so we can keep this a kidnapping? Or would you rather it become an assassination?"

Leigh took Myra's hand. "It'll be all right. Let 'em do whatever they are going to do. They want something and they seem to need us alive for it."

"I believe Leigh is right," Peg said. "Don't give them any reason to hurt you and I don't think they will."

They started toward the back of the truck when Nacho said, "Not you, Leigh. You're riding in front with me."

"The hell she is," Tristin growled, lunging forward.

One of the gang members spun, striking him in the gut with his rifle butt. Leigh heard the air rush out of him as he crumpled to the ground.

"Daddy!" Myra screamed as she ran to his side. Peg was already there.

Two men closed in and tossed Myra and Peg away. They began dragging Tristin to the truck.

"Easy," Nacho ordered. "Remember, they are to be unharmed."

He took Leigh by the elbow. "This way."

"Get your filthy hands off me," she said, jerking her arm away.

Nacho lifted both hands in surrender. "If you say so. I don't want to hurt you."

"You *are* hurting me," she said. "Worse than if you were beating the hell out of me."

She walked toward the cab of the truck.

Passing the bed, she saw that it wasn't a trailer rig. It was a flatbed with a shipping container loaded on top.

"You taking us to the shipping yard?" she asked.

"See," said Nacho as he fell in beside her, "that right there is your problem. You're too smart for your own good. We need to know what you know. What your father told you which, I believe, is nothing, but also what you found out on your own. If you would have left things be, it would have been better for all of you."

Leigh climbed into the cab. Behind her she heard Nacho giving orders. "Tie them up tight, but no need to be mean about it. We want them frightened, hopeless, but above all, unharmed. When you're done, load the car into the second truck and get it to the chop-shop. I want it disassembled and all the parts out of the country before morning."

He started to heave himself into the truck but Leigh refused to move. "In back," he ordered.

The truck had a sleeper compartment and, having no other option, Leigh squirmed through the gap between the seats. She yanked open the curtain separating the sleeper from the driving area and threw herself in.

"That for me?" she asked, nodding her head in the direction of a roll of duct tape on the floor.

"Not unless you make it necessary," Nacho said, following her in.

Leigh crawled to the farthest wall and glared at him. "You lied. I know you did."

Nacho's jaw clenched. "Lied? About what?"

"There's nothing to talk about, is there? You're going to kill me."

"Yes, I am. Sorry, Leigh. I mean that. I am sorry."

Leigh never liked silence, but was thankful for it on this ride. Her final ride.

When they arrived, Nacho ordered her out of the truck. Waiting to see that the job was done right, Nacho stood watching as the shipping container was lifted off the bed and added to the hundreds of identical containers that were surrounding them.

When Nacho gave the order to move, Leigh felt like a miserable hound kept under control by being chained to cinderblocks, forced to drag them along behind her. Every breath made her broken heart hurt more. Her eyes were clouded with tears. She couldn't see where she was going.

Stumbling along with the shambling steps of broken fighter whose been defeated, she tripped over her own feet and fell flat.

"I thought we were friends," she said, her voice cracking in despair as she pushed herself back up.

"We are," Nacho said. "Don't change what I gotta to do."

She whirled around, squashing the tears that sprang from her eyes with the heels of her hands, ignoring the gun pointed at her chest. "How can you say that? How can you care for someone then do to them what you're doing to me?"

"It's like being in different rooms of the same house, you know? In one room we're friends. In another, I kill you. Kinda trashes that first room but if I don't, the whole house gets burned down. Si?"

"No, I don't 'see'!" Leigh shrieked. " Who's forcing you? If this house of yours is built on killing your friends, how great can it be? How honorable is life living there?"

"Didn't say it was honorable. It's the way my life is, unless I want to go back to the one I had before. Broken. Terrified. Alone. I made a choice to never be that scared little kid again.

"I knew I'd always be that way with the cartels so I looked higher and fell in with the ones who were controlling *them*. Now everyone's scared of me. I took my life back and I mean to keep it. If that means I have to do some messed up things along the way, that's what I do. Besides, you're dead anyway. If not by me, then by someone else. Difference is, I'll be dead too, if I don't do it."

Leigh straightened. "I would have died for you."

"I believe it," Nacho said, nodding his head and grinning at her, "but I ain't dying for you or for anyone."

Half of Leigh's lip lifted in a sneer. "And you don't see how that makes you still scared and alone? And man, are you broken. So broken there's nothing left making you human."

She turned away from him and started walking again with steps more confident and self-assured. "So, where we going?" she asked. "I want to get this over with."

"Just like that?" Nacho asked. "Not even going to try to stop it from happening?"

"You said if you don't kill me, somebody is going to kill you. I meant what I said. Because you're my friend, I will die for you."

"The building on the left," Nacho said in hoarse tones that weren't there a minute ago. "Inside, then up the stairs."

"Why there?" Leigh asked.

"I do what I'm told."

"By who?"

"If I tell you that I might as well let you go, because I'll be just as dead."

Frustration filled Leigh hot as lava. "Who's making the rules?" she screamed. "Who is it that, in what's left of my five minutes of life, I can't find out about?"

Nacho nodded his head toward the stairs in reply.

"Here's good," he said when they reached the top and walked halfway down the mezzanine. "On your knees."

Leigh dropped to her knees. "Why my parents? Can you tell me that?"

Nacho shrugged. "No big secret there. Your dad was close to finding out about our organization. Closer than anyone since before my grandparents were born."

Leigh swallowed hard. "And Mom?"

"No way to know what he might have told her. You were supposed to go that night, too. For the same reason." Nacho shook his head. "You decided to go to the movies instead. Life's funny like that."

Having nothing left to say, Nacho started to walk around her but she shuffled her kneecaps over the concrete floor so that she remained facing him.

"What are you doing?" he asked in a tired voice.

"I said I'd die for you. I didn't say I was going to make killing me easy. The least you can do is look your friend in the eyes before blowing her brains out."

Nacho heaved a heavy sigh as he brought the gun up.

Leigh stared down the black barrel. A rivulet of sweat trickled down her back. She hated Nacho. In an odd way, she hated him more for betraying her than for killing her.

Tightening her teeth to keep from swearing at him, she forced her thoughts onto anything but him. She didn't want to die thinking of someone she hated. She wanted to think of those she loved. Keeping her eyes locked onto his, she began whispering their names. "Tristin. Peg. Ty. Myra. Little Bodie."

"Little Bodie," she repeated.

"Big Bodie," she blurted out. "Wait!"

Nacho lowered the gun. "It's no good begging. I've got to do this."

"No," Leigh said, "that's not it. I want to say that I...that I forgive you."

Her words made Nacho furious. "I'm about to kill you, and you're forgiving me? I murdered your parents -- caused you all that pain. You forgive me for that, too? Or is this some trick you're using to stall for time?"

She shook her head, too choked up to speak. Dragging her teeth over her bottom lip she croaked, "I'm so tired, Nacho. I know you know what that's like. I had Myra, Bodie, and the rest of the family. You had no one. If it weren't for them, maybe I'd be like you. I've carried this hatred and pain for so long, but I've seen what happens when you take it with you to the other side. I don't want that. Anything but that. So, yes. I forgive you for it all."

Nacho scowled. "You done talking crap?"

Leigh nodded.

The gun in Nacho's hand rose again. The black chasm of the barrel was shaking, not aiming steady like before.

"Damn it," Nacho growled.

He put his other hand around the pistol grip of the gun. The black barrel kept wavering.

"Damn it!" he said louder.

Leigh saw his eyes dart left and right. "We're being watched, aren't we? They're here to kill you if you fail. Then, they'll be the ones to kill me?"

The tension Leigh saw in his face made him look skeletal.

Leigh forced a thin smile onto her face. "It's all right, Nacho. You said it. I'm dead anyway. You go on and live. I'm ready."

An ear-splitting crack, followed by an acrid stink, forced her eyes to snap closed as she jerked her head away. Something sticky and wet splashed over her face. Everything went dead silent.

Chapter Twenty

The warehouse reeked of gunpowder. Leigh's ears were ringing from the report of the shot. Slowly, afraid to look into the afterlife, Leigh squinted just enough to see through her eyelashes. She was kneeling on the concrete floor. She was alive. Nacho missed.

Nacho's body lay three feet away, a puddle of blood pooling beneath his head. She wanted to scramble over to him to see if anything could be done for him but was too afraid to move. His eyes were open but not even the dimmest spark of life shimmered within them. His tongue hung limp over his teeth. He was dead and she knew it.

Light clicking footsteps came from the shadows to her left.

Leigh vaulted to her feet. To the right, the mezzanine ended at a brick wall. Racing to the railing she saw this second level was too high to jump down to the first floor. The only way off was back the way she and Nacho came -- from where the sound of footfalls was approaching.

With nowhere to run, she stared into the black. "Who's there?"

A dark figure was moving toward her through the shadows of stacked crates and containers. As it approached, entering the light, it gained more substance until, finally, it had an identity.

"Miss Tree!" Leigh shouted in surprise.

Miss Tree strolled into the middle of the warehouse floor, a heavy pistol dangling from one hand. Standing over Nacho's body, she used the toe of her red heeled shoe to roll his head over so she could stare at the bullet hole she put in his temple.

Leigh struggled to her feet. "Miss Tree! It was him. It was Nacho."

Words rushed out of her like racecars given the green light. "He was behind it all. He told me about how the cartels took over his village. How they forced people to join. He said he didn't but I guess he did. He must have. They want to use Simmons-Pierce Shipping to move illegal cargo around the world. He told me so. He killed my parents because Dad found out about them. He killed Mom because they were afraid Dad may have told her something. They were supposed to kill me, but I wasn't home, and...and..."

Miss Tree crossed her arms, the gun still hanging in her hand. An odd smile was tugging at her lips.

That cruel taunting grin stoppered Leigh's speed-talking. "Miss Tree?"

Miss Tree snickered. "That never gets old. Say it again."

"Miss Tree? This isn't funny!"

Miss Tree's mirth turned into laughter.

Her voice echoed off the walls as she mocked Leigh. "Miss Tree. Miss Tree."

Leigh cradled her head in her hands, confusion making her brain spin. "Miss Tree? What are you doing? Why are you being like this?"

Miss Tree raised her eyebrows. "Still haven't got it, dear? Say it again."

"Say what again?"

"My name, fool."

"Miss Tree?"

"Faster."

Leigh kept silent.

Miss Tree pointed the gun at her.

Anger twisted Miss Tree's features. "I said, say my name again!"

"Miss Tree," Leigh mumbled.

Miss Tree took a step closer and slapped the gun across Leigh's face. "Faster! Over and over!"

"Miss Tree," Leigh sobbed in pain. "Miss Tree. Miss Tree, Miss Tree, Miss Tree, Mystery."

Leigh gasped, her eyes bugging in her head. "You! You're behind all this?"

Miss Tree groaned and turned her back on Leigh in disappointment. She leaned against the metal barrier at the edge of the mezzanine and stood looking down at the floor below.

"That took for-*ever*," she groaned. "I kept hoping you would put it together so I could kill you and get on with my life. But no! I had to stick around and listen to you go on and on about how horrible your life is."

Leigh, too stunned to say anything sensible, stammered, "But, it can't be you. You were helping me."

Miss Tree wheeled back around. "No, stupid! I was trying to push you over the edge. To get you to kill yourself so I wouldn't have to. I wanted you dead along with the rest of your stupid family but," she waved the gun at Nacho's body, "this idiot couldn't even do that right. I had to come do the job myself."

"Me? Why? You had to have figured out I don't know anything."

Miss Tree scowled at Leigh. "Of course I did. You were a loose end, that's all. I was going to do you quick and that would have been that. Then, you made things difficult by coming to live with the Simmons's. After that, your murder would have been too risky. Too high-profile. We want Simmons-Pierce as part of our organization, but there's no way we are going to get it with the police swarming. That fool Tristin might have started talking about our pressuring him to let us in. So, I thought, why not get the girl to do herself. She's already tried once. All she needs is a bit of coaching and poof! All our headaches are over.

"But you! You had to start picking at threads. Some were to our benefit, like the discovery that Massy fool was double crossing us. He drew too much attention to himself so I had to kill him before he told the world about us. Some of your other meddling was dangerous to us, like ferreting out the drugs we were smuggling through the shipping yards. In either case, you had to die."

"Dante was involved!" Leigh exclaimed.

"That fool? No. He was too stupid to be part of anything as big as our organization."

"So, you work for Nacho and his cartel buddies?"

"Us? Work for them?" Miss Tree laughed in her face. "Leave it to you to get everything all back-to-front. They work for us, dear. The cartels. The Mafia. The Yakuza. All of them. They work for us!"

"You're lying," Leigh said. "Those organizations don't answer to anybody."

"You don't think so? Is it so outrageous to believe that, after decades of grooming and infiltration, we couldn't put our people in the highest of positions within those organizations? That we couldn't become silent partners in the biggest crime syndicates? In legitimate businesses? That we couldn't pack governments around the world with our own people? Naive child!"

Leigh spun away from Miss Tree. Her mind was in freefall. First, Nacho, now Miss Tree? How could she have spent so much time with both of them and not have known? Not suspected? Her thick-headedness was going to get her killed.

Pain blazed from her scalp. She realized her bangs were snarled around her fingers and that she was pulling them in her distress. She straightened her back and let her hair loose. Squeezing her eyes shut, she thought of Bodie and all the times he thought he was going to die as a child. She searched the memories he gave her of how he clawed, bit, and scratched to stay alive. So would she. She had to. She would have died for Nacho, but not for Miss Tree.

Nobody would ever know about Nacho or Miss Tree if she died here. Nobody would know about the organization she was claiming to be part of. Tristin, Peg, Myra — they would all be in danger under the control of Miss Tree if she didn't live to tell the tale.

With all the power she had, she wheeled back around and launched herself at Miss Tree. Like a well-trained matador, the woman twisted away. Leigh's high tops squeaked on the concrete floor as she dug them in and reversed course so hard her ankles and knees threatened to sprain.

With a loud thud, Miss Tree whipped the pistol against Leigh's temple. Her feet continued forward but her head snapped backwards. Her eyesight flashed white. Crunching to the floor, she landed flat on her back. All the air in her lungs rushed away like a retreating wave.

"Pathetic," Miss Tree scolded, looking down on her in scorn. "Haven't I been telling you? As long as you are too weak to stop me, you'll be too weak to catch your parent's murderers."

She let out a cackling laugh.

Leigh recalled the countless times Miss Tree taunted her with that. Knowing what she was actually saying, the double meaning, that she was being toyed with like a mouse under a cat's paw, bonfire rage consumed her. She rolled away, putting some distance between her and Miss Tree before scrambling to her feet.

"I can stop you," Leigh growled. "I *will* stop you."

"You think so?" Miss Tree asked. "Tell you what..."

Miss Tree sauntered to a large wooden crate. Slipping out of her high heels, she laid the gun on top of the box, "...you give it your best shot. I'm going to kill you with my bare hands. You can kill me whatever way you think you can. Come on! You can even use my gun, if you think you can get your hands on it."

Leigh's body trembled with the urge to lunge at the gun, but she knew Miss Tree would be ready for such an impulsive move. That path would end in a quick death.

She circled around, trying to get a better side angle on the gun. Miss Tree turned to keep facing her, but otherwise didn't move any closer to protecting the gun. Leigh tried the same tactic going the other direction. Miss Tree's reaction was identical.

Leigh began inching the other way again.

"Are we going to dance like this all night?" Miss Tree sneered. "Or, are you wasting time hoping somebody will come and..."

Leigh lunged straight for Miss Tree. Her mind flashed to a time when Bodie threw himself feet first at a burly man who was beating him to death with a riding stick. The instant the memory came to her she pushed herself off the ground and soared feet first at Miss Tree.

Miss Tree screamed obscenities, crossing her arms across her torso, letting her forearms take the brunt of the blow, but the force of it sent her staggering backwards. Leigh struck the ground hard but scrambled to her feet and made another lunging move for the gun.

Fast as she was, Miss Tree was quicker. Leigh felt an explosion of agony in her head as Miss Tree grabbed her hair and slung her back toward the protective railing where she fell to the floor.

"You've been holding out on me," Miss Tree said. "Did dear old ex-Marine, super-cop Daddy show you a trick or two? Whatever he showed you, it won't be enough."

Using the railing behind her for support, Leigh struggled to her feet. Without warning, she lunged again. Miss Tree swung her fist, but Leigh managed to duck under it. If she kept moving toward the gun, Miss Tree would have her. Spinning around she rammed her fist as hard as she could into Miss Tree's kidney. The blow made Miss Tree scream and stagger, but she managed to twist fast enough to grasp Leigh's arm and Judo-throw her back against the railing.

Making use of the distance, Miss Tree pressed her hand into the small of her back and used it as a brace to straighten herself.

Encouraged by the look of pain on Miss Tree's face, Leigh clambered to her feet with the railing's aid. "Little by little," she gasped through her own pain, "I can stop you and I will stop you."

"This may not mean much to you," Miss Tree said, "but it seems I've underestimated you again. You're right, the longer this goes on, the worse it will go for me. Oh, I'm going to kill you, but the long, drawn-out death I had planned doesn't seem worth it anymore. I'm going to get it over with."

Leigh pushed off the railing, her fingers stretched out like claws, searching for Miss Tree's eyes. How Miss Tree avoided the attack, Leigh didn't know but, with expert precision, Miss Tree's fist struck an upward blow to Leigh's diaphragm. Her lungs emptied and she couldn't manage to refill them. Choking, she dropped to all fours.

Not giving her a second's rest, Miss Tree kicked Leigh in the gut, lifting her off the ground and sending her flying onto her side. Bodie's memories warned her a follow-up kick was coming. Leigh rolled away. Miss Tree's foot whizzed past, a centimeter from her cheek.

Leigh scrambled back to the railing. She knew she was out-classed and about to die. Not knowing what else to do, she balled up as tight as she could as Miss Tree closed in and started raining down blow after blow. As she was being beaten, another memory came to her. Not one of Little Bodie's, but one of her own. In her mind she was watching the killer on the stairs being lifted and dropped to his death, over and over and over by Big Bodie.

With a primal scream, Leigh sprang upwards, her hands clutching for Miss Tree's clothing, hair, flesh -- anything she could get her hands on. With all the strength she had left in her, Leigh lifted and twisted, throwing her stomach against the railing so hard she nearly flipped over the top of it. Miss Tree did go over and, with a sickening crunch, landed on the concrete floor below.

Leigh tore herself away from the gruesome sight. Her body heaving with panted breaths, she squeezed her eyes shut trying to slow down the whirlwind in her mind. Not sure of her next move, she took three staggering steps toward the gun before falling to her knees, retching.

"You...can't...stay here," she said aloud in-between gasps.

Reeling, she pushed back up onto her feet. She took a deep breath. Let it out. "Myra. Tristin. Peg. My family. I've got to get to them."

Lurching to the gun she snatched it off the crate and shoved it into her hoodie pocket. Wincing against the pain, she straightened her back and forced herself to walk to the steel steps leading down.

Walking gave her a sense of control. If she gave in to her desperation and ran, hysteria would overtake her. What lay ahead required a cool head and she knew she was closer to insanity than to a calm mind.

Weaving like a drunkard, she staggered out of the warehouse and into the shipping yard. The smell of fuel polluted ocean and rusting shipping containers hit her nose like a blast from a firehose. Her stomach, still squeamish, lurched into her throat forcing her to swallow hard to pull it back down.

Panic-sweat blanched her face. Her eyes darted in all directions, searching for some place to hide until she could pull herself together. Leaning her shoulders into the shadow of a three-tier stack of containers, forcing her legs to follow her weight, she sank onto her ankles and pressed her fingers into her temples attempting to stop the spinning in her brain.

What was her plan? Where was she going? How was she going to save her family? How many of Miss Tree's goons were there? Should she run for help? If she did, would she be able to bring help in time or would she arrive too late?

Frustrated, she banged her head against the container. She had no answers. Looking left she stared into the yellow maze of the shipyard. Somewhere in that chaos was her family.

To her right, she could see the path to the main gate. A thirty-second sprint would get her to somewhere she could call for help. She knew she couldn't stay where she was and that she had to make her choice.

A gravel crunching whisper came from the shadows of the shipyard. "What's taking so long?"

"I don't know," another voice rasped. "Something must be wrong."

Silent as a panther on the hunt, Leigh moved toward the voices. Keeping out of sight by using a meandering path, she crept to where she thought the talking came from. Turning a corner, she stood in plain sight of the two. Faster than thought, she darted back behind the container. Without stopping, terrified she was seen, she went around to the opposite side. By pressing her feet against the container and its neighbor, she inched her way to the top. Laying on her back, she stared at where the night sky should have been. No starlight penetrated the sick yellow glow of the shipyard lights.

"You're right," she shouted. "Something is wrong. Tree, or whatever her real name was, is dead. I killed her. Whatever her plan was, it's over."

She heard the men swear over the metallic clicks of their guns being brought to the ready. "You know your organization wants control of Simmons-Pierce Shipping," she shouted. "With that woman dead, that can't happen without the Simmons family alive. Best thing to do is to retreat, regroup, try again later."

In the distance she heard an ambulance siren scream. Her dad taught her the difference between emergency vehicle sirens. Squeezing her eyes shut and grimacing at the risk she was taking she prayed these men weren't that smart.

"You hear that?" she shouted. "I called the cops. That's them coming. Do you hear it? Think about it! Nacho's dead. Tree's dead. Their bodies are sure to be found and I swear I'll tell them you two did it. Murder? Kidnapping? Maryland may not have the death penalty, but you will go away for the rest of your lives."

One of the men grumbled.

"Shut up," the other shouted.

The two started to whisper between themselves and all Leigh could do was clamp her teeth shut and wait. Silence fell over the shipping yard. The place was too quiet. Where were all the longshoremen, the forklift drivers, the security details? Something wasn't right.

She closed her eyes and slid her hands into her hoodie pockets. The cold gun gave her a sense of reassurance as her fingers wrapped around the grip, her trigger finger pointing down the barrel and was kept off the trigger like her dad taught her. In the distance, another siren joined the first. This one was a police car.

Leigh shouted into the night, "I'm telling you! They're coming!"

Like an ice maker pumping out crushed ice, a voice above her said, "And we'll be long gone before they get here."

Leigh tucked her chin to her chest, lifting her head and shoulders off the roof of the container. Beyond her feet stood one of Miss Tree's goons, his rifle pointing down at her. She thought about pleading, arguing, begging for her life. A whirl of Little Bodies memories blew through her mind like a desert storm leaving her with one clear impulse. Don't think! Act!

Her finger slipped off the barrel of the pistol and onto the trigger. She exhaled and squeezed.

The only clue that she'd hit him was the widening of his eyes and his mouth moving to form soundless words. He stumbled sideways, teetered at the edge of the container. Lurching to the side, he disappeared over the side. Leigh heard the thud of his body hitting the ground.

Curses erupted from below. Eardrum shattering explosions rang through the night as sparks flew off the edge of the container where wildly shot bullets ricocheted off the metal. Leigh curled into a ball, rolling her back to the sparks and screaming in terror.

Muffled by the ringing in her ears, she heard the receding flap-flap-flap of running boots. Opening her eyes, she saw the second man dart behind a stack of containers. Leigh unfurled and crawled on her stomach to the edge. The man she'd shot was lying on the ground below, moaning but otherwise unconscious. The sirens roaring in the distance multiplied from two to several. From where she was, she could see a steady stream of workers as they evacuated the shipping yard. The cat was out of the bag and no one remained guarding the container where her family was imprisoned.

She leapt to her feet and dashed to the other side of the container. Reversing her chimney-climb up, she rocked her feet between the neighboring container and the one she was atop, lowering herself back to the ground. Despite feeling her blood pulsating in the veins of her neck and temples, terrified Miss Tree had more henchmen in the area, she sprinted to the container where Myra, Tristin, and Peg were imprisoned. Fear was crippling her movements and she flailed at the container's locking mechanism. Her fingers and knuckles, raw and bleeding, kept working until the door yielded to her frantic efforts.

Inside she found her family trussed hand and foot with thick duct tape. Large strips encircled each of their heads, ensuring their mouths would stay gagged.

Hurling herself toward Myra, she picked at the tape binding her wrists. "There's no way to do this without hurting you."

Myra grunted, her wide eyes urging her to work faster no matter how painful.

Leigh picked and picked until a corner of the tape pulled up. Pinching it between her fingers, she rolled her hand round and round, unwrapping Myra's wrists like a mummy's. Reaching the point where the adhesive clung to the skin, Myra shrieked behind her mask of tape, but Leigh kept working, repeating over and over, "Sorry. Sorry. Sorry."

Once Myra's hands were free, Leigh moved to Tristin, leaving Myra to free her own ankles, mouth, and hair. As Leigh worked on Tristin, Myra, tape dangling from her hair, lunged over to help her mother.

The door behind them slammed wide. A crowd of men and women stood in the doorway with guns drawn. Leigh grabbed Myra by the shoulder and, spinning around, shoved Myra to the floor behind her. In the same fluid motion Leigh wrenched the pistol out of her hoodie and stood pointing it at the crowd.

With tears streaming down her cheeks she screamed, "You're not taking them. Not again. Not again!"

"Hold fire! Hold fire," a voice yelled. "Nobody do nothing."

Ty shouldered his way to the front of the crowd. "It's okay, baby girl. It's all gonna be okay. Nobody's taking anybody away from you. Not today."

"Ty?" Leigh's hand, still gripping the gun, dropped to her side. "Oh, Ty! It was Nacho. And Miss Tree. They...they fooled us all and...and...and they lied to get us out of our home and...and..."

She crumpled to her knees, her butt flat on her heels. Tears streamed down her face.

"I know," Ty said calm and slow. "They're gone. I need you to put the gun on the floor and slide it away from you. Can you do that for me, baby girl?'

Leigh looked at the gun in her hand. Lifting her head, she blinked at the tense crowd in the container's doorway, their own guns drawn. She laughed. She didn't know what was so funny, but she couldn't stop laughing. Myra's arms reached around, encircling Leigh. Leigh let Myra take the gun from her hand and fling it across the container floor where Ty stopped its slide with his shoe. Leigh leaned her head back against Myra's shoulder and the world turned black.

Chapter Twenty-One

In the hallway, Leigh heard the familiar sound of Ty's voice arguing with the Interpol officer who spent the last three hours asking the same questions in a million different ways. Their words were too muffled to make out, leaving Leigh to stare at the back of her hospital room door waiting, trying to gauge from his tone of voice the degree of Ty's anger.

"Hey, Ty," she said with false cheerfulness when he entered. "I didn't expect to see you."

He stood in the door eyeing her.

Her happy facade evaporated. "You stop by to chew me out, too?"

He flashed a wry smile at her. "Aw, is somebody giving baby girl a hard time?"

Leigh answered with a sour look and a huffy shift in her hospital bed but inside she felt relieved. If he were mad, he wouldn't be teasing her.

"Actions have consequences," Ty said coming to the side of her bed and taking her hand. "You acted and the world *consequenced*. That's how it works. Every time."

A tear rolled out of her eye and she ground it away with her palm. "So Nacho being killed *was* my fault."

"No. It wasn't your fault. That was the consequence of his actions. His decisions. None of the innocent died this time and that *is* down to you. Ain't gonna lie, you did some pretty stupid things. You also did some very brave things, too. The line between those two can be pretty stinking thin."

Leigh tightened her grip on his hand. "Any sign of that woman?"

"Miss Tree?"

"That's not her name. Don't call her that."

"All right. That Woman. No, we didn't find her body."

"Promise you'll keep me posted this time?"

Ty chuckled. "I'll tell you what I can, when I can. But I already know that won't be good enough for you."

"Please talk to me from time to time. Let me know there's still hope."

"That I can promise. Might be a bit thin to start with, though."

She looked at him in shock. "You're not still thinking about quitting the force, are you?"

"Never was," Ty said. "That letter you found was part of a cover story. You know what that is?"

"You were going to pretend to quit?"

"That was the idea. Plan was to make it look like I was chucking it all in before what happened to your folks happened to me and mine. Like I was switching sides because the other side is winning at the moment. I would have told you all this, if you would have asked. Communication has to run both ways, baby girl."

Leigh fiddled with the TV's remote cable that lay across her chest. "Are they?"

"Are who what?"

"The bad guys. Are they winning?"

"I know better than to lie to you so here it is: No, they aren't winning. They aren't losing either. See, there'll always be good and bad in this world. But it ain't about that. Those big wars between good and evil? They exist to force us to pick a side. That choice makes you the person you are. After all, look at the fine young woman your choices are making out of you!"

"I'm a mess," Leigh protested.

Ty countered with a chuckle. "Show me a youngster that isn't. Thing is, your messes are in the right direction. And you aren't sitting on the bench either, that's for certain! Don't beat yourself up too bad."

Ty's words made Leigh feel better about herself and she didn't want to at the moment. Changing the subject she asked, "So why might it be difficult for you to keep in touch?"

"You took away any reason I might have had to go undercover and expose their organization. You dragged them into the light. Thanks to you, we can get to work on snuffing them out. To do that, I'll be spending a lot of time in Washington on special-assignment at Interpol headquarters. I'll also be traveling to Europe and anywhere else the leads take me."

"That's wonderful," Leigh said, unable to put any enthusiasm into her words. She'd miss him.

They shared a moment of silence before Ty asked, "You ready to get out of here?"

Leigh's eyes bugged in her head. "Hell, yes!"

Ty's eyes narrowed.

Leigh bowed her head and corrected herself. "I mean yes, please, sir?"

Ty grinned. "That's why I'm here, to take you home. Your Uncle Tristin is still making his statement and he's got a posse of lawyers making him revise every word of it. Peg's refusing to leave his side. As for Myra..."

"Myra? How is she doing?" Leigh grew angry. "Once again. Nobody is telling me anything!"

"She's fine. She's back at the manor with strict orders to take it easy. That's why she can't be here. She pitched a fine fit when she was told that."

"Why'd she get to go home and I had to stay overnight?" Leigh asked with a tone of indignation.

Ty stretched his neck to the side and shifted his weight from foot to foot. "Easiest way to put it is that your health background isn't the same as hers. Doctors wanted to make sure you were in a good spot to be released."

"A good spot?" Leigh grumped. "*A good freaking spot?* Who do they think they are?"

"Doctors," Ty said. "Doctors who only got to read a report about a fragile young girl who once tried to kill herself without the benefit of getting to know the supercharged dynamo that girl has become."

The stern look in his eyes told Leigh to drop it.

It took another two hours before the discharge papers were drawn up and signed. Leigh was prescribed medication for her nerves which she had no intention of taking. Ty let her know he had no intention of filling the script. As long as she didn't mention it to her aunt and uncle, he wouldn't either.

When they arrived at the manor, Leigh went to the kitchen and brought back a soda for herself and a cup of coffee for Ty. They sat in the library not talking about anything of significance and, in the end, sat not talking at all.

Ty rose to leave and Leigh gave him an unexpected, clinging hug. "I decided. It'll be easier to live with the organization that killed my parents going unpunished than it would be to have anything happen to you. Please remember that and be careful."

"Ain't nothin going to happen to me, baby girl."

"If there's one thing I've learned, it's that nothing ever happens to anyone, until it does."

Ty kissed her forehead. "Look at you, growing up right in front of my eyes."

As he left, he turned in the library's doorway. "As long as we are making promises to each other, promise me you'll make better choices?"

She smiled mischievously. "All my decisions are perfectly reasonable...at the time I make them."

He jabbed a playful finger in her direction. "That right there? You get *that* from your old man."

They said their goodbyes and he was gone.

Leigh untied her high tops and slipped her feet out of them. Tucking her toes beneath her, she curled into a chair and lay Bodie's journal open on the arm. She began re-reading, not only what Bodie wrote, but also her first entry. He hadn't given her permission to write in it but she knew, or at least hoped, he wouldn't mind.

"Officer Milbanks's take off?" Myra asked from the doorway.

"Left about ten minutes ago," Leigh said, her attention still focused on the book.

"Did he have anything useful to say?" Myra persisted, taking a seat.

"Not really." Leigh closed the book. "He talked about how he is going to be working on assignment with Interpol to track down the organization that had my parents killed."

"That's good, isn't it?"

Leigh sighed. "It is. But, with him gone, it'll be hard for me to keep up with progress. Or lack of, if that's the case."

"You're not thinking of getting involved again, are you? Not after what happened? What nearly happened?"

Leigh's face flushed with anger. "I never wanted to be involved in the first place! All I wanted was to know what was going on and no one would tell me. Not knowing was driving me nuts and nobody understood that."

"Okay. Okay. Calm down," Myra said, looking out the door to make sure no one heard her outburst. "You know I believe you, but I'm afraid nobody else does."

"Well that's freaking great," Leigh grumped as she slapped the journal open again.

Leigh knew Myra was waiting for her to say something but she wasn't about to. Myra wasn't the one she was mad at -- she wasn't mad at anyone -- but she was so frustrated with how everything turned out, leaving her feeling guilty of either doing too much or too little. She didn't know which and that uncertainty left her angry. It was that directionless anger that splattered onto Myra.

"I've been meaning to ask," Myra said cautiously, as if the sound of her voice would set Leigh off, "what's that book? I've seen you carrying it around for months."

Leigh took a deep breath and, puffing her cheeks, blew it out slowly. Part of her selfishly insisted the journal was her secret but another part didn't want there to ever be secrets between herself and Myra. She knew she was being a brat and hated the way it made her feel.

Committing herself to openness, she whispered, "It's Little Bodie's journal."

Myra slid to the edge of her seat. "It's what?"

Leigh closed the book and hugged it tightly. "Bodie's journal. I found it under that loose floorboard in my closet not long after I arrived."

"I've been in that closet a million times over the years. How come I never found it?"

"I don't think he wanted you to," Leigh said as gently as she could.

Myra pouted.

"What I mean," Leigh tried to explain, "is that I don't think he ever thought you needed to find it. Certainly not in the way I needed to."

That answer seemed to soothe Myra. "Can I take a look?" she asked.

Leigh hesitated. Reluctantly, she handed the book over. While her cousin flipped through it, Leigh shifted her eyes around the room. If Bodie didn't want Myra looking at his journal, he'd let her know.

The room remained quiet and still which brought a slow smile to her face. Bodie didn't throw a tantrum when she wrote in his journal. He wasn't making a fuss over her letting Myra see it. A comfortable warmth settled into her chest as she sensed Bodie didn't share his journal with her. He *gave it* to her.

"You've been reading this all summer?" Myra asked, turning pages without reading.

Leigh nodded. Feeling embarrassed but willing to take the risk she said, "The last entry is mine. You can read it, if you want."

Myra used her thumb to flutter through the pages to find the last entry. She looked at it with an odd expression on her face. "You wrote this?"

Feeling self-conscious by Myra's tone, Leigh nodded.

Myra handed her the book. "Read it to me."

"Now you're being mean," Leigh said.

"No, I'm not! Please, just read it to me."

Leigh groaned and read, "When I first came to Simmons-Pierce Manor I had lost everything I ever loved. As much as I didn't want it at the time, I found a new family to love and who loved me. Especially..."

Leigh looked out the top of her eyes at Myra, embarrassment making her heart flutter, but she refused to stop. "Especially my cousin, Myra. If she hadn't been so kind on that first day, and every day since, I think -- no -- I know! I'd be dead by now."

Leigh stopped reading.

Myra sniffled and wiped her eyes. Holding out her hand she whispered, "Can I see the book again?"

Leigh handed it over. Myra inspected the page she read from. "Is that really what it says?"

Her voice tainted with hurt and anger Leigh snapped, "Read it for yourself."

"I can't," Myra said. "This whole book is written in Japanese."

Leigh's mouth dropped open.

Myra flipped to a random page. "Can you read this?" she asked, handing the book back to Leigh.

Leigh looked at the page. "Of course I can. It's written in plain English. Why are you being like this?"

"Close your eyes," Myra said.

Leigh scowled.

"Please."

Leigh, on the verge of losing her patience, did as she was asked. "There!"

"Now, when you open your eyes, I want you to look at the book, not like you would expecting to see words you want to read, but like you would a painting, or a scene out the window. See the whole page, don't focus on the words."

Leigh opened her eyes. Her vision was cloudy and she had to blink several times to bring the book into full focus. As the fog lifted, she discovered Myra was right. Beautiful Japanese script filled the pages.

"Do you see it?" Myra asked, excited by Leigh's expression of confusion.

"I...I...You're right. It's all Japanese!"

"Can you still read it?"

Leigh turned to the first page and read aloud, *"My name is Ichabod Peirce and I'm ten years old,"*

Myra's soft gasp made Leigh pause and look up. Myra's expression was a mixture of shock and fear.

"What?" Leigh asked breathlessly.

"You were reading it in Japanese!"

"That's impossible," Leigh said. "I don't know Japanese."

"Bodie does. Did he show you how to do it like he did all those other things you told me about?"

"No. I don't know. Maybe?"

Myra laughed at her. "Well that made everything clear."

Serious again she said, "Turn to the last page. To what you wrote."

Leigh did. It, too, was written in Japanese.

"How is this possible?" Leigh hissed, feeling both elated and scared at the same time.

"I told you," Myra said, "Bodie! Has to be."

Leigh sat staring at the book. "I don't know what to think."

Myra sat back, her brows knitted in thought. "I don't think he'd do anything that would hurt you." She chuckled. "My advice is to just go with it."

Leigh pulled an expression of exaggerated skepticism. "You don't seem too put out about my best friend being a ghost."

Myra shrugged. "I grew up believing in them. Knowing they were here. Even if I never saw them, I knew they were there, looking over my shoulder. Little Bodie even saved my life once, remember?"

Outside, tires crunched in the gravel. Myra's face lit up and she sprang to her toes, pushing herself up to see who was pulling into the drive.

"Let me guess," Leigh groaned. "Marcus?"

Myra shot her a shocked look. "How long have you known?"

"I started to suspect when you were terrified of what could be found on your phone the night the SEC was here." A wicked smile spread across Leigh's face. "But I didn't *know* know until just now."

Myra lips tightened and her eyes narrowed, but Leigh saw straight through the scathing look to the underlying grin.

"How did it happen?" Leigh asked. "I thought you hated the guy."

"After being busted at the party he sat me down and talked to me. I found out he's covered for Theo loads of times. Tessa, too. He even managed to keep Ralph's police record clean, though how, I've no idea. After that, I started seeing him as someone besides head of security and, I don't know! We just started talking more. When I finally kissed him..."

"Ew!" Leigh squealed.

Myra 's face contorted as if she sucked on a lemon. "Done?"

A mischievous smile twisted Leigh's lips. "Not even close, but go on."

"Well, it felt totally different than doing research. I still think he's an ass when working his security role but he's really sweet otherwise; always thinking of others before himself. He's like two different people, if that makes sense."

Leigh's eyes darted to the portrait of Big Bodie and she smiled. "More than you know. Still, ew!"

"Write this in your book," Myra said. "On this date I, Myra Simmons, predict that within a year, you, dear Leigh Howard, are going to meet someone who is going to pull your world inside-out, and you are going to love every minute of it."

Leigh laughed and started writing. "Got it," she said but continued scribbling.

"What else are you writing?" Myra asked.

"The Japanese equivalent of calling bullshit."

Myra patted Leigh on top of her head like an obedient dog. "We'll see, little sister. We'll see."

Myra rushed out to meet Marcus. Leigh rose and stretched and sock-skated to one of the big bay windows. Looking out, she watched Myra stroll over to where Marcus stood talking to Tristin and Peg. Walking around her parents, Myra slid her hand into his. Leigh could see a smile brighten Peg's face. Tristin shifted on his feet but didn't object. When Myra and Marcus strolled off toward the garden patio, Peg threaded her arm through Tristin's and watched them go.

"If I still ate food that performance would make me vomit," a hollow voice said at Leigh's elbow.

"I think it's sweet. I hope it works out for them. Um, don't tell them I said that."

Big Bodie let out a loud groan only a ghost could make, one that echoed throughout the manor. "To think, I rescued her all those years ago so that she could grow up to throw herself at men beneath her station."

Leigh turned on him. "You're such a snob! And when did you rescue her?"

Her brow furrowed for a moment. Thinking back on his words, her eyes grew wide with understanding. "It was you and not him? You carried her back to the house from the river when she was a child. After she fell out of the tree and hit her head."

Bodie growled and walked toward his painting. "She was foolish then and she's being foolish now."

"Foolish? For swimming in the river alone?" Leigh asked.

Bodie's head twisted around backwards so she could see his look of impatience. "Of course not. I swam in that river right up to the day I died. But I can assure you I was never fool enough to fall out of a tree."

Leigh put her fists on her hips and taunted, "If she's such an embarrassment to the Simmons-Pierce name, why'd you save her?"

His body spun to match the direction his head was facing. "It's my duty to protect the family. That, unfortunately, includes her."

Making a sour grimace he snarled, "And him."

Leigh dropped her hands off her hips, confused by his answer. "Little Bodie? What are you protecting him from?"

Big Bodie lunged at her, his face decomposing as he drew near. Bone, flesh, and sinew glistened, oozing wet in his purple aura. One watery eye glared at her. An empty socket shimmered grotesque with hues where the other eye should have been. He was revolting to look at and cruelty radiated off his presence like heat from a stove-top burner. Leigh wanted to turn away, to run out of the library screaming but she defiantly refused, knowing that's what the ghost wanted her to do.

She clamped her teeth so tight her molars ground together. Her neck muscles strained against the impulse to look away. He was so close to her that the dark purple mist that always surrounded him swallowed her. His presence felt stifling. Big Bodie's aura was the heat of hatred and malice. Her breath caught in her lungs as she imagined the torturous heat of Hell.

"From turning into me," the horrifying apparition yelled in fifty voices at once, ranging in pitch from a lion's roar to a hawk's screech.

A wail of rage and anguish filled the library as Bodie turned himself into a bodiless skull and soared around the ceiling. Hurtling across the room, his skull collided with Bodie's painting and, as though struck by a nightmare water balloon, purple goo splattered across its surface. As it streaked down the painting it began to be absorbed into it.

"Please sit," a smooth voice said from the chesterfield behind her.

Whipping around, Leigh found Big Bodie sitting with one knee suavely draped over the other. She inched across the room and, keeping a cautious eye on him, lowered herself into a chair.

"You're not right in the head," she said. "You know that?"

He let out a charming chuckle that left Leigh blinking in surprise. Still old, something about him looked more vibrant and youthful -- more sane.

"We shared with you the abuse we suffered while held captive," he said without preamble.

She couldn't focus on what he said, too flummoxed by how he said it. "You said 'we'. Not me and not him. Are you two together now or what?"

Big Bodie smiled and gave a patient nod of his head. "More unified than usual but not one. Not...whole."

Leigh shook her head and scowled. "You two are the ones who should be seeing a therapist, not me."

Bodie inclined his head in recognition of her observation. "Maybe, if we were still alive, but as it is," he shrugged, "it's too late for us."

"*Too late*," he repeated as his eyes glazed with long-past memories. "I thought I was doing all I could to keep what remained of our humanity, some tiny spark of our innocence, alive. In life, I failed miserably. My fear and zealousness did what our captures couldn't. Everything that was kind or joyful, everything that is still him, was lost to me. In death, we found ourselves split into what I had become," he laid a hand on his breast, "and what I was trying to protect. What I am still trying to protect."

"You once told me you can't move on because he won't," Leigh said. "Is that why? You feel you have to stay and protect him? Or is the truth to protect what innocence is left in you?"

"That's exactly it. I will not risk him doing anything that would tarnish that innocence should any of the family be in jeopardy. That's how I started my decline into wretchedness. Now, I do what needs be done so he will never have to."

"But what keeps him here?" she asked.

"There are repercussions in the afterlife for the things we do in this one. Though torn apart, the piece of us that is him knows, on some level, the horrible things we've done -- that *I've* done. Given the abuse we suffered as a child, is it any wonder he is terrified by the possibility of being punished for all eternity?"

Leigh's heart wrenched. "That's the saddest thing I've ever heard."

Without acknowledging her words Bodie continued, "There is, after so many years, hope."

"What?" Leigh offered. "I'll do anything to help."

Bodie's face turned grim. "Never say that. 'Anything' encompasses everything and you need limits; moral boundaries you will not cross no matter what. Lines I never had the courage to set for myself."

"I think I understand, but I want to help."

"Help him?"

"Both of you."

She reached out her hand to touch his knee. Like always, her hand slipped through his image but her fingers felt as if they were passing through water instead of empty air.

The ghost smiled at her valiant effort. "When you first came here you were broken and so close to death you reeked of it."

He bounced his walking stick off the floor and outside, thunder cracked. "Now you are brimming with life!"

Leigh blushed and moved the topic away from herself. "So, how can I help?"

"You've proven you would sacrifice yourself for the family. That makes me believe you will protect him as well. Convinced of that, I can let go -- fade away -- rest."

Confused, Leigh asked, "I thought you couldn't go as long as he remained?"

Bodie gave another patient smile. "The living mind can't ever grasp the dead's world. The closest you can get to understanding is to know that I can't move on, but I no longer have to stay here."

He rose to his feet with such an unexpected and quick movement that it made Leigh's heart skip a beat. She sprang out of her seat, prepared for anything.

"Goodbye, Miss Howard. You are an extraordinary young woman and I am glad you came into our after-lives."

He leaned in and, as his freezing cold lips grazed her cheek with a kiss, he disappeared.

She turned in every direction searching for him.

A small piece of the back wall shimmered blue. The light turned to mist. The haze swirled and became a hallway leading out of some other world. Little Bodie wandered towards her, hair tussled, wearing nothing but his long breeches underwear.

"I'm going swimming in the river. Want to come?" the boy-ghost asked.

Leigh smiled and gave him a shrug. "Sure."

The End

About The Author

Shawn's life mirrors the adventures he likes to write. He has been a skydiver, scuba diver, bungee jumper, and martial artist. Shawn would be the first to tell you, being a husband and father is by far the wildest and most rewarding part of life. Before professionally turning his hand to writing, Shawn was a paratrooper, a pediatric therapist, and an engineer.

The first books Shawn remembers reading were the adventures of a horse named Blaze and his youthful owner, Billy, written and illustrated by Clarence William Anderson in the mid-1930's. Billy and Blaze always found themselves in the middle of some crisis and, with courage and heroics, never failed to save the day. Hooked, Shawn tried to write adventure stories of his own. Shawn was four and has been writing ever since.

Note From The Author

Word-of-mouth is crucial for any author to succeed. If you enjoyed *Leigh Howard and the Ghosts of Simmons-Pierce Manor*, please leave a review online—anywhere you are able. Even if it's just a sentence or two. It would make all the difference and would be very much appreciated.

Thanks!
Shawn M. Warner

We hope you enjoyed reading this title from:

BLACK ROSE
writing™

www.blackrosewriting.com

Subscribe to our mailing list – *The Rosevine* – and receive **FREE** books, daily deals, and stay current with news about upcoming releases and our hottest authors.
Scan the QR code below to sign up.

Already a subscriber? Please accept a sincere thank you for being a fan of Black Rose Writing authors.

View other Black Rose Writing titles at www.blackrosewriting.com/books and use promo code **PRINT** to receive a **20% discount** when purchasing.